THE
IMMORTAL
GENE

OTHER BOOKS BY JONAS SAUL

The Future is Written (*Books 1-3 of the Sarah Roberts Series*)

Sarah Roberts Series
Dark Visions
The Warning
The Crypt
The Hostage
The Victim
The Enigma
The Vigilante
The Rogue
Killing Sarah
The Antagonist
The Redeemed
The Haunted
The Unlucky
The Abandoned
The Cartel
Losing Sarah
The Pact
The Terror
The Chase
The Betrayal
The Threat
The Specter

The Threat (*A Drake Bellamy Thriller*)
The Specter (*An Aaron Stevens Thriller*)
A Murder in Time (*A Marcus Johnson Thriller*)
Sharp Fear (*A Mafia Thriller*)
Twisted Fate (*Tales of Horror*)

THE
IMMORTAL
GENE

JONAS SAUL

The Immortal Gene

Copyright © 2018 Jonas Saul
All rights reserved.

Cover Credit: Original Illustration by Sam Shearon
www.mister-sam.com

ISBN: 978-1-944109-58-5

VESUVIAN BOOKS

Published by Vesuvian Books
www.vesuvianbooks.com

Printed in the United States of America

10 9 8 7 6 5 4 3 2 1

PART ONE

THE INCIDENT

CHAPTER ONE

Jeffrey Harris knew murder in its many delicate forms. To Jeffrey, it wasn't murder. That was a man-made word to describe something the populace hadn't come to terms with. People murdered themselves every day as they drank and smoked their way to the grave. Jeffrey was no dullard. He knew how the world turned and murder wasn't vile or wrong. Murder was a blessing.

Apart from that, he knew the art of aiding in the soul's passage. The pleasure it afforded him was a trifle of the pleasure it afforded the travelers as they left this plane and made their journey home. All Jeffrey wanted was a family in return and a family was what he got.

Each and every time.

He had parked his Honda Civic by a large tree, which offered him an unobstructed view of the Marcello farmhouse in the distance. Their plain, nondescript home looked like any other rural Ontario family domicile. A wide expanse of an old cornfield spread out from the left side of his car, covered in an early-winter dusting of snow. The closest home in the area was almost a kilometer behind him. Another farmhouse was two kilometers north.

This particular family dwelling housed the lovely Marcello clan, consisting of mother, father, and twelve-year-old son, who had just returned from school on a large, lumbering yellow school bus.

As the sun settled early over the distant trees in the cool temps of mid-November, Jeffrey ran through his checklist to make sure he had everything for tonight's family get-together. He blew into his cupped hands, then rubbed them. He had turned off the car to stake out the Marcello home. The interior temperature had dropped to match the outside. A cloudy frost formed on the windows, blocking most of his view, but he didn't mind. It blocked views from the outside as well.

The family get-together—or *Gathering*, as he'd called it since he'd begun doing these over a decade ago—was imminent. It was a simple mission. One his parents had taught him well. Family was something you *take*, not something you make. Being born was the only thing we were all given equally, and even then, some died in birth. Once we were born, the families we were dropped into by some karmic fate didn't need to be our only kin. Fate could be a fickle bitch, because sometimes families could be horrid. He'd learned years ago that once a boy became a man, he could choose his family—a man could *take* his family.

So, Jeffrey Harris took his family.

At will and often.

At least once every two years or so.

And the Marcello family was his for the taking. He'd admired them from afar. He'd driven up on Sundays to attend their church and offered generous donations to the collection plate. He'd even talked to them on several occasions.

Jeffrey's story was usually the same. Lost his wife to cancer. Never had children. In the last weeks before the family get-together—the Gathering—Jeffrey would prepare by shaving and waxing his body smooth. At church last week, he'd told Stephen Marcello he was undergoing chemotherapy for lung cancer. It would probably be his last visit to church for a month or so as his strength was waning.

Once Stephen had talked with his wife, Melissa Marcello, they'd invited Jeffrey for dinner on Friday night.

Friday night had arrived, and Jason was home from school. Jeffrey's new family waited for him. He could only imagine what Melissa was cooking. He would probably smell it the second he entered their home. A fine meal she would never get to eat.

He pulled on latex gloves and wrapped plastic around his shoes. The steering wheel made it hard to maneuver, but he managed. He peeked through the small hole of frost on the windshield. The sun had dropped far enough that he would be unobserved by anyone other than the Marcellos as he approached their farmhouse.

He slipped on his thick reading glasses, keyed the ignition, and the engine came to life. In the hour he'd watched the house, only one vehicle had passed his position other than the school bus. Another reason to choose this house, this family. They were out of the way. There wouldn't be any witnesses, and no one would hear a thing if the situation got out of control. Although it never did. Jeffrey Harris maintained control. After a decade, the authorities were baffled by what he left behind, cold cases piling up after each Gathering.

Jeffrey would remain organized. He would remain diligent and he would never stop. He would never stop because no one *could* stop him.

No one knew his real name. He didn't need to present ID to engage in church activities. The Marcello family, along with everyone else he'd met at the church, knew him as Jeffrey Harris, Jeff for short. He wore glasses, had a thick beard, and a full mane of hair. But now it was just the glasses. Everyone would remember the beard, the hair. Identifying him would be difficult if suspicion ever pointed toward the guy at the church.

His month-long surveillance of the Marcello family had revealed them as home bodies. In that time, only one friend had visited Mrs. Marcello and it had only been for an hour. None of the boy's friends ever came to the house. On Saturdays, the family went shopping in Orillia. On Sundays, they visited their local church and then returned to spend the week at home. Online research, including all social media, revealed the Marcello family lacked friends and were generally antisocial. The invite to dinner had surprised Jeffrey as it had been out of character. But Jeffrey had been quick to accept.

That was why Jeffrey needed them. They, as a family, were unfulfilled. Within the next hour or so, Jeffrey Harris would fulfill their purpose and the Marcello family would be whole again.

He closed the gym bag on the seat beside him and zipped it up. A small ax and handsaw were buried at the bottom of the bag.

With the heaters warming him and clearing the windows, he started up the road toward the Marcello family domain, already fantasizing the Gathering as a fitting end to the Marcellos' stagnant life. A gallant passage from one plane to another, delivered with love and caring. When he was done, Jeffrey would collect his family mementos and head home to start anew.

The Marcello family.

It had a nice ring to it.

He would be part of the Marcello family for a while. At least until Mrs. Marcello had his baby.

Oh, the things people get to do while dead.

CHAPTER TWO

Ontario Provincial Police Detective Jake Wood stood next to his partner, Detective Kirk Aiken, while studying the dead man felled by a washing machine.

"Weird fucking luck," Kirk whispered. "A Maytag." He turned to face Jake. "How would that look on his epitaph?" He snapped his fingers and bounced his head once, his usual beginning to a short rap. "Here's John Doe, a tag on his toe, wrapped in a bag, after eating a Maytag."

"No." Jake gave Kirk a friendly punch in the arm. "No, can't see it saying that." He cleared his throat and looked away from the man's dented skull. He had seen enough. He couldn't imagine how the wife felt being the one who had found him.

The wife had been away on a week-long trip to Calgary where she had buried her mother after a long illness. She hadn't been able to get a hold of her husband just before the flight back and had begun to worry but brushed it off as funeral jitters. When she'd walked in the door and seen her husband under the washing machine, she had screamed and run from the house, collapsing on a neighbor's front lawn two doors down.

Local O.P.P. showed up and homicide was called in to secure the scene and ascertain whether there were any signs of foul play.

Jake entered into the kitchen, leaned on the counter and stared out the window.

"Kirk," he called.

"Yeah?" Kirk shouted from the laundry room.

"C'mere." He waited until Kirk entered the kitchen. "Assessment?"

"Death by washing machine. The man's old, feeble. He had to use a walking stick. When the Maytag slipped off its moorings, he had the unfortunate luck of being in the way."

"Short of an autopsy, cause of death?"

"Compression asphyxiation."

Jake turned to face his partner. "Did the wife do it or have anything to do with it?"

"Absolutely not. She was out west." He narrowed his eyes. "Wait a second. Are you suggesting she wasn't out west at her mother's funeral?"

"Absolutely not. That's easily verifiable."

"Then what?"

Jake shrugged and shot his hands out at his sides. "Homicide or not? Suicide? Accident? C'mon, does this death need us to conduct a homicide investigation? Or does it just need a coroner and a clean-up crew?"

"Ohh, I see, said the squirrel in the dark."

"The what?"

"Nothing." His face tightened as he grew serious again. "Um, yeah, no homicide. Not in my opinion."

"How did you come to that conclusion, Detective Aiken?" Jake asked in his official devil's advocate tone.

"Because the washing machine dropped on him."

Jake looked out the window again. "Kirk, have you considered that the wife rigged the washing machine before leaving for Calgary? When her husband pulled the laundry room door open, the shelf let go, slid his way, jammed into him in the confined space, and came tumbling down on his diaphragm."

6

Kirk let out a small chuckle. Jake spun to look at him.

"What?" Kirk asked, looking comically offended. "There's a rhyme in there somewhere."

Jake crossed his arms. "How about this? Wifey hired a couple of thugs to come here and make it look like an accident. Positioned the man in front of the machine and forced it to crush his head."

"Nice theories, but naw. No sign of forced entry. Once we canvass the neighbors, we'll learn whether any theory like that held water. Life insurance policy? There are a number of things to look at, but at first glance, this was an accident, through and through." Kirk opened the fridge, moved something aside, grunted, then closed the fridge and met Jake's eyes. "Where are you going with this?"

"Nowhere, other than to say this wasn't a homicide. Therefore, we're not needed. Agreed?"

"Of course. I agree. Even before we saw the body I concluded we weren't needed because I'm such a good detective."

"Sure you are," Jake placated. "Once the coroner gets here, we'll sign off on this, console the wife, and head home." He checked his watch. "It's almost twenty-one-hundred hours. I wonder what Cindy's up to." Jake started for the front door. "Let's talk to the wife now."

Kirk followed close behind. "How is Cindy now that you're engaged? Anything changed?"

Jake shot him a sidelong look, then scowled. "What's that supposed to mean?"

"Women change, Jake. Especially once you're married. All that nice shit ends."

"Oh really? And you know this, how?"

They made it to the front door and nodded at one of the uniforms on the way out.

"C'mon Jake, every guy knows how women are. They seduce,

offer sex freely, are the best girlfriends, and act all lovey-dovey until they're married. Then they've got you. The honeymoon is over. Try getting sex even twice a week two years from now. Good luck."

"You done?" Jake asked, a smile playing across his lips. Kirk only understood women on a one-night stand basis. He'd have a girlfriend for a month or two and then when it wasn't fun anymore—which translated to having to work at the relationship—he dumped her. His most recent girlfriend had really done a number on him, so understandably he was still raw.

"Yeah, I'm done," Kirk mumbled.

As they walked down the street toward the neighbor's house and the grieving wife, Kirk moved away from Jake.

"Touchy subject, eh?" Kirk asked.

"Nope."

"Then why do you look all offended?"

"Not offended. You're just wrong. You know what Cindy and I have is different. Been with her since grade eight. We're going to make it all the way. Biggest speed bump we've ever encountered is whose family we're spending Christmas with each year."

"Oh my shit," Kirk said as he angled back to walk beside his partner. "Are you ever in for a world of hurt."

"Famous last words."

They hopped up the porch steps of the neighbor's house and knocked. After seven years as partners in Toronto, they now worked out of the O.P.P. Orillia detachment, where less homicides were committed. There had only been three murders last year and two the year before. It kept them busy with paperwork and court dates, but the pace was a lot more laid back than their days in Toronto. When Jake had put his transfer request in, Kirk had done the same and they'd been together since.

The neighbor let them in and directed them to the living room where the distraught wife lay sprawled on the couch. An untouched cup of tea cooled on the coffee table beside the woman's head. At least a dozen scrunched up tissues were balled up on the carpet.

Her face glistened from tears, her eyes red and puffy.

Jake sat in the chair closest to her and offered his condolences. In a soft, gentle voice, he told her what she needed to know and that the death would be ruled an accident.

"He never does laundry," she managed to choke out in a nasally voice. "Why would he try the day before I come home?"

Jake didn't answer. Nor did he want to stay longer than needed. He patted her shoulder, got up, and headed for the door.

"Officer?" the sobbing woman called.

Jake turned back and Kirk almost bumped into him.

"Are you married?" she asked.

"About to be. I'm engaged."

"Good luck."

The woman set her forearm over her swollen eyes and started to sob softly.

Jake walked out, Kirk close behind. Once outside, Jake retrieved the car keys from his pocket.

"What do you think that meant?" Jake asked. "Good luck?"

"Exactly what I've been telling you. That woman knows relationships."

"Oh, fuck off," Jake said good-naturedly as he shoved Kirk's shoulder.

In the car, Jake stared out the windshield at nothing.

"What's on your mind?" Kirk asked.

"Just had a thought."

"And?"

"Why was the washing machine on the shelf above the dryer? People put dryers above the washing machine. Why was the heaviest one on top?"

"No idea." Kirk snapped his fingers and tilted his head.

"People are strange. They won't change, then they die. Who am I to feel remorse? But of course, then there's Jake, here to take, all—"

"Okay, okay," Jake cut in. "Got it."

Kirk laughed as Jake started the unmarked cruiser down the street.

"Marriage is tough, bro."

Jake eyed him hard for a second before looking back at the road.

Kirk raised his hands in surrender. "Just saying, man. Just saying."

"You're always *just saying.*"

CHAPTER THREE

Jeffrey Harris backed into the Marcello driveway and got out, gym bag in hand. Once the car door was closed, he paused to stare out at the field beyond. He pushed his glasses up to the bridge of his nose. Something large bounded across the field behind the fence attached to the side of the house. The Marcellos had two huge black horses. Jeffrey figured something must have spooked them. He had no idea horses would run like that in the dark unless they were startled. One of them whinnied as it came up to the fence and stopped to look at him.

"Don't worry about Gracie," a soft voice echoed from the house.

Jason Marcello, his head stuck out his bedroom window, watched Jeffrey as he watched the horse. He would have to remember that about little Jason. He was sneaky and popped up wherever he wanted. A good boy getting up to little boy antics. Jason would make a fine son.

"Gracie," Jeffrey said, rolling the name off his tongue. "And the other horse's name?"

"Mary. She's shyer. My parents went with religious names. You know, Amazing Grace and Mary Magdalene."

"Of course," Jeffrey replied, not surprised.

The front door opened and Mrs. Marcello stepped out. "I thought I heard you pull up, Mr. Harris. Please, come on in."

"Jeff is fine," he said as he started up the long driveway, his polished black shoes clunking on the cold cement with each step, even through the plastic booties.

"Then Jeff it is. Call me Melissa."

So fake sounding. Her tone, her smile. Underneath it all, this ceremonial dinner was because they thought he was dying and they ought to do the good Christian thing. It would be awkward if he were a normal guest without the cancer tag. But Jeffrey was no normal guest.

He wiped his feet on the welcome mat at the door and stepped inside, admiring the large foyer that opened up to a center staircase. Little Jason was already on the stairs, watching Jeffrey remove his shoes.

He stood to his full height, pushed his glasses up, and addressed Mrs. Marcello.

"I want to thank you for the invite," Jeffrey said.

"Oh nonsense." She glanced downward, then looked up too fast. Mrs. Marcello had seen the clear plastic booties clipped over his shoes but had diverted her eyes to be polite. No doubt feeling awkward, she moved around Jeffrey to slip through an alcove to the right.

"Anything for a fellow Christian," Melissa said as she moved away from him. "Stephen should be down any second."

Jeffrey smiled at Jason. He pointed at his bag and jerked his head in a come-over-here gesture.

"Wanna see what I brought?" Jeffrey asked, his tone softer, more approachable.

Jason's face lit up as he scurried down the last steps and ran over to Jeffrey. Once Jason stood by the bag, Jeffrey unzipped the side pocket and pulled out a bottle of red wine.

"Take this to your mom," he said. "It's a small thank you for their generosity."

Jason bounded away to the kitchen.

"You shouldn't have," Melissa called from the kitchen. "Would you like a drink before dinner?"

"Sounds nice. Whatever you're having."

Jason returned and stopped in front of Jeffrey.

"Want a new toy?" Jeffrey asked the boy.

"A toy?" Jason squinted and looked at him sideways. "I'm a little old for a toy. I'm already twelve."

"Not for this kind of toy."

Jeffrey pulled out white twist ties.

"What are those for?" Jason asked.

"An advanced version of Hide 'n' Seek. Turn around. I'll show you."

Jason shrugged and turned around. Before Jeffrey could place the ties on Jason's wrists, Mr. Marcello stepped into the foyer. With Jason in front of him, Jeffrey was able to drop the twist ties back into the bag unnoticed.

"So glad you could make it," Stephen said. "I had to take a call in my office." He shot out his hand.

Jason moved to the side as Jeffrey shook hands with his father.

"Easy drive up?" Stephen asked. "Easy to find?"

"Very easy. Your directions were perfect."

Stephen placed a hand on his son's shoulder. "What were you two up to?"

Jason playfully squirmed out from under the hand. "We were going to play an advanced version of Hide 'n' Seek."

"You were?" Stephen appeared surprised.

"An old trick I learned years ago," Jeffrey said. "You wanna play?" he asked Stephen in a child's voice.

"You two go ahead. I think I'll look in on Melissa and see how she's doing with dinner."

"It smells amazing, whatever it is," Jeffrey said.

"Roasted duck with an orange marmalade and soy sauce glaze. Melissa's version of it is simply delicious."

"Then I cannot wait for dinner."

"C'mon, Mr. Harris." Jason pulled lightly on his sleeve. "Let's play."

Jeffrey pretended to be pulled sideways and made an apologetic gesture to Stephen as the boy led him toward the stairwell. Little Jason seemed younger than his age. Like his mental growth had been stunted along the way.

"I'll be in the kitchen," Mr. Marcello said.

Then they were alone. Just the boy and his new father. About to play a game.

Jeffrey brought the white twist ties out of the bag again and held up two.

"Place these on first," he whispered.

"How?" Jason asked.

"Turn around. I'll do it."

Jason turned around and offered his hands to Jeffrey. One final look toward the alcove that led to the kitchen, then with deft hands, Jeffrey wrapped the boy's scrawny limbs tight and clamped the ties so nothing short of a pair of scissors could release them.

"Ouch," Jason cried. "Too tight."

"That's needed," Jeffrey whispered in Jason's ear.

He spun Jason around, walked him over and sat him down on the second stair. Jeffrey moved behind him.

"Hey, what are we doing?" Jason asked. "Aren't we going to play the game?"

"Soon. First, I have a game for your parents."

"You do?" Jason twisted his head as he tried to look at Jeffrey. "What kind of game? It better be good, because my parents don't play many games."

Jeffrey rifled through his gym bag until he came up with the

14

Magnum. It was the deadliest weapon in the bag and one he had never been forced to use. He removed four more twist ties and two ball gags, then placed everything on the stair beside him.

"Oh, they'll play this one. It's a family game called The Gathering."

"How do you play that?" Jason asked.

"You'll see."

He was ready. The safety on the gun was off. Twist ties beside him. Gym bag open. Child secure. Reading glasses high on the bridge of his nose. All was well in the family that he was about to make his own. Now he just needed the parents so he could begin the game.

So he could make them his family.

"Mr. and Mrs. Marcello," he called. "Could I see you out here a moment?" He leaned down to whisper in Jason's ear. "You're going to love this part."

CHAPTER FOUR

Jake dropped Kirk off at his car behind the O.P.P. building and drove home, the image of the Maytag man's face scrawled on his mind the entire way.

Cindy's car was in the driveway. He pulled up behind it and cut the engine. In the silence that followed—except for the intermittent tick from the cooling engine—Jake thought about their upcoming honeymoon.

The wedding was planned for the end of March. They would fly to Rome immediately after the ceremony. For two weeks, they would tour Rome, Pompeii and Venice. Since Jake didn't have his parents around and Cindy's dad had died years ago, the entire cost of the wedding and the honeymoon was coming out of Jake's pocket. That cost had ballooned, but he'd agreed to go forward with it as this would be his only wedding.

The bank had the paperwork for a second mortgage on the house but he had to wait until the end of the week to learn if it would be approved.

If it wasn't, there would be no honeymoon until after the summer, possibly September or October. There just wasn't enough money in law enforcement. After living expenses, there was enough left to live comfortably and go on vacation once a year. But a large wedding with a hundred guests and a honeymoon was simply too much to tackle all at once without a little help from the bank.

How would he break the news to Cindy if the loan wasn't approved? The biggest dilemma he faced was whether or not he should tell her now or wait until he heard from the bank. If they approved his request, there was no reason to worry her.

But what about full disclosure? He'd never kept anything from her in the past. This was a big deal. This was her wedding, her honeymoon, as much as his. Yet she hadn't been brought in on the small details, like whether or not they were even going to Italy.

He opened the car door, the cool November air rushing against his face. He shivered as he headed for the front of the house.

Cindy should know. He had to tell her. They could learn the bank's position on Friday together. She'd understand. It was only fair. The policy of truth had to always trump any debate he had on whether he should talk to Cindy or not. She was going to be his wife. If they couldn't handle something as trivial as money now, how would they handle terrible news from a doctor later in life?

Athina, their German Shepherd, bounded toward him as he stepped inside, tongue hanging out the side of her mouth. Athina had been in the K-9 Unit before she'd retired with full honors to live out her life with Jake and Cindy. She was a good dog, well-trained, and kept watch over the house, but her eyesight was fading. It pained Jake to watch Athina deteriorate. After all the service she had given the department, the least he could do was love her until the end.

Once Athina had moved in with them, Cindy had grown even more attached than Jake as she was the one who spent the most amount of time with her. It made Jake's heart swell to watch Athina lope around the house, following Cindy wherever she went, sleeping at her feet. But Athina recognized Jake as the alpha, which afforded Jake a different kind of love, even though he was home less than Cindy.

Two large front paws connected with Jake's chest as Athina

jumped up and tried to lick his face. Her past police training wasn't always evident when excitement took over.

"Okay, girl." Jake wrapped his arms around her and knelt down. "Daddy's got you."

Cindy stepped out of her home office where she designed knitting patterns for magazines. She'd been doing this off and on for years, until suddenly two years back, her work had gotten noticed and *Vogue*, along with a few other publications—Jake couldn't always keep them straight—had called upon her for sweater and scarf designs, and socks that could handle stone floors. Scandinavian wool had come in last week for that project.

"Hey honey," Cindy hugged his neck while Athina dropped back to all fours. "Missed you. Late night calls?"

"Is that wine I smell?"

"Red." She kissed him, long and hard. "Want some?"

He nodded, staring at her eyes, then her lips.

She kissed him again, easing her tongue out. He tasted the wine immediately. Then she pulled back.

"There," she said. "You just got some."

"I thought maybe I'd use a glass, you know. Although the method you chose works just as well."

She turned and stomped to the kitchen. When she looked over her shoulder, he caught the glint in her eye. She loved to toy with him. There was no denying its effectiveness.

By the time he'd hung up his jacket, she was back with a goblet half full of red. He followed her into her office, which consisted of an easy chair for her knitting, a TV where she watched her tutorials, and a drafting table where she planned and created her designs.

"That Scandinavian wool working out for you?" he asked.

"You remembered," she cooed. "I love that about you, Jake Wood. You listen."

"What else is a future husband supposed to do? A man needs

to be a good listener."

She held up her wine and they clinked glasses. They drank. Should he tell her or wait until Friday when he would know if the loan was approved? In his heart, he felt she needed to know, but didn't want to cause undue worry.

"I love the sound of those words," Cindy said. She dropped into her easy chair. "Future husband." She stared off into space, lost in thought, a blank expression on her face. "We're getting married in four months and we're going on the best trip of our lives." She blinked, then faced him. "Remember, I want to tour all the knitting stores in Rome I can find. At least two per day." She waved a dismissive hand. "Don't worry. I'll research them and plan it into our daily itinerary. All you'll have to do is join me."

"Looking forward to it," Jake said, watching her from the door. He realized in that moment he wouldn't say a thing until Friday. He just couldn't. When he knew whether they were going or not, that would be when she would know.

"And Jake, don't worry. This isn't about me and what I do. This trip is our honeymoon. It'll be about us. I just want to visit a few stores, see how they do it over there."

"I'm looking forward to it, too. When I think about you wandering through a knitting store, touching everything, I see myself wandering through a large bookstore, touching all the books. That's passion. I love that about you."

"As I love that about you," Cindy whispered.

She set her glass aside and got up from her chair. In two steps, she stood in front of him, her hands on the top button of his shirt. The image of the Maytag man's face flashed in his mind and he blinked. Cindy stopped.

"You okay?" she asked.

"Yeah. Just work. And Luke."

"Luke?" She continued unbuttoning his shirt, then stopped.

"What about Luke?"

"You remember he asked me to join him?"

"In Brazil?" Cindy took a step back.

Jake nodded. "Did he call today?"

She shook her head. "Isn't he working for that ultra secret company up north or something?"

"Fortech Industries. And they're not ultra secret, per se, they just handle government contracts."

"Which means top secret. Anyway, what about Luke?"

"I hadn't given him an answer yet."

"We have the money?"

It was Jake's turn to ease back. With the wedding coming, how much did she know about his money situation?

"Luke offered to pay for everything. Three days in Brazil, then back."

"You want to go?" she asked.

"Not really. But I got from Luke that he wanted me to. More like, he needed me to. And I owe him."

Cindy stepped back inside his personal space and placed her hands on his shirt. "Let me help you with that," she said, without waiting for a reply. "I have an idea. I think I can get your mind off work with what I have planned."

"I'm sure you can."

She opened his shirt. He sipped from his glass, feeling a little guilty that she didn't know their exact financial situation. He should've told her. She needed to know that a second mortgage was necessary. Even after their honeymoon, his mortgage payments would increase for a while. How would she handle that?

His pants opened at the waist. Cindy slid them down past his knees, then stopped at the ankles. His libido hadn't responded yet, but he was sure she could change that soon enough.

As she opened her mouth and applied it to him where he stood in the doorway of her home office, she proved him right. After a minute, he lifted her off the floor and carried her to their bedroom where they moved rhythmically until they finished together, their fingers entwined in a tight grasp, skin glistening in the nightlight by the bed.

"I love you, Jake Wood," she whispered in his ear as he lay spent on top of her. "I will always love you."

Somewhere in the house, Athina barked once.

CHAPTER FIVE

Stephen and Melissa Marcello emerged from the alcove by the front foyer and stopped when they saw their son sitting on the stairs in front of Jeffrey, Jason's hands behind his back.

"Glad you could join us," Jeffrey said. He raised the .357 Magnum so they could see it, but kept it behind Jason, out of his line of sight. "We're going to play a little game."

Melissa gasped and held a hand over her mouth. She stepped toward her son, but Stephen grabbed her arm and steadied her. His face had hardened, turned to stone, awash in an angry red. Classic case of a hysterical mother and a thinking, planning father. Jeffrey had seen it several times.

"My baby," Melissa called out. "Don't touch my baby."

"We're going to play a game," Jason pleaded in his good-natured voice. "It's okay, Mom." He tried to turn around to look at Jeffrey, but Jeffrey stopped him. "It's okay, right, Mr. Harris?"

"Of course, Jason," Jeffrey said. "It's just a little game. Everything will be fine if your parents are interested in playing along."

Melissa looked down at the plastic booties on his shoes by the door, then met Jeffrey's eyes.

"What do you want us to do?" Stephen asked.

Jeffrey dug in his bag and pulled out a handful of twist ties. He threw them toward the Marcellos. Then he took off his glasses and set them on the stairs beside him, careful to keep the gun handy while doing so.

"Put the twist ties on Mr. Marcello. Wrists and ankles. Do this, and nothing happens with Jason. He doesn't disappear like in Hide 'n' Seek. He doesn't go away." Jeffrey waved the gun behind Jason's head. "That's how this game starts."

Melissa's eyes moved from the plastic twist ties to her husband, then back again.

"It's okay, honey," Stephen said. He offered her his wrists. "Go ahead. Do what he says."

"You'll need to be on the floor," Jeffrey added. "Otherwise you'll fall when she does your ankles."

Jason looked over his shoulder. "How will he look for us if he can't walk?"

"Remember, this is an adult version of Hide 'n' Seek called The Gathering. They're setting up the gathering part."

"Ohhh," Jason moaned as he turned back.

Mrs. Marcello tentatively picked up the plastic twist ties, then dropped one as her hands shook uncontrollably. Mr. Marcello nodded for her to do it as he got down on the floor and lay on his back. It took her a minute to secure his ankles and wrists. They were tight, but not tight enough to cut off circulation.

"Very good. Now, Melissa, do your own ankles."

Melissa stood and faced him. "No way. Let Jason come to me first."

"Honey," Stephen cut in. "Just do as he says."

Jeffrey waved the gun by Jason's head. "A lot of parents would go above and beyond for their kids. It's true. I know this. What I also know is that parents will do anything to save their child's life." Jeffrey set the gun on the stair beside him and pulled the Taser out of his bag. "This isn't a negotiation. The plan is mine and it is created with everyone in mind. The plan is not to be changed in any way. Are we clear?"

"Let him go," Melissa stammered. Her lower lip quivered and her whole body shook. Tears bubbled up on her lower eyelids and dropped off her cheeks, lost to gravity.

"As soon as your ankles are secure."

Melissa tossed aside the twist tie. "No deal. Let him go."

Jeffrey brought the Taser to Jason's neck. "Last chance."

Jason stomped a foot, not knowing how close he was to being tasered. "C'mon Mom. Play along. It'll be fun."

"Listen to your boy."

Melissa leapt from where she stood and ran for Jason.

Jeffrey pushed the button. Jason jerked and seized in front of him. The second the volts took over Jason's small body, Jeffrey dropped the Taser and picked up the Magnum.

Jason fell away from the stairs and landed on the floor, his body wracked with spasms. His mother dropped to her knees beside her son and pleaded for it to stop.

Jeffrey stood and placed the muzzle of the Magnum against her temple.

"Don't," Stephen yelled from the other side of the foyer.

"Get up," Jeffrey ordered.

"Shoot me," Melissa shouted. "Or let me tend my son."

Jeffrey shrugged, none of this bothering him in the slightest. Each family resisted in some way as he tried to make them his own. He liked a tough mother figure.

"Fine, have it your way, but you have totally ruined the game."

He spun the gun around in his hand, drew it back, then slammed the butt of the weapon down against Melissa's temple. The woman collapsed like she'd been clipped by the corner of a freight train passing by. Sprawled out beside her son, her eyes fluttered, her body spasmed.

As Stephen muttered angry threats, Jeffrey put the gun back

on the stair and grabbed a small bottle from his bag. He opened the bottle and dabbed some of the liquid on a white cloth. Once the cloth was applied over Jason's mouth and nose, the boy went peacefully to sleep. He wet the cloth with more liquid, then held it over Melissa's mouth until her shuddering ceased.

"What's that?" Stephen asked.

"Chloroform. They'll be out until this is over."

"A blessing," Stephen said.

"Depends on your definition of a blessing."

"How's that?" Stephen asked as he struggled with the twist ties, grunting and moaning.

"It's hard to watch this," Jeffrey said to him. "I'll spare you the trouble. It's the least I could do for family."

Before leaving Melissa's side, he bound her ankles and wrists a little too tight. Then he tied Jason's ankles, too. With everyone tied up, secure, and asleep except for the father, the hard part was done. Always get the kid first. Once the kid was his, the parents would do anything he asked.

Most of the time.

Near the bottom of his bag of tricks, he found the ropes.

"We need to get you tied up before I finish here and leave." He walked over to Stephen as the man squirmed like a worm on a hook.

Jeffrey made a loop with the rope and wrapped it around Stephen's ankles. As Stephen protested and did a mockery of sit-ups trying to reach Jeffrey, Jeffrey dragged him into the large living room near the side of the staircase.

He changed direction and started up the stairs, keeping the rope over the railing while Stephen stayed on the level below. With each step, Stephen's ankles lifted higher until the man was on his back, feet and legs pulling him upward. Then Stephen was on his shoulders, and finally the tip of his head. At last, Stephen was suspended upside down and bucking like a hooked fish against the wall below the banister. That was where, with as much strength as Jeffrey could muster, he tied the rope to the thickest post. Stephen faced the wall below, his back exposed. Once Jeffrey had checked the rope and was certain Stephen couldn't escape, he returned to the foyer to deal with his new son.

Jeffrey grabbed a pair of scissors from his bag and clipped a lock of Jason's hair. After zipping the hair into a plastic baggie and stuffing the baggie in his gym bag, he grabbed Jason's feet and dragged him to his bedroom down the hall. When he was done with the boy and had taken his memento, Jeffrey took Melissa, his new wife, by the ankles and dragged her into the kitchen.

"What are you doing?" Stephen yelled from where he hung from the banister.

"Preparing for The Gathering," Jeffrey yelled back. "Just wait. Your turn is coming."

"What are you going to do with us?"

Jeffrey expelled an exasperated sigh. "Enough questions. I'm making you my family."

He headed back to his bag. The wound on the side of Melissa's head had bled a little, leaving traces on the floor. Since it was the mother's blood, it wouldn't connect him to this house when forensics did their cleaning.

After pulling the plastic sheets out of the side pocket of his bag and unfolding them, Jeffrey grabbed the scissors. Back in the kitchen, he laid the sheets on the linoleum floor beside his new wife. He cut off her shirt and pants, then rolled her naked body onto the plastic.

"Now, for my official taking of the female of the house."

"Don't do it," Stephen shouted, his voice strained, pleading. "You don't have to do this."

Jeffrey looked over his shoulder, even though Stephen

couldn't see him from here. "It's how I take a family. Don't worry, your turn is coming."

When he was done with his new wife, he got to his feet and admired his work. "There, all mine," he said between breaths.

It was Mr. Marcello's turn.

Jeffrey went to his bag and snatched the hammer and the small ax. The final moment was upon him. He would collect the rest of his mementos and do the cleanup with gasoline wherever he'd touched a surface, acid wherever he'd left any of his bodily fluids. The plastic under his new wife would collect whatever DNA he'd left behind. Being completely hairless went a long way in reassuring him that taking a family would never be his undoing. If anything, this episode would continue to baffle the authorities as it had for over a decade.

Back at Mr. Marcello's side, watching him struggle and sway upside down, Jeffrey found his peace. It was in this moment he felt the most clarity. This was the final act of making a family his. The final moment when the soul of the family was captured, the necessary rendition of this Gathering.

Jeffrey slipped the scissors inside the neck of Stephen's shirt and cut upward toward the man's waist while Stephen squirmed.

"What are you going to do?" Stephen shouted, his voice heavy, thicker. He bucked against the wall and tried to worm his way out of Jeffrey's grasp.

"It's a small procedure the Vikings used to do about a thousand years ago. It'll prove painful and may paralyze you if you're moving around like that. Just hold still. It won't take long."

Stephen pushed, bucked hard, and swung away from the wall.

"I had a feeling you'd be like this," Jeffrey said, disappointed. "I'm going to do it anyway."

With the father's shirt stripped from his back, Jeffrey lowered the tip of the ax until it touched the vertebrae by Stephen's waist.

He applied pressure to the spine and dragged the blade of the ax downward in a straight line, splitting Stephen's skin open. At the shoulder blades, he stopped, the skin split all the way now.

Stephen roared in pain but stopped struggling. His neck arched in a way that didn't look natural as he bellowed. The gash had to have gone an inch deep. Blood oozed out the entire length, running down Stephen's neck, met his hair where it disappeared briefly, and then reappeared as it dripped on the floor. The blood had rushed to his head, his bloodshot eyes bulging.

"This'll only hurt for a few seconds. Then the pain will end."

"Why?" Stephen asked, his voice soft now, almost as if he was sleepy.

The roasted duck must be burning in the oven. The smell in the air had changed. He would have to remember to turn the oven off before he left. Wouldn't want the house to burn down.

"No more questions," Jeffrey said. "Your family is mine for the taking."

"You won't get away with this."

"I always do."

"God is watching."

Jeffrey stopped and looked down at the back of Mr. Marcello's head, contemplating what he had just said, the ax in one hand, its tip red with Stephen's blood.

He knelt to be close to the father of the house and whispered. "There is no God. Religion is man-made. Even the Bible is a bunch of lies. How would a man named Jesus find men in the Middle East named Simon, Paul, Matthew, Andrew, James, and John? The Bible is an archaic criminal and moral code. Someone found it and said, 'Hey, got a new religion here.' Well, it's all bullshit." Jeffrey leaned in closer. "There is no God. If there were, why make people like me?"

Jeffrey placed the ax blade inside the cut in Stephen's back,

28

making sure it was just right. Then he raised the hammer and brought it down on the back of the ax to complete his masterpiece.

When he had finished the Viking Blood Eagle on Stephen's body, The Gathering was complete. He cleaned all traces of his presence throughout the house, even remembering to turn the oven off.

As he left the Marcello house with his mementos, his new family, and the soul of the Marcellos along with it, he had a spring in his step. He couldn't be happier. New pictures, new memories, and a new lease on life. His extended family would be so happy for him.

Jeffrey Harris was a new man and he would stay that way for a while.

At least for two years.

CHAPTER SIX

Jake Wood rolled over to cuddle his fiancée, but she wasn't there. Instead he was greeted with the smell of bacon and eggs, and Athina at his feet. The large shepherd moaned when Jake bumped his foot against her.

"Sorry, bud."

He stared at the bedroom ceiling and blinked sleep away. Dreams had assaulted him through the night. After dealing with dead bodies, his dreams were of a dark, brooding nature. They would last a few days then wane. It was part and parcel of being a homicide detective. Seven years since his transfer to the Orillia detachment and the dreams still came, murder scene after murder scene.

He rubbed his face and rolled out of bed.

Disturbed, Athina bounded off and ran out of the room, dog tags clanging as she hustled down the stairs.

"I gotta use the toilet, too," Jake said.

Once he was dressed and had splashed water on his face, he made his way downstairs to the kitchen. At the table, Cindy was pouring coffee into his cop mug, a large black cup with O.P.P. stenciled at the top and Naughty by Nature written below.

"Morning," he mumbled and moved to kiss her cheek.

She angled her head and accepted the kiss with a smile.

"What makes you so cheery today?" he asked. "Spill the beans.

Let me in on it so I can be happy, too."

Cindy placed the coffeepot back and grabbed a plate off the counter which brimmed with eggs, bacon, and toast already buttered.

"You. Last night."

"You must think I'm hungry." Jake snatched up his fork. "That's a lot of grub."

"You're always hungry," she teased and lunged in for a short peck on his cheek.

He jammed eggs in his mouth and bit off the tip of a piece of bacon. With a full mouth, he asked, "What about me last night?"

She sat in the chair across from him, her grin wide enough to show teeth. Something was obviously making her too jolly for the early hour.

"Tossing and turning in your sleep—"

"And that's funny?" he gasped in mock frustration. "My nightmares amuse you?"

"After you calmed a bit and I was about to fall back to sleep, we were spooning."

"Okay," he said between mouthfuls. "I'm following the story but not the humor."

"Your hips." She raised her coffee cup—pictures of kittens on it—and sat back in her chair.

He stopped chewing and stared at her. "Gyrating again?"

She nodded, that smile of hers wider somehow.

"In my sleep?"

Another nod.

"Sorry." He resumed chewing.

"Don't be. It's cute."

"Whew. Close one. Thought I'd be in trouble there."

"Silly." She drank. "We're going to be married in a few months. You think that would bother me?"

The thought of the marriage, the honeymoon, and the cost of everything came back and turned his stomach. He sipped from his mug.

Worried she would see a change in him, he looked at her and smiled.

"What's wrong?" she asked.

"Nothing."

"Jake Wood." She leaned forward and rested on the table. "Tell me."

He took another bite of eggs and shrugged. "Just work."

"I mentioned the wedding. That caused the change."

He debated telling her about the second mortgage again. But how could he tell her there might not be a honeymoon? No trip to Rome. No fancy getaway. Everything could still be a go.

"A man was killed by a Maytag last night."

Cindy frowned. "A Maytag?"

Jake nodded and resumed eating. "Washing machine."

"How does someone get killed by a washing machine? And how does that relate to our wedding?"

Jake set his fork down. "When you mentioned marriage, my thoughts went to the wife I had to talk to last night. She's married. To the dead man. It had no relation, really. Just, you know, I deal with so much death and crime every day, how is it possible we could be so happy?"

Cindy studied his face a moment too long, then looked away. "I guess I can see the correlation." She drank the last of her coffee. "A Maytag?"

"Yeah. Some idiot put the washing machine above the dryer. The shelf gave way and pinned the old man against the wall, under the machine. The weight was just too much. Ruled an accidental death."

"Is that what you dreamed about last night?" she asked.

He nodded. "Probably. Don't remember though."

"You never do."

He scooped up the last of the eggs with a desire to finish eating and get in the shower. "Plans for the day?" he asked. Time to change the subject. They'd both know in a few days if the money would be there. No more pussyfooting around her after that.

"Knitting, knitting and more knitting. Oh, and a little designing. You know, the usual."

"It's barely eight in the morning. You're up early when you don't have to be."

"The only difference when running your own business is you get to *pick* the fifteen hours a day you work. I still work as much as everyone else. I still need to put the time in."

"True." He wiped his mouth. "I, on the other hand, have to report for duty whether or not there's another dead body."

"Lovely." She got up from the table and smacked his arm before taking his plate away. "You're always so chipper in the morning discussing your macabre job."

"Macabre job? Really?" He acted stunned, like she'd offended him. "I solve crimes and put bad guys in jail where they're supposed to be so people like you are safe to sleep in their beds at night."

"Okay, Colonel Jessup. Got it. While I'm knitting, you're on the wall and I can't handle the truth." She lowered her voice and recited Jack Nicholson's lines. "You want the truth? You can't handle the truth." Then she laughed.

Under normal circumstances, he would get up, wrap her in his arms, and kiss her until she protested. But this morning, he wondered if she was hinting at *his* untruth. There was no way she could know about the second mortgage. The house was in his name. He'd gone to the bank on his own time. On Friday when the money was approved, he'd tell her everything and the honeymoon would be on. If the money didn't come through, he'd tell her everything and they'd work together to make things right.

It was that look she'd given him, though. That extra pause. Then the quote about truth from a favorite movie of theirs.

The other possibility was he was reading into it too much.

Cindy bent to wipe the table with a cloth, still smiling. Jake smiled along with her, feeling like a shmuck. Money problems stressed her out. He was doing her a favor by excluding her until he knew the results. At least that's what he told himself when he chose not to say anything.

His cell rang upstairs. Athina barked from the front door.

"Gotta get that," Jake said as he ran for the phone.

It rang four times before he seized it from inside his jacket on the closet door.

"Wood here."

"Morning, partner."

"Hey, Kirk. What's up?"

"Bodies."

"Bodies? As in more than one?"

"Three."

"What? Where?"

"Farmhouse. Outskirts of town. It's bad, Jake."

He plopped on the edge of the bed, bouncing twice. "How bad?"

Cindy entered the room and stopped, concern on her face.

"A whole family."

"Directions," Jake said, his voice granite-like.

Kirk told him where to go. Jake showered, dressed, and exited without a kiss goodbye from Cindy. His mind was on other things. Like what his nightmares would be like tonight.

A whole family?

"Fuck me," he mumbled under his breath as he ran for his car, the cold November air chilling him to the bone.

CHAPTER SEVEN

As Jake drove up to the Marcello farmhouse, he counted at least a dozen cars parked out front, scrambled in disarray. There were so many emergency vehicles, they obscured Kirk's car. Jake parked for an easy exit.

The sun peeked between soft, fluffy clouds, but did nothing for the chill he felt. After all the years of dealing with dead bodies, it never got any easier. The only thing that changed was the job, the paperwork, the investigation, the court room testimonies. But seeing more dead bodies, especially two in two days, would cause a week's worth of nightmares.

Kirk had said this was an entire family. Three people murdered. Grotesque fashion. The morning eggs and bacon Cindy had prepared weren't sitting well.

As he strode across the lawn, he watched two horses running around behind a fence, agitated by all the people and vehicles. They would've never seen this much activity unless the Marcellos threw large Christmas parties.

After he examined the bodies, he would see if he could calm the horses down a little. Officer Tammy Feltz met him at the front door.

"Need you to sign in," she said.

Jake took the pen from her and hesitated before signing. He always liked to scan the names of the people who'd trekked through his crime scene before him. Maybe an officer from another detachment was here, trying to snatch his case from him or connect it to another.

To make the pause less obvious, he tried to sign in the wrong spot on purpose.

"Not there," Officer Feltz said. "Here."

She pointed at the empty spot below the last name.

"How did I not see that?" Jake said jokingly.

He signed his full name and added the time and date as per his Tissot watch. Kirk Aiken had signed in just over an hour earlier. Two hours before that, Detective Keri Joslin had signed in. Joslin was from the Toronto detachment. He'd worked with her on a few cases a decade ago. They'd never gotten along.

The first signature was two and a half hours ago.

He handed the pen back to Officer Feltz and stared out at the vehicles scattered in front of the Marcello farmhouse, sunlight reflecting off the roofs. Two and a half hours ago, the authorities had begun to show up. How had Joslin, out of the Toronto detachment, gotten here that quickly? Her home and office were over an hour's drive away.

A crime scene lab tech walked out and kicked his booties off.

Whose crime scene was this, then? Geographically, it was his. Unless it was connected to other ongoing cases. Then it could be whoever was deemed in charge.

He donned booties and gloves offered by Officer Feltz, who also handed him a small vial of Vick's VapoRub for under his nose.

"You might want this," she said. "The smell."

"Fresh bodies or stale?" he asked.

"Fresh. I've been at my post for over two hours, but someone said time of death was last night."

"Then why the vapor rub? It shouldn't be too bad yet."

"Take it anyway. You decide for yourself."

Something in Officer Feltz's expression warned him not just about the smell, but what he was about to see. It was probably something he would never be able to un-see.

"Detective Wood," a woman shouted from inside the house. "So glad you could join us."

He stepped up to the door and looked inside. Detective Joslin stood beside his partner, Kirk. She had a half smile pasted on her face. The kind of smirk that preceded a belittling remark about one's attitude or lack of taste in clothing. He hated that look. It occurred to him that was probably the reason they had never gotten along well. Professionalism aside, Detective Joslin was not someone he worked with willingly. She was crass, rude in a tell-it-like-it-is way. No soft edges. But she was one of the best detectives Ontario had ever seen and everyone in law enforcement knew it.

"What have we got here?" Jake asked, addressing his partner.

"What we have here," Joslin said in a raised voice, "is a failure to communicate." A few of the crime scene techs turned her way. They were local. She wasn't.

"How's that?" Jake asked. "Seems to me you're a long way from home."

Just inside the Marcello farmhouse front door and he couldn't see a single body yet. To the left behind a stairwell banister, a congregation of techs swabbed something. Other techs roamed in and out of the kitchen and several EMTs came down the hall that probably led to the bedrooms.

"Jake Wood," Joslin said, slowly swiveling her head back and forth, an appearance of distaste in her eyes.

"*Detective* Jake Wood," he said. "Orillia detachment. You're stomping around on my crime scene. You want to tell me why? Actually, what I would love to know is how you're one of the first officers on the scene when this farmhouse is at least an hour and a half from your office." Throw her off balance. Offer her no quarter.

Run roughshod over her before she could corner him and take the case.

"I will do you the courtesy of answering your questions." Joslin moved closer to him, her face masked in amusement. "We received the call when an early morning paperboy came by to drop the newspaper off and the front door was sitting wide open. The boy wandered in and discovered the bodies. The responding officer recognized the murder scene for what it is and called Toronto. They called me."

"Why would he do that? What does that even mean?"

"Just listen to her, Jake," Kirk said. "Let her have the case. You don't want this one with the wedding coming up."

"What? Why?"

Joslin said, "I had the authorities up here post an officer at the front door until I could get here."

"You haven't answered the most important question yet." He stepped aside to let two lab techs squeeze by, his anger brewing. He hated the politics of the job. The jurisdictional bullshit. Geography played a role in his job and this was his territory. That was one of the reasons he'd left the Toronto detachment all those years ago: to get away from people like Joslin and their bullshit. How could she not see they were all on the same side?

"I have been granted the authority to take this case as it pertains to other known cases from previous years. Cases I'm lead detective on." She scrunched up her face and sneered like a little girl who wouldn't give him back his candy. "Safe to conclude this is now my case, irregardless of geography."

"Irregardless? Don't you mean, regardless?"

She offered him a blank stare.

He let the nonstandard word go as it all came together quick in his head. "You're saying the Marcello family killer has done this before? And you know this already? In all of two hours?"

Detective Joslin nodded once, then turned away.

"Come," she said, waving her hand over her shoulder. An image of Meryl Streep's character in *The Devil Wears Prada* popped into his head. That was who Joslin reminded him of. "Follow me and you'll understand," she added.

Kirk leaned in close. "I'm warning you, man," he stammered under his breath. "Let it go. Give her the case without a fight. It's bad." His voice broke. "Steel yourself."

Jake frowned. What could be so bad that it unsettled Kirk? His partner had seen dozens of dead bodies in his time. Those who had been raped and mutilated. Kirk's warning only ramped up Jake's curiosity.

With each step into the farmhouse, something tickled his nose, like it was suddenly running. He sneezed twice rapidly. Stars hovered in his eyes for a brief moment.

"Hey, you okay?" Kirk placed a hand on his shoulder.

"Yeah. Fine." He took another step, then sneezed three times in succession.

"Whoa." Kirk was beside him. "Got a cold? Allergies?"

"Don't contaminate my crime scene," Joslin yelled from beside the staircase.

Jake wiped his nose with the back of his gloved hand. "Don't have allergies that I'm aware of. It's nothing. Just something in the air."

Detective Joslin was staring at him. "You coming?"

She acted like he'd delayed her on purpose, as if she hadn't heard him sneezing. Without answering, he made his way around the base of the stairs and looked at the body hanging upside down from the banister.

"The father," Joslin said, emotionless. Maybe she was the better detective for this case after all.

"What happened to his back?" Jake asked, happy his voice

didn't betray how he felt on the inside.

"It's called a Blood Eagle."

Jake glanced at Kirk first, then Joslin. "*This* is the work of the Blood Eagle Killer?"

"You've heard of him?"

"There've been rumors that he's tied to the Orangeville, King City, Hastings, and Bowmanville murders. Haven't these cases been going on for quite a few years?"

Joslin stared at the suspended body. "And now Orillia," she said, ignoring his question. Since she was lead detective, and the case was ongoing, recognizing the length of time would embarrass her.

Jake stepped back to allow a tech dusting for prints to ease by him. It gave him a moment to breathe and collect himself.

"What happened to him?" he asked again. "Why the Blood Eagle?"

"He's an invisible killer," Joslin said.

It was as if she were in her own world, not listening to a word Jake said. He turned to Kirk who shrugged. He felt another sneeze coming on.

"Invisible because we can never gather a single DNA sample from the house he performs in," Joslin continued. "There are never any witnesses and he travels within a geographical radius of one-hundred-fifty kilometers from downtown Toronto." Joslin faced Jake. "That leaves us with an extremely large number of people to sift through. He wears gloves, caps, masks, the whole enchilada. The hunter—"

"Wait," Jake cut in. "Hunter?"

"Detective Wood, the man I seek is a hunter first, killer second. He deems his subjects as prey. Then he takes the family, soul and all."

"The family? Where are the other bodies?"

Joslin nodded somberly. "Before we leave the father's body, I'll explain the Blood Eagle." She pointed at the exposed vertebra. "With a sharp knife, the killer cuts the skin along the spine. Then he severs the rib bones on either side, detaching them from the center and spreads them apart as he's done here." Joslin waved a hand beside the ribcage that had been pulled back, exposing the man's chest cavity. "He then reaches in"—she emulated the performance with both hands squeezing, pretending to grasp— "takes a hold of each lung"—she snapped a look at Jake, then turned back to the corpse— "and forces the lungs out of the body to place them on the exposed ribs where they flutter with the dying man's last breath."

Unexpectedly, Jake sneezed violently. He reached for his partner and found his forearm as another sneeze took hold.

"Turn away," Joslin yelled. "Don't contaminate my crime scene."

After another sneeze, he wiped his nose with his arm and gathered himself.

"What's this Blood Eagle signify?" Jake asked, his voice taking on a nasally tone.

"The taking of the enemy's soul. The bones and skin are pulled outward to give the appearance of wings. The lungs flutter until they stop, offering a semblance of wings attempting to give flight. The victim is unconscious while the bones are being pulled back due to the blood loss and pain. Our killer suspends his victims to simulate flight." Joslin stepped back from the body. "It's an ancient Viking ritual that some dispute actually ever happened. Whether it did or didn't, it's happening now."

"Why is the killer after his soul?"

"He's stealing the family."

"How do you know that? Is the father the only dead body and the rest are kidnapped?"

"No. All dead."

"How does he steal the family then?"

"Come. I'll show you."

Jake followed Joslin to the kitchen where a naked woman lay on the linoleum. More white-coated crime scene techs worked on her.

"The mother. If she's the same as in the previous cases, she has died of compression asphyxiation. Our hunter uses chloroform to subdue and then applies pressure to the woman's diaphragm so it can't move, making it impossible to take on air. She dies as if someone is choking her."

"What happened to her crotch?" Jake asked, a part of him not wanting to know.

"Our killer has sex with the corpse, then cleans out her insides with acid to leave no forensic clues." She turned to face him, her eyes roving between Jake and Kirk. "Our killer is invisible. At least that's how we've perceived him since he started. His semen would be all we need. But not this madman. We go over the bedsheets, the corpse, underwear, clothing, the floor, anywhere a tiny drop of semen could be left behind." She blew out an exaggerated huff. "Never a single drop of DNA is left at the scene. Not even a hair."

"How is this possible?"

"He is careful. Very careful. Probably does his deed on a bed of plastic and takes it with him. The acid ruins any evidence. The autopsies of all of the females have always come back without any semen available."

More tickling in his nose. He gripped his nostrils to suppress the sneeze.

"The son is in his bedroom," Joslin continued. "Compression asphyxiation as well."

"Nothing else?" Jake asked, hoping the boy wasn't tortured in some way. "I mean, he didn't do anything vulgar to the boy?"

"He killed him. That's horrid. Also, he's missing a lock of hair." Joslin shrugged, a hardened air about her now. Maybe the job made her the way she was. Maybe, deep down inside, she was a good woman, burnt out by the job, her psyche down for the count.

"Hair?"

"The killer steals the father's soul, simulates having a baby with the mother, and takes a lock of hair from the children in the home. In this case there was only one child. In the other homes, he kills all the children in the same fashion. Then he steals the wedding rings from the parents and leaves nothing behind for us. Ever."

A man stepped into the kitchen and nodded at Joslin. He seemed too calm for the setting. Like he was entering the room to let them know dinner would be served in five minutes. The eyes of a professional who dealt with death daily, nine to five. The bald man wore a white lab coat and gloves and waited to get Joslin's attention.

"Jake, meet our resident medical examiner, coroner and whatever I need him to be, Dr. Gavin."

They shook hands.

"Dr. Gavin handles all the bodies in this case for me. We thought it would be better to keep everything in-house once we saw a pattern forming at the second crime scene years ago."

"Been doing it since the Reilly family in Hastings back in 2008."

Jake sneezed twice before he could stop himself. He needed Kleenex and he needed out of this house. Something was definitely bothering him. He hadn't sneezed this much in a long time, if ever.

"Sounds like you're coming down with something, Detective," Gavin said.

"Might be." Jake's voice sounded like it was coming out of his nose.

"We're done here," Joslin said. "We can continue outside."

Jake nodded at Officer Feltz, who still guarded the front door as he walked by her.

"You doing okay?" Kirk asked as they approached the fence.

"Yeah." Jake placed a hand on Kirk's shoulder. "Just something in the air. Bothering my nose something awful."

"I'll expect your full cooperation on this case," Joslin said as she came up to them.

He was beyond fighting with her. If there was anything he could do to help catch the Blood Eagle Killer, he would do it without pause. A killer like that didn't deserve to be free, out there on the streets with the rest of society. He didn't deserve to live.

"You will have access to our full resources." Another sneeze overwhelmed him. He cleared his throat and sniffled. "How often does this hunter strike?"

"About every two years."

"There's your window. Catch this guy in that time frame before another family has this done to them."

"We're doing everything we can. Right, Gavin?"

The M.E. nodded. "Absolutely. We'll scour for any signs of DNA that doesn't belong to the family. I will personally conduct the autopsies. We won't miss anything, I assure you. We'll catch him this time."

"I'd stake my career on it," Joslin added.

"You might have to," Jake countered. "A decade of murder and not a single suspect. This could end up like the Ripper, or the Zodiac Killer."

Joslin leaned in close, saw he was about to sneeze again, then reared back. "It'll never happen," she said. "I'll catch the asshole who's doing this. Before he strikes again. He's human. He'll make a mistake. He has to."

Jake sneezed so violently that he gagged. Kirk held him up as Detective Joslin trudged across the lawn, her medical examiner heading back into the house.

Jake ambled toward the fence. One of the horses, a gorgeous shiny brown specimen with beautiful eyes, trotted over.

Jake collapsed in a fit of sneezing and coughing until Kirk shouted something. Before he could stop his partner, Kirk asked for the ambulance guys loading up their equipment four cars over to come tend to him.

"It's okay—" Jake sneezed. "It's just a cold or"—another sneeze— "something in the air."

"Fuck that," Kirk said matter-of-factly. "You're all red around the neck and I think that's hives breaking out on your face."

"What?" Jake managed to get to his feet. "Hives?"

What the hell was happening to him? Why a sudden violent reaction to this house? If it was something in the air, how come no one else appeared to be sneezing?

Two paramedics ran up. "What have we got here?" the man on the right asked.

"My partner can't stop sneezing and he's breaking out in hives and a rash."

"Sir?" the paramedic leaned down to Jake. "Can you hear me?"

Jake nodded as he let go of the fence and dropped to the ground. The horse whinnied behind him.

"Sir, do you have any allergies that you're aware of?"

Jake shook his head, then sneezed again, a headache already started.

"Sir, do you suffer from asthma?"

"He doesn't," Kirk answered for him.

Jake shut his eyes and focused on his breathing, which seemed shallow, difficult.

Is my throat closing? Like what happens to people with a bee sting?

"Get the Epi-pen," Jake overheard the paramedic say to his partner. "Fast."

His nose was clogged now. He breathed through his mouth, but that proved more and more difficult. Everything itched, too.

Something cold touched his right ear. He jerked to the side and banged his head on the fence.

"Sorry, sir. Need to check your ears."

"For what?" Kirk asked. It sounded like his partner's voice was far away.

"Looking for fluid behind the eardrum. It tells me if this is an allergic reaction."

"Can't we do this in the hospital?" His partner, always standing up for him when he was down.

Then Jake went swimming. His consciousness floated out as if he was about to sleep and was already dreaming. In his semi-somnambulistic state, Jake felt his body being lifted, then carried. Frantic voices shouted at each other. Car doors slammed somewhere. A siren. Someone took his hand. A needle pierced his flesh.

The rest became a blur as he sank lower, breathing still a chore. Until it all stopped.

CHAPTER EIGHT

"**P**aging Dr. Clemens to the ER. Dr. Clemens to the ER."

Voices drifted in and out. Sounds and smells. Hospital smells. Heavy eyelids that refused to respond. Darkness, then light across the backs of his lids. Breathing rough, but easier now. Itching in several spots, but overall not as bad as mosquito bites.

Jake tried to pull himself up and out of the semi-conscious state, swimming higher until things around him were clearer, the sounds less filtered, crisper. Someone stood close by.

He was in a hospital. But why? Because he'd had a sneezing fit? And why was it so hard to wake up, open his eyes? Had he been drugged?

"He's coming to, doctor."

Cindy's soft voice. The voice of reason, understanding. His future wife. Happy she was nearby, he tried to smile.

Someone moved close to his side, their clothing brushing along his right hand. Something cold tapped his inner ear, then retreated. That same device edged in his right nostril, then retreated. He had enough strength to pull his head back at the intrusion.

Fluttering his lids, he opened his eyes slowly, then closed them. The light was too bright.

"Cindy?" he whispered.

"I'm here, baby." She wrapped a hand around the top of his

head as she came down close to his face. "I'm here."

Jake closed his eyes. "Where's here?"

"You're in the hospital."

"Why? Because I sneezed?"

She pulled away. "I'll let the doctor explain. He was just about to tell me everything anyway."

Jake opened his eyes until he could see the room well enough, then focused on the doctor, a pit of dread welling in his stomach.

"What happened to me? A tumor? A stroke?"

The doctor wore the proverbial white lab coat and had a thin, white beard. He reminded Jake of Sean Connery.

"I assure you it's nothing like that, Mr. Wood. As far as we can tell, anyway."

"Good, then I'm sure we can handle the news. Bring it on, Doc."

The doctor didn't appear to have a sense of humor. Not a single muscle moved in his face as he stared down at a clipboard in his hand.

Cindy stopped leaning on the bed. She stood beside him, her hand in his.

"Early results suggest you had an allergic reaction," the doctor said.

"That's all this was?" Jake asked. He looked from Cindy to the doctor again. "Bit violent to be just an allergic reaction. What am I allergic to?"

"Based on the skin test we did since you arrived, I suspect you have an allergy to horses. We pulled some blood and sent it off for a RAST test, but those results might take a few weeks."

"Horses? How could I be allergic to horses? That's weird."

The doctor set the clipboard on a hook and approached Jake. "It happens." He pointed at Jake's ears. "You have fluid in the ears, behind the eardrum. The pale, swollen mucus membranes in your nose also suggests allergies. You have allergic shiners in just a few short hours, too."

"What are allergic shiners? And what's a RAST test?"

The doctor checked his watch, then adjusted the sleeve of his white coat back over his wrist. "RAST stands for Radio Allergo Sorbent Test. Basically, they'll do this test on your blood to determine exactly what it is you're allergic to." He edged closer and pointed at Jake's eyes. "Allergic shiners are the dark circles under your eyes that are due to nasal congestion."

"It happened that fast?" Surprised, Jake stared at the doctor, then turned to look at Cindy who offered him a comforting smile.

"You've been here since this morning," Cindy said. "It's mid-afternoon. I was getting worried you wouldn't wake up."

"Your condition precipitated a response similar to asthma. A horse allergy is caused by a blood protein called albumin. It can cause urticaria, which are hives, angioedema, which is the swelling that accompanies hives, and anaphylaxis, which is a life-threatening reaction caused by your own body's defenses to the allergen."

"Which means what, exactly?"

"When your body produced the necessary histamines, leukotrienes and tryptase from mast cells—"

"In English, Doctor. I have no idea what you're saying."

He checked his watch again, then moved backwards a few steps. It was obvious he had to leave.

"Okay," the doctor said. "When your body began to fight the allergen, you had a shortness of breath, wheezing, sneezing and coughing. Your heart rate accelerated and you experienced low blood pressure, in addition to the itchy skin, hives and swelling. Next would've been nausea, vomiting, diarrhea, and abdominal cramps, but the attending paramedics got you away from the horses fast enough to avoid further symptoms." The doctor moved steadily toward the door. "We'll be checking you out of the hospital within the hour and sending you home with Zyrtec to help you handle the rest of the symptoms. You'll be fine as long as you stay away from horses."

Then the doctor disappeared out the door. Jake turned to Cindy.

"Who knew I'd be allergic to horses?" he asked. "That's insane."

"I know, baby. But now we know what it was. No horses for you."

Jake turned his gaze toward the hospital's ceiling. "It's funny. I can't remember a single time in my thirty-five years where I've been that close to horses."

"Makes sense. You would've had this reaction then and learned of your allergy years before."

Images of the crime scene came back to him. The Blood Eagle Killer. Detective Joslin.

He scanned the room. "Where's Kirk?"

Cindy looked at the door. "He's right—"

"Here," Kirk said as he stepped inside the room. "And the zombie wakes." He held two coffees and two muffins. "Had to run to the cafeteria." Kirk handed Cindy a coffee and a muffin.

"What happened with Joslin at the crime scene?" Jake asked.

"Wait," Cindy interrupted. "I'll step out while you two talk shop."

"Okay, honey. Don't go far. I want out of here."

Cindy took her coffee and muffin and headed for the door. When she was gone, Kirk closed the door and approached Jake's bed.

"Nothing happened with Joslin." Kirk shrugged and bit into his muffin. It looked like oatmeal. Jake was suddenly hungry. "Joslin walked away," Kirk added, his mouth full. "I got you in the ambulance and rode with you here, calling Cindy on the way. I know nothing else and don't want to know anything else. It's her case."

There was a moment of silence as Kirk finished his muffin.

"Ever see anything like that before?" Jake asked, images of the Marcello family bodies floating through his head.

Kirk studied his face for a moment, then walked over to the window. "Never. And hope I don't again."

"Me too."

Jake closed his eyes and scratched at an irritation on his arm. "Today we saw what madness can produce. It's contagious, like getting a cold. Witness the results of insanity enough and a sane mind could slip to the other side."

"Agreed," Kirk added, peeked at him over his shoulder, then continued looking out the window. "Reminds me of that murder in Toronto. The Bowling Alley case that we got assigned to."

"I remember," Jake said. "We never caught the guy."

"*We* didn't catch him, but he got caught through a DNA match while in prison."

"That's right. It's coming back to me." Jake tapped his chin. "This case does remind me of that. Brutal murders. Killer walks away and would've stayed gone if he didn't have an argument with his girlfriend and try to beat her to a pulp." Jake eyed his partner. "We have to treat this case like that one and not give up."

Kirk walked back to Jake. "Easy there, big guy. We're not treating this case any which way. This isn't our case."

"Joslin can't handle it alone. She's been lead on it since—what did she say, 2006?"

"Something like that."

"And the Blood Eagle Killer is still at large. The reason she said she would stake her career on finding him is because she is out of a job if he strikes again after this. No way she stays on as lead if she doesn't solve it now."

"So?" Kirk watched him suspiciously. "What are you saying? You want the case?"

"Why not? Talk to our old bosses in Toronto. Let them know we're interested. We have the experience and the knowledge of the terrain up here to handle this kind of case. Or at least to help in some capacity."

Kirk stepped away, switching his coffee from one hand to the other. "I don't know, bro. Too intense. It's not for me."

"What is then? A Maytag killer?"

Kirk spun around. He drank from his coffee, the slurping sound rather loud for the private room.

"Sorry," Jake said. "That was uncalled for."

"Yeah, it was. You're a dick. Always been a dick. But it's okay with me. I'll protect you from the world. If they knew how much of a dick you were, you wouldn't be able to survive out there with your dickness." Kirk laughed at his own humor.

"Hey, thanks. Happy to hear you've got my dickness covered."

"That's what partners are for?"

The door popped open and Cindy slipped into the room. "What are partners for?" she asked.

"Sickness," Jake said quickly. Probably too quickly. "You know? In case I get sick. I've got you and I've got Kirk when it's about the job."

Cindy turned to Kirk, who smiled wide and shrugged. The door opened behind Cindy.

Luke Mercer stepped inside. He nodded at Kirk, then stopped to hug Cindy.

"Luke," Jake said. "You're here? At this hospital?" He hadn't seen Luke in weeks. When he had taken the new job at Fortech Industries months ago, Luke had disappeared, no doubt staying quite busy.

"I heard you were brought in," Luke said, moving to the side of the bed. "Wanted to check the condition of my best friend."

"Horse allergy," Kirk said. "Can you believe it?"

Luke suppressed a grin. "There goes the best name you had in college."

"What was that?" Cindy asked, sounding eager for dirt on her man.

Luke turned to her. "He was often called the horse's ass."

Kirk chuckled under his breath. Cindy smiled and shared a glance with Jake.

"When do you leave for South America?" Jake asked.

"Now. As soon as I leave this room. I'm on my way to Toronto to fly out this evening. A short layover in Miami, then I land at the Manaus airport in Brazil after seventeen hours of traveling."

"Wow," Cindy said, moving closer. She sat on the edge of the bed. "What's in Brazil?"

Luke glanced at her, then back to Jake. "Just work stuff." He grabbed the clipboard and scanned a couple of pages. "Sure wish you could come, Jake. All expenses are paid."

Kirk moved closer. "You worried about something specific, Luke?"

He shook his head. "Not really. Just need to do a one-day trip into the jungle, collect samples, then fly back. Just never been to the Amazon Rainforest and Jake always said we'd do it together." He set the clipboard down and refocused his attention on Jake. "In truth, I don't want to do it alone."

"I can understand that. I wouldn't either."

"Then come." Luke tilted his head sideways and wrapped an arm around Cindy. "She'll let you get away. You'll be back before the weekend. Not only will I pay for everything, I'll throw in spending money. And if you don't buy anything, bring it home. Spend it on this lovely woman."

Swallowing a ball of emotion that rose in his throat, he shook his head. "I really shouldn't. We've got a new case, too."

Luke dropped his arm and checked his watch. "I understand. Look, I have to go if I want to make my flight." He moved toward the door. "If you change your mind, I've already bought your ticket. It's at the Air Canada desk. You fly out later today, or if you miss that one, tomorrow afternoon." He thrust his hands in the air to ward off Jake's protest. "Don't worry. That doesn't fall under coercion. I never tap into my expense account." He opened the door. The sounds of the hospital broke through the tension Jake felt. "If you change your mind, text me. I'll send you the hotel details. We'll do a jungle adventure together and head home. Deal?"

Jake nodded. "I'll think about it."

Luke eased out of the room, the door closing on him with an audible click.

Cindy turned back to Jake. "He really wants you to go."

Jake pushed himself up in bed.

"He sounded worried to me," Kirk added. "Maybe you should consider it."

Jake had thought about it already and had declined. He had no idea why Luke wanted him on the trip other than companionship, which was fine, but the timing wasn't good. And the days off with the department weren't feasible.

Cindy checked her phone. "It's time to leave this place. One last talk with the doctor, then we'll head home."

"That's a good idea," Kirk said as he headed for the door. "I'll go to the station and see if there's anything Detective Joslin wants us to do since you offered full cooperation earlier."

"Do that, Kirk, and get back to me at home. Call me later. I want to talk more about this case."

Kirk opened the door and looked back over his shoulder. Cindy gathered Jake's clothes for when he climbed out of the hospital gown.

"No, you don't want to talk more about the case," Kirk muttered. "We don't want to discuss this case other than to help the lead detective solve it. We are only going to *assist*."

"Kirk, we need this. I need this. After what we saw at that farmhouse"—Cindy stopped what she was doing. Jake felt her eyes on him— "I won't rest until the perp's caught."

"Think about what you just said. Think long and hard. Make sure you know what you're asking for." He paused. "Maybe you do need to go to Brazil for a couple of days. Clear your head. Shit, you could get the rest of the week off after your little episode with the horse allergy. Call it in. Then head to Toronto. Come back after the weekend. I don't want your shit and I don't want this case. Think about what you're saying."

"Fuck you, Kirk." Jake snapped his fingers. Cindy jumped at the volume of the snap. "There. Thought about it. Done. Kirk, how long have we been doing this? What we saw today was the worst for us. Even if Joslin runs with this to its conclusion, I want to see it through, too. Get in touch with her. Find out what she wants from us. Tell her we'll be there every step of the way."

"You tell her when you get home. I'm going to the office."

"Are you with me?" Jake asked.

Cindy stared at Jake. Jake watched Kirk. Kirk looked at the floor. Over five seconds passed before Kirk raised his head. He started to let the door slide shut but stopped it before he was completely out. Jake met his eyes while Cindy remained immobile beside the bed, his clothes draped over her arms.

"You know I'm always with you. Don't ask me shit like that. We're partners. All the way. Until the end. You're my brother. If that's what you want, I'm in. But until you're sure, I'll fight it and pick holes in your idea. I'm only in if you're a hundred percent."

"I'm sure. I'm a hundred percent."

The door closed.

"Fuck you, bro," Kirk's muffled words came through the closed door.

"Hurry, baby," Jake said. "I need to get home. Where's that prescription shit the doctor told me I'd get?"

"We have to buy it in the pharmacy downstairs before we leave."

"Then let's go."

Jake hopped out of bed and stripped off the gown. He stood completely naked before Cindy.

"What?" he asked when she stared at him. "Gimme the pants," he pleaded.

"Are you sure we need to leave so fast? There's a lock on the room door."

Jake looked at the door, then back at Cindy. He offered her a sly smile. "I could use a good nurse to do a once over. You know. Check things out. I might've pulled a muscle."

She smiled. "Pulled muscles are my specialty."

Jake ran for the lock.

CHAPTER NINE

Half an hour later, Jake was out of the hospital bed and getting dressed. Breathing had progressively gotten easier and the sneezing hadn't returned. His body was coming back to itself, which helped since he had so much on his mind, so much to do.

Yesterday, a serial killer had been in his city. That unknown subject took the lives of an entire family under the nose of Jake Wood, the ranking homicide detective in Orillia. Detective Keri Joslin was hard to get along with at the best of times, but she would need all the help she could get and Jake was determined to see this case through to the end—even over the needs of his friends.

"Baby." Jake jammed several things into a small bag Cindy had brought. "This allergy thing is over. As soon as we get home, I need a shower and then I need to get back to work."

Cindy exited the small bathroom attached to his hospital room. "I don't think so. You're taking the rest of the day off."

Jake shook his head. "Can't. Last night." He zipped up his bag. "Somebody killed an entire family in a farmhouse out in the concessions just west of the city."

"Kirk mentioned something about it. Said I'd read about it in the papers."

"He told you?"

"I asked how you happened to be near horses." She shrugged. "He had to give me something."

Jake lifted his bag and swung the strap over his shoulder. "Fair enough. Let's get those pills and leave. I hate the smell of hospitals."

"Me too, but you're staying home for the rest of the day."

He stopped by the door and turned back. "Honey," he said, his voice drawing the name out.

"No honey," Cindy stated firmly. "Don't honey me." She walked by him, opened the door, and stepped into the corridor. "Health first, then job. Or I'll pull the wife card even though I'm not the wife yet."

"No, don't pull the wife card." He lowered his head. She was the only one who could talk to him this way successfully. It wouldn't be all that bad to take the day off. He had been admitted to the hospital with a severe allergic reaction. Taking the day off would be good for him. Home time, couch time, rest time, was always good. Helping Joslin could come tomorrow, the day after. Maybe after the weekend.

Could a side trip to Brazil be worked in there somewhere?

Cindy was right, though. The job had gotten into his soul years ago and he just couldn't let go. Jake lived and breathed the job. So much so that when he took too much time away, it took days to get back into the rhythm. He needed to be doing it steadily to stay on top. Leaving the crime scene yesterday to return to the job tomorrow felt like a colossal waste of time. But it was either that or argue more with Cindy. And the wife card was her trump card. Pull that and *he* was not part of the discussion anymore. Any further negotiation was nixed. Better he just agree and go home and rest before he paid a greater price—one he couldn't afford.

They made it to the elevator. "Did Kirk leave?" He scanned the hallway.

"Not sure." Cindy followed Jake's gaze. "He didn't say."

They waited fifteen minutes for the prescription at the hospital pharmacy. Outside, the small amount of snow that had accumulated over the past week was almost gone, driven away by milder temperatures and rain. Dark clouds hovered above Orillia's Soldiers' Memorial Hospital as they strode toward Cindy's car. The rain had fallen, the air damp, but none dropped on them now.

While he waited for Cindy to unlock the passenger door, a man yelled Jake's name. He spun around. Kirk was in their cruiser, headlights on, gesturing for Jake to join him.

"Not today," Cindy warned.

"I know, but I have to see what he wants." Cindy's car door unlocked in front of him. Jake tossed his bag in the backseat and shut the door. "I'll be right back."

"Jake," she said, a warning in her tone.

"Let me at least tell him I'm off until tomorrow. Drive around and pick me up at his car."

Jake scurried to his partner. "What's up?" he asked. "I thought you left."

"I did. I was on my way to the office when I got a call from Detective Joslin."

"About what?"

"Looks like they lifted a solid print. A different one from the family's prints. And they may have a witness. Apparently the Marcellos had a dinner guest scheduled for last night. A man named Jeffrey Harris from the Marcellos' church. One of the fellow worshippers overheard the dinner invitation last Sunday at church. The witness might be able to work with a sketch artist to give us a face."

"Joslin must be happy to have that much. It's more than the other murders." Jake glanced over his shoulder as Cindy's car approached. "Look, I have to take a sick day. Fill me in tomorrow."

"No can do. You asked for this. I called Joslin and she wants us in Toronto ASAP. She wants to apprise us on the other murders, cover how this predator hunts the families he takes so we know what to look for up here. We're officially working this homicide from Orillia as of ten minutes ago. I came to pick you up, bro. I know Cindy is going to hate me, but we gotta go."

"Go where?" Cindy asked as she pulled even with Kirk's car.

"Jake has something to tell you," Kirk bellowed, his voice gleeful.

"Oh he does, does he?" Cindy eyed Jake.

He met her gaze, mustering up a stone-like expression.

"Cindy, baby, there's been a break in the case."

"Great. There are a lot of detectives that can work that break in the case while you heal at home. Get in."

"Detective Joslin requested we head to Toronto for a briefing." He leaned in her window. "Don't be mad. Don't use the wife card." He leaned farther inside the car. "I love you, honey. And I'll rest all the way there, rest in the briefing room, and then rest in the car all the way back. In the passenger seat of the cruiser is the same as if I'm sitting on the couch at home."

She glared at him. "It's not the same and you know it." She hesitated a moment, then said, "Go, do your job. I understand, I just wanted you all to myself to nurse back to health."

"Hey, there's a rhyme in there somewhere, Cindy," Kirk muttered.

"No Kirk, no rhyme. That's your talent, not mine."

"See," he shouted. "You did it again!"

"No *see*," Jake said. "Don't say *see*." He kissed Cindy on the cheek, then pulled his head out of the vehicle. "Baby, I'll be home soon. You're the love of my life. I don't know what I'd do without you."

She grabbed his collar and dragged him to within an inch of her face. "Come home and be ready for relaxation and rest and plenty of intimacy. You need a few days to heal. And promise me, no horses."

"No horses."

"I mean it."

"I know."

They kissed long and hard until a car horn disengaged them.

"Sorry." Kirk shrugged, an innocent expression on his face. "Bumped it by accident."

Jake stepped away from the window as the first drop of rain hit his cheek. "See you soon, babe."

"Love you," Cindy shouted as she rolled up her window.

Then she was gone and a hole opened in Jake's heart. He had been looking forward to spending the day at home with her.

He got in the passenger side of the cruiser as the rain came down harder. By the time they left the hospital parking lot, Kirk had the wipers on full.

On Highway 11 heading south toward Toronto, the traffic backed up as the rain turned to sleet.

"Take it easy," Jake said. "Slow down. If we have an accident, Cindy'll kill me."

"Don't worry. I got this. No hurry. Ride in bliss."

"Okay, Kirk. You can stop anytime you want."

"I'll stop when I'm dead."

Jake adjusted the lever on his seat and reclined until it was almost lying flat. His head back, he closed his eyes. "That can be arranged."

"Nice. My own partner just threatened my life. Great."

He had slept enough in the hospital and wasn't tired, but kept his eyes closed. They headed south through the traffic. He wanted to be a part of this case, help solve it, see it to its conclusion. But he also wanted Cindy, and nothing bothered him more than hurting her feelings. He knew her intentions were clean. If he really needed to work, she never stood in the way. This was different and sometimes a man needed a mother. Cindy was everything he could ask for—a wife, a girlfriend, a mother. And one day, when they had kids, he knew she would make an exceptional mother to them.

That was the one piece of advice from his father that he would never forget. When looking for a life-long partner, if you wanted children, your first goal is to look for a woman who would make a good mother, wife second. Children were more important long term than your selfish needs, his old man would say.

Cindy would be a perfect mother. And lucky for him, she would make an excellent wife, too.

When he got home later that night, he would be tired and need his knitting nurse of a fiancée to tend to him.

Or maybe he would tend to her.

The cruiser's wheels offered a steady hum with the sleet and moisture on the road sounding like cymbals rattling in the background.

Jake rolled sideways and stared at the door handle, trying to get the image of the man's torn back out of his head.

A ding sounded from his cell phone. He pulled it out and saw a text from Luke.

"What is it?" Kirk asked.

"Luke."

"Asking you to reconsider and head off to Brazil?"

"Something like that."

"Read it."

> *Jake, I need you man. I realize how unorthodox this is, but I'm afraid for my life. Come to Brazil. Your plane is waiting. When I check into the Hotel Amazonias, I'll tell them to expect you in case I'm out.*

"That's it?" Kirk looked at him, then back at the road. "He's afraid for his life? You think he's okay? What could he be talking about?"

Jake stared out the windshield at the traffic ahead. "I don't know." His voice was barely above a whisper.

His cell dinged again. When he read the message, he checked his seatbelt, then shifted in his seat.

"Turn around. Take me home. Now."

"Take you home?"

"Yes," Jake snapped. "Turn around. I need my passport."

Kirk hit the turn signal to exit the highway. "What the fuck, man? You going to Brazil?"

Jake stared out the rain-soaked window, looking at nothing. "I have to."

The car slowed as Kirk made the turn that would take them over the highway and back onto it, heading north.

"What did the second text say?"

Jake looked down and recited it for Kirk.

> *Jake, I'm being followed. They'll kill me if I don't go. Don't respond to this text. They'll find you, too. I'm throwing this phone away. See you in Brazil. You know I wouldn't ask if I thought my life wasn't at stake.*

"Holy shit, man. What the hell's going on?"

"I have no idea, but I intend to find out."

CHAPTER TEN

Jake had packed a bag, spent too long reassuring Cindy, and ran back to the car. Kirk got him to the Toronto Airport and dropped him at Terminal One inside two hours. Once he'd picked up the ticket Luke had left for him, he waded through thick merging lines that led to security. On the other side of security, his blood pressure calmed. He'd made it. He was through security, near his gate, and ready to fly to South America.

But why? What could be going on that Luke feared for his life?

He shouldered his carryon and headed to the Starbucks. Inside his bag were two paperbacks. With approximately sixteen hours of flight time ahead of him, he wanted to read as sleep was usually elusive for him on long flights.

After ordering a coffee, he checked his phone to see if Cindy had texted, but she hadn't. Understandably, she was upset. One minute he was in the hospital and the next he's about to fly to the Amazon Rainforest. He thought about texting her something nice, something to remind her he's fine, but chose to wait. He'd text her in Miami at the first layover.

Coffee in hand, he turned away from the Starbucks and bumped into a tall man standing too close.

"Sorry," Jake muttered.

A quick step back and to the side wasn't enough. The man matched his movements, mumbling something. Not willing to engage anyone in friendly banter, Jake slipped around a woman waiting by the counter, then walked between two round tables to escape the Starbucks traffic.

By the time he reached his gate again, something bothered him about that encounter. He stopped walking, stared along the length of the concourse, then pivoted on his heels and looked back at the Starbucks. A dozen people milled around, oblivious to his stare. The man he'd bumped into was gone. Was the man wearing sunglasses? Was he clean shaven? Did it matter? He was tall and had worn a black overcoat. That seemed like a heavy jacket to travel in.

Jake took a sip of his coffee, eyes roaming the travelers. As far as he could tell from the hundreds of people sitting at surrounding gates and travelers walking by toting and pulling small pieces of luggage, no one wore a black overcoat.

He shrugged, and let the odd feeling go. Luke had claimed someone was following *him*, that *his* life was in danger. Not responding to Luke's text wouldn't matter. If in fact someone was following Luke and these people were professional, they'd already know who Jake was. Which meant someone could be following Jake.

Or maybe I watch too much TV ...

He turned back toward his gate and stopped abruptly. Fifteen feet away, leaning against an exit door, the man in the black overcoat stood statue still, watching Jake. Coolly, he lifted his cup and let the hot liquid ease down his throat while he considered his next move.

The man's glare didn't waver.

Outside, the sun had descended behind clouds, the sky dark, yet the man in the overcoat wore large dark sunglasses. His taut cheeks narrowed down to a pointy chin that, from this distance, looked cast from stone. They stared at each other a moment longer, then Jake stepped forward, headed in the man's direction.

The man smiled, adjusted his weight, leaned sideways, and slipped through the exit door.

Jake lurched forward, held his coffee up to avoid spilling it, and got to the exit door too late. It clicked shut with finality. He tried the latch, but it remained locked. A sign on the door said Authorized Personnel Only. It would only open with a special keycard.

He hustled around the corner and found a window that looked out onto the tarmac and the back of the door, which led to the outside. The empty metal staircase descending from the exit door stopped by a truck parked near the underside of a plane. Crews were unhooking a large hose from under the wing. Near the rear of the aircraft, other teams were loading luggage onto a conveyor belt that fed into the belly of the aircraft.

The odds of missing the man were low. At least a dozen steps led to the cement. From there, the man would've been in the open until he walked the length of the plane and Jake had gotten to the window fairly quickly.

So where the hell is he?

Beneath the window, a vehicle eased into the open. With his forehead pressed hard against the glass, he tried to look directly downward. The area he stood in jutted out over an access road of some sort where the airport employees traversed without being in the way of arriving and departing aircraft. The man in the overcoat must've had a vehicle waiting for him.

But why pay attention to Jake in the first place? Was it connected to Luke?

He turned and watched the people closest to him. Could the threat to Luke be credible? If so, then the man in the overcoat had to be involved in some way.

That led him to another question: What the hell could Luke

be working on at Fortech Industries that was so important?

A woman's voice came over the loudspeaker announcing the flight to Miami was initiating boarding by zones. Business class would be first. Then zones would be called out by numbers after that. Zone numbers were located on individual boarding passes.

Jake took one more look out the large window, then moved toward his gate and fished out his boarding pass. He would get to Manaus, Brazil. He would find his friend, and he would determine what the threat was. Together they would work it out. Then he would return to help with Joslin's murder case.

In the meantime, if he saw Overcoat Man again, he would persuade him to speak on why he had been following him. Jake had a way with making people talk.

That odd feeling struck him again. What bothered him was the bump protruding from the man's coat. Everyone had gone through airport security to be in that area, so how was it Overcoat Man still had a shoulder holster? Jake had been a cop for decades. He could tell when someone was carrying a weapon under a coat and the man with the chiseled face and dark sunglasses had definitely been packing a piece.

CHAPTER ELEVEN

Jeffrey Harris entered his house, closed and locked the front door, and exhaled.

"Hello," he called out. "I'm home."

Overwhelmed with joy, Jeffrey strode into the living room and set his eyes upon the wooden easel. Soon, within the hour, he would begin his drawing of the new family. His wife and son would love it. Once the drawing was painted, he would frame it and hang his portrayal of the Harris family above the dining room table for all to see.

The bag in his hand grew heavier with each passing minute. He set it on the table and slid out the scrapbook.

"Honey, I got a great deal on the scrapbook from the store. They had a pre-Christmas sale and I just couldn't resist."

He glanced at his wife on the couch, his smile widening until his cheeks lifted with the effort.

"You see that?" he asked. "This is a Duchenne smile, the only authentic smile in the eighteen known versions of the smile known to man." He stepped closer to her. "I'll explain the differences. With a real smile, the Duchenne, it uses two of the major muscles in the face. The zygomatic and the orbicularis. The zygomatic raises the corners of the mouth like so." He pointed at the corners of his mouth for her benefit. "And the orbicularis raises the cheeks enough to cause what people refer to as crow's feet. See?" He pointed at a spot by his temple. "That's a real smile from a guy who is really happy. Are you happy, honey?"

He detected a slight nod.

"Good to hear," Jeffrey whispered as he stepped back and retrieved the scrapbook. "Inside this book is where I'll place Jason's lock of hair and a few of the pictures we have of him. I'll keep the scrapbook in his room."

Jeffrey set the scrapbook on the table and reached into the bag. "The store had a sale on watercolors, and I picked up some great brushes as well. Our family portrait will be stunning."

He turned to her on the couch and offered his Duchenne smile again, white teeth showing, cheeks and mouth lifted as high as they could go. After holding the smile for several seconds, he rummaged in the bag one more time.

"I also bought a few extra frames for the pictures we took recently."

Jeffrey trudged over to the couch where his new wife sat on the middle cushion. Beside her were other pictures laid out of a family she had once maintained. A man Jeffrey recognized as Stephen Marcello was in a few. That would have to be taken care of. Once all traces of Stephen Marcello were removed, the pics would be placed in the new frames, at which point the family photos of his new kin could be hung throughout the house.

"It's going to be so grand to have you all to myself. You and Jason are going to love it here. Tonight's a pizza night to celebrate our first day as a married couple." He stopped as the light reflecting off the wedding band on his finger caught his eye. "I'm so happy to have found you, baby. We'll make a good team." He glanced at her and saw the image he'd been talking to since walking in the door. A moment of raw lucidity offered clarity on a day otherwise filled with fantasy and daydreams. He drew his head back in surprise.

Since entering the apartment, he had been talking to a 13x19 photo of Melissa Marcello plucked from the Marcello farmhouse and placed on the middle cushion of Jeffrey's couch.

He closed his eyes and shook his head to clear it. It couldn't be. He was married to her now. They had a son named Jason. Stephen Marcello had pretended to be hers, but Jeffrey had taken the role of father of the house when he'd taken the man's soul.

Jeffrey opened his eyes and saw the truth. His new wife sat on the couch smiling at him. She loved him. She would make love to him every day and together they would raise Jason as *their* son until Jason left for university.

When Jason left, Jeffrey and his new bride would only be a married couple and that wasn't enough. He got bored easily. He would preempt that, needing a new family in eighteen months, maybe in two years. But none of that mattered now. He had his wife and he had his son.

He caressed the edge of her cheek, touched the ring on her finger, then rubbed his own.

"It's time to start the family portrait."

Jeffrey rose from the couch and set up his tools by the easel. He disrobed and tossed his clothes on the chair beside the couch.

"I always paint in the nude," he said to Melissa. "At least until our son returns from school, which gives me a few hours."

He lifted an HB pencil, pushing his 4B and 6B aside for shading later.

"Once I've done our portrait, it'll hang nicely by our table." He held the pencil, suspended in the air, hovering by the blank page. "And so begins our time together." The picture on the couch smiled back at him. Her lips parted wide as if she was trying the Duchenne smile, too. "Thank you, darling. That means so much to me."

With his free hand, he touched his flaccid penis where his new wife's vaginal secretions had left white flakes of crust near the base. Thoughts of her last night, how it felt to be inside her, making a new family, came back to him.

"What a night we had, eh honey?"

The pencil touched the canvas and Jeffrey began creating family memories that would last as long as he allowed.

CHAPTER TWELVE

The layover in Miami was uneventful. The second leg of travel would fly him directly into Manaus' international airport.

While waiting for his next flight, he texted Cindy, but got no response. She was probably sleeping. He texted again, this time a longer message to let her know he was feeling much better and would be home within a couple of days. Once it sent and he checked email to see if there was anything from Kirk on the Joslin murder case—there wasn't—he turned off his phone to conserve the battery.

Within a half hour, he boarded the flight, settled into his seat with a blanket wrapped up over his shoulders, and promptly fell asleep, the Lee Child paperback in his bag all but forgotten.

The bump on the tarmac snapped him awake. In a brief moment of delirium, Jake wondered where he was, grasping at his armrest. Then it all came rushing back and he opened the window shade to look out at Manaus, Brazil. From the tarmac, as the plane slowed and began to taxi into the terminal, he couldn't see much. A perimeter of thick trees lined the outer edge of the airport property. The surrounding terrain was prairie flat, with no hills of any kind towering above the tree line in the distance. In the blue sky above, white fluffy clouds floated by. From the inside of the aircraft, it looked like a gorgeous day.

He retrieved his cell phone and powered it up. He wondered

if his roaming would offer him cell coverage in Manaus. While he waited for his phone to connect, Jake stretched his limbs, allowing a small grunt to escape his throat.

The two seats beside him were empty. Across the aisle, a small child watched him. He smiled at the little boy, then looked up at the child's mother, who offered him a welcoming smile in return.

He probably looked like shit. He'd left the Orillia hospital in a hurry. Fueled up on caffeine, he forced himself to stay awake, which hadn't lasted long on the second flight, then slept the rest of the way. Hair unkempt, eyes bloodshot, smiling at random children, did not beget welcoming smiles from mothers. He must have misread her grin because now she had placed a comforting arm over her child and looked away.

The plane stopped abruptly, jolting everyone. As the passengers jumped from their seats and voices rose to be heard over one another, Jake checked his phone again.

Nothing. No cell coverage, no service. He frowned. Maybe he should have checked that out before he'd left Toronto.

After stuffing his phone into his pocket, he snatched his bag from the overhead bins and joined the line exiting the plane. Within twenty minutes, he had made it to customs, cleared through without an issue, and stepped outside into the warmth of the Manaus sunshine.

On his way to the taxi line, he opened the text from Luke. Hotel Amazonias. Luke said he would tell them to expect Jake.

The taxi driver spoke Portuguese, but his English was passable. He understood the name of the hotel without an issue and they were soon en route.

The man in the overcoat at the Toronto airport haunted him. Jake turned in his seat and watched the buildings sweeping by the vehicle's windows. Whatever that man wanted, it would have to wait. Jake had a feeling he'd meet him again soon enough.

Less than ten minutes later, Jake paid the driver in what little Canadian currency he had on him—overpaid in order for the driver to take the money and do the currency conversion on his own time—and entered the main lobby of the small Hotel Amazonias. It was a tiny, quaint lobby that had a tropical feel to it. Evenly spaced tropical plants surrounded the outer wall of the lobby. Some with thin leaves, others with fat, wide green leaves.

A string of lights hung from the ceiling along the back wall, directly above a small seating area. Jake moved farther inside until he stopped at the empty main desk. Someone was talking in the back room attached to the main desk, but Jake couldn't understand what they were saying. He assumed they were on the phone. He waited a moment, then hit the bell for service, suddenly exhausted.

The male voice said a couple of more words, then stepped out.

"Good afternoon. *Olá*. How can I help you?"

"My friend is staying here. He's expecting me."

"Your name, sir?" The clerk's English sounded British.

"Jake Wood."

The clerk typed on a keyboard and stared at the screen in front of him. "Passport please?" he asked, without looking up, his hand outstretched.

Jake fumbled in his bag to retrieve his passport, then handed it over. Once the clerk checked his name, he grabbed a keycard, swiped it through a reader, and handed it to Jake.

"Room 204. Your friend has you listed as a guest. You're welcome to the continental breakfast over there"—he gestured toward a set of double doors— "and the brochures for tours and shows at our opera house are on that rack there."

"Thank you." Jake grabbed his passport and started for the stairs.

On the second floor, he found room 204 and knocked. After no one answered, he knocked again, then slipped the keycard in and opened the door a crack.

"Luke?" he called. "You here?"

When no one answered, Jake stepped inside and closed the door. The room was small, but it had two beds. They were both made up. It was obvious that Luke had used the one closest to the window as his bags crowded it and his laptop sat on the end table.

Jake dropped his bag on his bed and entered the bathroom to splash water on his face. When he stepped out of the bathroom feeling refreshed, he saw a note taped to the TV. Jake snatched it up and read.

I'm on a tour of the Amazon with a company that does, "Tours by Locals." I will be gone for three days. Please join me. Once you've rested and had dinner, call the number below and tell them who you are. The "Tours by Locals" people know where I am. I've arranged for you to join me in the Amazon Rainforest. They will send a guide and a tracker. These two men have already been paid for and are expecting your call. They will explain everything. Meet them at six in the morning and the guide will take you to my location. Once you're with me, I will update you. Two days from now, we can head back to Canada with all the evidence we need, but I can't speak on an open phone line or in public. Just meet me in the Amazon Rainforest and everything will make sense. I sure hope you're reading this letter and you made it safely to Manaus.

Remember, call the number below. They're

expecting you. Have dinner and charge it to
the room. Or order in—doesn't matter.
Just meet me. I'll explain everything when we
get together.
I'm sorry to drag you into this in such a
manner, but there was no other way. They
were watching me and now I suspect they're
watching you. But don't worry, they'd be
stupid to go after you—you're a cop.
So many people have died. You're the only
one who can fix this.
Be careful,
Luke

Watching him? Of course they were watching him. But Jake
suspected the man in the overcoat hadn't traveled to Manaus just
to follow him. He hadn't seen anything untoward since leaving
Toronto.

Was Luke paranoid? What could he possibly be working on
that was so important?

Jake folded the note and stuffed it in his front pocket.

So many people have died. You're the only one who can fix this.
What did that mean? Who had died?

Jake slipped his passport into his bag, grabbed his bank card
and what cash he had left, then snatched up the phone in the room
and dialed the number Luke had provided. A man answered on the
second ring and explained in fluent English how he was waiting for
Jake's call.

"It was unorthodox for your friend to pay in advance," the
man said.

"Luke is an unorthodox kind of guy."

"I have two men who will meet you at the pier at six in the
morning. Can you make it to the pier on your own or would you

like I send a taxi?"

"Send a taxi with instructions for the driver. That way I won't get lost, as I'm sure the pier is a large place."

"I understand. Okay, taxi at your hotel at 5:45 a.m. Everything is paid for as well. Please dress for the jungle. All the supplies you will need my men will have."

"I'll be ready." Jake hung up the phone and headed for the door, excited about meeting up with Luke in the morning.

He exited the room and retrieved his cell phone to see if there was any coverage yet. A small piece of paper stuck to the outside of the phone. He frowned as it floated to the carpeted floor, not remembering putting anything in his pocket.

He grabbed it and read.

> Stay in Toronto. Don't go to Brazil. You will die down there.

"What the hell?" he whispered.

Staring at the note, it all came clear to him. The man in the overcoat had bumped into him at the Starbucks at the airport. He'd slipped the paper in Jake's pocket and watched him to see if he'd read it. But Jake hadn't read the note, so the man in the overcoat continued to watch him, then slipped out the exit.

"You won't make it home," Jake said as he started toward the lobby.

What was Luke messed up in? People had died? And now an Ontario Provincial Police Homicide Detective was being threatened. There was something intriguing going on here. It was what made him a cop—a damn good cop. This sort of thing spurred him on.

Whoever was after Luke, or trying to stop him, had now come on Jake's radar and like a predator with its teeth sunk deep in flesh,

Jake would not let go until there was a resolution.

When he entered the lobby to ask the desk clerk where the closest bank machine was, a smile was pasted on Jake's face.

He had a lot of questions for the man in the overcoat.

He would be seeing that man again.

Soon. Real soon.

CHAPTER THIRTEEN

Jake left the hotel and secured money from a bank machine. Prior to dinner, as the sun began its descent, he decided to wander the streets of Manaus as it would be his only chance to see some of the Brazilian city. Within three days, he'd be on a plane bound for home.

The streets were busy, cars and busses vying for tarmac as they forged their way through wandering pedestrians. Men walked by in droves, pushing shopping carts, some empty, some offering wares for sale, while other carts were filled with the owners' earthly possessions.

At a street market, he was struck with an odd sense of déjà vu. The sellers stood in front of their small square stalls offering everything from trinkets, jewelry, and souvenirs, to soccer balls and Frisbees. Just like Mercado 28 in Cancun, Mexico, an outdoor market he'd visited on a trip to Cancun several years earlier.

A quick walk through the market took him to a less busy area. He crossed the street at the light and wandered into an open park with freshly cut grass where couples strolled in the dusk, arm in arm. It made him miss Cindy. He wondered what she was doing at that moment. When he got back to the hotel, he'd have to get his phone working on their WiFi in order to at least email her. Or maybe he'd use the room's phone and just call her.

A large building loomed to his right, the windows aglow with an amber light from inside.

"The Amazonas Opera House," a man said to his left.

Jake spun around. A uniformed police officer stood five feet away. The man was tall and thick, his chest covered in a Kevlar vest with small pockets overloaded with supplies. Pepper spray was attached to the vest in a small pocket on the man's left, and a thin wire ran up to an earpiece tucked away in his ear. The light-blue uniform was dappled with insignia on epaulets, sleeves, and chest. A small caliber firearm rested in a holster strapped to the officer's thigh.

"I was just admiring the architecture," Jake said, turning slightly back toward the building.

"It's a gorgeous building with many parts of it coming over from Europe."

"Europe? I'm surprised."

"French windows, Italian marble."

Jake studied the edifice with renewed respect. "Manaus is a beautiful city."

"Don't placate."

Jake turned back to face the cop, who had moved a foot closer.

"Garbage litters the street," the cop said. "After the money wasted on the 2014 World Cup here in Manaus, security became an issue. Our favelas are out of control."

"Favelas?"

"What you call slums in America."

"I'm not from America."

"Do you have slums where you're from?"

Jake shrugged. "Yeah, I guess."

"Then does it matter where you're from? You understand the word slums, yes?"

Jake nodded.

The cop fixed his gaze on two teenagers with skateboards, then turned back to Jake. "We have been called a crime-ridden hell-hole by a British newspaper." He gestured at the couples walking by. "Yet romance still finds a time and place in this hell-hole."

"I'm sure that description was a bit of an exaggeration."

The cop eyed him. "Who are you here with?"

"A friend."

"Male or female?"

"Why do you ask?"

"You are walking alone. You are a foreigner. The sun is almost gone and the thieves and pickpockets are emerging from the cracks they hide behind throughout the day. You might think about walking with this friend of yours or staying near your hotel."

"I'm sure I'll be fine."

The cop tilted his head and straightened his belt line. "What do you do? What is your line of work?"

"I'm a homicide detective."

The man's head righted and his eyes widened. "Ahh, a fellow law enforcement man. And you are here on business? As a professional courtesy, have you let my superiors know that you're here investigating something?"

"I'm not working a case here." *Were all Manaus cops this concerned with foreigners?* "I'm here with a friend. Tomorrow, we're doing a rainforest tour. Then flying home in a few days."

The cop nodded. "Just watch yourself out here. Danger lurks behind every corner."

He touched his earpiece as if someone spoke into it, then started away, but not before hitching his pants up at the waist again. Jake stared after the cop until he stopped at the corner of the building thirty feet away and turned back to face Jake.

"Remember," the cop shouted. "Watch yourself out here, Jake Wood. Danger lurks behind every corner."

Before Jake could think, he broke into a run toward the cop, but the officer stepped sideways and disappeared behind the building. As Jake ran for the corner, his mind raced. How had the cop known his name? Once he'd registered at the hotel, had it gotten sent to a police database? If so, had he been followed on his walk, or was this man with the man who had watched him at the Toronto airport?

At the corner, Jake came around, giving it a wide berth, unsure of what was waiting for him, being mindful of the 'danger lurking behind every corner' comment.

The sidewalk was empty. Along the wall, a door led into the building, but it was locked. Wherever the Manaus cop disappeared to, he had planned his exit well.

Jake turned back the way he had come. How many people were watching him? Were the men who had threatened him after Luke as well? Luke's claim of being followed didn't seem so paranoid now.

Jake started back to the hotel, knowing Luke was okay. He'd made it to Brazil. Otherwise, who left him the note in the room? Who had paid for the room and the tour guides that he was to meet in the morning?

Thoughts of food forgotten for now, Jake retraced his steps, wanting the security of his room.

Another thought struck him. If that was in fact a Manaus cop, and he was in league with the man in the overcoat at the Toronto airport, then their reach was far and wide—too wide. It had to be a simple case of Jake's passport being reported to the authorities when he'd checked into the hotel. Nothing else made sense.

As he hustled around vendors packing up for the night, another idea came to him. Were they watching him, keeping tabs on his movements so they could access his room? All he had on himself was his ATM card and the cash he'd withdrawn. Everything else was in the room. Everything.

Jake broke into a run.

CHAPTER FOURTEEN

Jake ran through the front doors of the lobby of his hotel, slowed to catch his breath, and leaned against the front desk. The clerk from earlier, the one who had given him directions to the bank machine was gone, replaced by a man in his mid-forties.

"Where's the ..." Jake panted, "... other clerk from ... half an hour ago?"

The man looked up from the computer, an expression of boredom on his face.

"What is problem, sir? I can help, no?"

Jake shook his head, strode through the lobby, and headed for his room. On his floor, he dabbed sweat out of his eyes and reached for the keycard.

The door opened to a mess.

The room had been turned upside down. Every drawer sat open. The bedsheets were ripped from the beds, the mattresses lay askew. The curtains were torn off the rail and thrown to the floor and the closet door that held an extra pillow and a small ironing table, had been wrenched open so hard, it had separated from the wall.

Jake rushed inside, shoved his back against the wall beside the bathroom door. After two quick breaths, he pivoted into the bathroom, hands up and ready.

The bathroom was empty. Whoever had ransacked his room

was gone.

The Manaus cop had to be involved. He had followed Jake, letting the ransackers know Jake's location at all times. When the cop heard they were done with the room through his earpiece, the officer had walked away, then turned back to offer his cryptic warning.

That had to be it.

But why ransack his room? What were they looking for? And who were *they* in the first place?

He stumbled over the bed sheets and snatched his bag from under them. The zippers were all open, the bag empty. Everything he had brought with him, his change of clothes, ID, and passport were gone—stolen.

"Shit."

He tossed the bag across the room and jumped over a mattress, heading for the door. The lock appeared untouched. Whoever had gained access to the room had a keycard.

Back in the lobby, he found the desk unmanned. When no one answered, he banged on the bell incessantly.

"I'm coming, I'm coming," the mid-forties man said as he emerged from the back room. "What is emergency?"

"Who has access to my room?"

"What room are you in, sir?" The clerk turned to the computer and typed something.

"When someone checks into your hotel, how many keycards are made?"

"I'm sorry, sir?" The clerk turned maddeningly slow until he met Jake's eyes. "I'm not sure why you appear so hostile. Please calm down. Everything will be okay, no?"

"No." Jake slapped the countertop with both hands, open-palmed. "Everything will not be okay." He raised his voice, more out of frustration than anger. "My passport has been stolen. My

ID is gone."

"I'm sure we can figure out what happened. Your embassy will help as well. Please." The clerk turned back to his computer. "What room number, sir?"

Jake kept his hands on the top of the desk. He forced himself to breathe slower, easier.

"I am in room 204."

The clerk typed quickly, then frowned. He eased in closer to the computer and guided his eyes with a finger on the screen.

"Are you Luke Mercer, sir?"

"No. I'm his friend. I was to meet him here. I checked in earlier. My name is Jake Wood." He gestured with his right hand. "Check again."

The clerk typed something else. "I'm sorry. I only see one guest in room 204—"

"I'm in room 204," Jake shouted. He yanked the keycard out of his pocket and held it up. "How did I get this, then?"

The clerk narrowed his eyes at the card, then laid his palm out flat.

"Please sir, let me check that card."

The clerk swiped it and glanced at his screen. "It is registered to room 204 at the moment—"

"For fuck's sake. *I'm* in room 204. It has just been ransacked. My belongings were stolen. I want to know who has access to my room and I want to know now."

The clerk had stepped back at Jake's outburst, keycard still in hand. His cheeks paled and his lips parted, but he said nothing.

Jake was getting nowhere with the clerk. It was late. He was tired and there was nothing he could do to get a new passport until after his trip into the Amazon concluded. He needed to calm down before the police were called and he ended up spending the night giving statements that would lead nowhere as he suspected a member of the Manus authorities had a hand in the robbery of his room.

In a quick gesture, Jake lunged over the top of the front desk, snatched the keycard, and dropped back to his feet.

"Are there cameras in the lobby? Just tell me that. Cameras in the corridors?"

The clerk shook his head. "No cameras."

"Fine. Forget it. I will report it to the proper authorities myself."

He stomped back up to room 204, let himself in, and started to make the bed. Inside the minibar, he found six cans of beer, two small bottles of wine, and several snacks, which he ripped into right away.

With no passport, he wasn't going anywhere fast. Even the front desk didn't have him down as a registered guest. He had his phone and the money he'd taken from the bank machine. He had a taxi coming in the morning and a trip into the Amazon Rainforest all paid for. He would take that trip, locate Luke, and then decide what to do next.

In the meantime, he tried to call Cindy with the hotel's phone, but only got Cindy's voice mail. He didn't leave a message. On his second beer, he called Kirk, got his voice mail, and decided to not leave a message. He would try Kirk again before he met the taxi in the morning.

On his third beer, Jake yanked the ruined curtains out of his way, and plunked down in the chair by the window.

Feeling sorry for himself, pissed that he'd lost his passport, he decided to have the rest of the booze in the mini fridge. It was past one in the morning when he fell asleep, the alarm set for 5:00 a.m.

CHAPTER FIFTEEN

A buzzer sounded from a distance. Jake thought of the siren in his cruiser. He moved to switch it off, the sound splitting his head. The button disengaged, the siren continued unabated.

He flicked it off again, but then someone pounded on the door.

His eyes popped opened. He was on the floor of the hotel room at the base of the chair by the window, his neck kinked at an odd angle. A moan escaped his lips as he rolled over and got to his hands and knees.

Someone pounded on the door again.

"Mister, your taxi is waiting," came the muffled voice through the door.

"Coming," he managed to say loud enough. The pounding on the door stopped. "Give me a few minutes."

He got to his feet, leaned against the wall as the full force of his headache rushed in, then started toward the bathroom. After urinating and splashing water in his face, he felt marginally better.

The word *coffee* rolled off his lips as a mumble. Outside the room, Jake headed to where the continental breakfast was set up on the first floor. After stuffing three butter croissants inside a small stack of napkins and loading up two coffee cups, he lumbered outside to the waiting taxi.

Once he was situated in the back seat, the ride was quick.

Within five minutes, the cab had stopped at the pier. The driver stared at him in the rearview mirror, waiting for Jake to exit. He'd kept his eyes closed on the ride over to avoid bolstering his headache as the sun rose in the east. Eyes open now, he looked back at the driver in the mirror.

"You're paid already?" he asked.

The driver nodded.

Jake shouldered the door open, pivoted on the seat, and dropped his legs out of the car. With his free hand, he pushed off the back of the seat and stood. As soon as he was clear of the car, the small yellow cab shot forward, gravity slamming his door closed for him, and disappeared around a corner a dozen feet away.

"What the fuck?" Jake mumbled to himself. "What's the hurry?"

He examined the area around him. A railing spanned the length of the street on the other side of the sidewalk. Beyond the railing was a drop-off, a small landing area, and then the Negro River where boats were parked tight-knit near the shore. He ambled over to the railing and leaned on it while stuffing one of the croissants in his mouth. If the tour guys didn't arrive soon, he was going to set off in search of headache meds.

Jake watched as hundreds of men and women busily loaded and unloaded various sized vessels at this early hour on the ground below. They moved like soldier ants, toting their bounty on their heads and shoulders.

Jake surveyed the busy crowd, devouring the rest of the croissants and drinking his coffee.

He asked himself how he could have consumed that much alcohol on the night before he was to take a tour of the Amazon. Looking back on the night, he wondered how he got so drunk on six beers and a couple of small bottles of wine, the size of the ones offered on airplanes. Maybe it had hit him harder because of the jet lag. Perhaps it had something to do with the change in environment, or barometric pressure—something he wasn't too knowledgeable about. He shrugged, feeling better by the minute, and bit into the last croissant.

Several minutes later, when he was finished eating and was working on the last bit of coffee two men approached. Each man had a warm, welcoming, expression.

"Mr. Wood?" the man on the right asked.

Jake nodded, then stopped moving his head abruptly when a spike of pain shot through it. He whispered, "That's me."

They shook hands. More pain burst in his head.

"Follow us."

The men started toward a stairwell that descended to the pier. Jake didn't move. "And you guys are?"

The men turned back around. "Oh, sorry. We're with Tour by Locals. I'm Milton Paulo, your guide, and this is Eduardo, your tracker." The men looked at each other, then back at Jake. "Sorry, we thought you were informed already."

"I'm not feeling well this morning, so go easy on me." He offered them a sheepish grin. "Long flight yesterday and an extra drink last night." He paused, swallowed, then added, "Or two."

"It's no problem, sir. We were told to take you to your friend. You should be with him before sundown. Overall, it's an easy ride and several hours walk—nothing too strenuous." They started down the stairs. This time, Jake followed them.

Last night's break-in, combined with his identification being stolen, weighed on him. When he returned to Manaus with Luke, he'd have to go through the monotonous struggle of identifying himself and getting travel documents made up so he could fly home. It's not that it would be difficult, but it would certainly be a hassle—one he could do without.

The men led him to a small boat with an outboard motor. On

board, Eduardo fired up the engine and steered them out into the river. Once away from the pier, Eduardo increased their speed. The buffeting wind refreshed Jake. At first, he breathed in deep, closed his eyes, and let the wind caress his cheeks. After several minutes, he leaned sideways and watched the trees race by on the right. Every so often, he checked the boats stern in search of followers, but none were present. The river to the rear was empty. Only the sun glinted off its surface reminding him of the nagging headache's insistence in sticking around.

An hour later, the rest of his coffee gone cold, Jake's bladder about to burst, Eduardo piloted the small craft toward an inlet on shore. After he cut the engine, they drifted up onto the bank. Milton hopped out, grabbed a rope, and secured the front of the boat to a nearby tree. The pungent smell of aquatic life and dead fish wafted up.

"This is where we start walking," Milton said. "Your friend came this way as well. Eduardo will show us the route. It's at least a five-mile walk. You okay for this?"

Jake nodded. "I can do it."

In the distance, emanating from the interior of the foliage, the susurration of hundreds, if not thousands, of creatures' mating calls came to him all at once in a daunting cacophony. Soon, they would enter the giant canopy of trees and completely immerse themselves within the undulating din.

Once the men had emptied the boat of their meager supplies, they began an inventory. Jake leaned against a small tree and watched as they organized three backpacks loaded with small foodstuffs, medical supplies, lotions and creams. Eduardo and Milton carried long machetes, wore hiking boots, and bore the signs of years in the sun with dark, leathery brown skin.

Jake pointed toward what looked like a path into the dense rainforest. "Are we going that way?"

Milton glanced over his shoulder as he finished packing his backpack. "Yes. That path takes us to our first stop where we'll have lunch. Then we continue until we hit basecamp where my colleagues took your friend."

Milton and Eduardo exchanged a furtive glance, then continued their tasks. He detected there was something they weren't saying.

"What?" Jake asked. "What was that look for?"

"We think they are at the basecamp."

"I don't understand. You *think?*"

Milton shouldered his pack and then held one out to Jake. "Our other team had GPS tracking. We use something similar to Find My Phone on your iPhone to locate one another."

Jake took the proffered pack and slung it over his shoulder. "Then it won't be too hard to find them."

"That's where the trouble comes in."

Eduardo strode past them, headed for the trail that invaded the vegetation. Milton watched him go for a moment, then said, "We lost their signal last night." He met Jake's gaze. "They were supposed to offer us coordinates today, but they didn't." He pointed at Eduardo. "That's why he's with us. Eduardo is one of the best trackers in Manaus." Milton arched an eyebrow. "It cost extra to bring him, but my boss is worried about your friend and our team."

Jake leaned in close, a knot forming in his stomach. "How worried? Couldn't it just be an accident? Like the GPS thing got wet and stopped working?"

Milton shook his head. "Waterproof. Also"—he pointed back toward the bank where their boat was tied to a tree— "where's their boat? Yesterday at this time, they called in that they were safely ashore. We always tie our boats up here." Milton started after Eduardo. "Something might be wrong, Mr. Wood. Today we learn what that is."

Jake stood alone on the shore, staring out at the large Negro River for another minute. Back home, he'd call in backup, assess the situation better. But here, in Brazil, he was heading into the rainforest unarmed, with a guide and a tracker, both men untrained civilians—at least untrained in law enforcement.

What are you involved in, Luke?

Jake turned away from the river and started after Milton, each step heavy with worry, the sun beating down on the back of his neck.

CHAPTER SIXTEEN

A t lunch, Milton tore a palm leaf off a tree and proceeded to fold it into a sturdy flat surface that would serve as a plate to hold their food. Eduardo gathered small branches and kindling, and then started a fire. Jake watched from the base of a tree where he sat to rest.

When Milton was finished with the palm leaf, he handed it to Jake. "Mr. Wood—"

"Jake's fine." He took the leaf that was now the size of a rectangular dinner plate.

"Why was your friend out here?"

"Why does anyone come to the rainforest? As a guide, Milton, you'd know that better than anyone else."

Milton fixed his eyes on what Eduardo was doing near the fire for a moment, then nodded. "I suppose so."

Moments later, Milton used his machete to remove a piece of bark and then sat beside Jake, carving the bark into something the size of a hand.

Jake leaned in closer. "What are you making?"

Without looking up, Milton said, "A spoon. For lunch."

Jake watched as the guide planed off enough wood near the center of the piece to form an indent where liquid could be safely held. The fire by Eduardo raged as he set about placing small chunks of chicken on spears of wood he'd carved.

"We make as much as we can from the land, only bringing food with us. When we leave to head back to Manaus, you can tell we were here, but we've left no rubbish." He held up the wooden spoon, examining it with a careful eye. "This wood was here when we arrived and it'll be here long after we are gone." He glanced at Jake with a crooked smile, like he was in on an anti-garbage conspiracy of some kind. "Much less to carry this way."

Being raised in Toronto and spending his entire life in the city, Jake lived a vastly different life than Milton and Eduardo. Out here was their land, their terrain. He realized in that moment that his life depended on them. If he got lost or something happened to his guides, his odds of survival would be greatly reduced.

Jake checked his arms, then surveyed the tree line. "Why are we not being eaten alive by mosquitoes?"

Milton set the wooden spoon aside and began carving another.

"There are no mosquitoes in this part of the rainforest as the water is too acidic to breed in. The mosquitoes spread malaria elsewhere, but not here."

Birds squawked overhead. Jake glanced up, trying to catch sight of them.

"Tropical birds bring us music," Milton said, also looking skyward. "Sometimes, when watching the tops of the trees, you'll be able to spot spider monkeys loping by. They are extremely agile and go tree to tree as if they have wings." He lowered his head and continued carving.

Fifteen feet away, Eduardo turned the three small pieces of chicken he was roasting and stirred a pot he'd placed above the fire.

"Why'd you ask about Luke?" Jake turned his attention back to Milton. "Is one's purpose in the Amazon to be stated prior to receiving a tour? Or can a foreigner hire your company for a tour, no questions asked?"

Milton didn't miss a stroke with his knife as he worked on the second spoon. "I asked because of the gear he brought with him."

"The gear? You saw it?"

Milton nodded.

"What kind of gear?"

"Two black cases were carted with them." He finished the wooden spoon and set it aside. "I caught a glimpse of the inside of one of the cases."

Jake waited for Milton to go on. After a moment, he did.

"Small vials of liquid were suspended in black foam. Evidently, the vials were filled with antivenin."

"Antivenom?"

Milton wiped sweat from his brow, then faced Jake. "No, it's called anti*venin*, not venom. A common misconception."

"How could you tell what was in the vials?"

"They were labeled."

Jake scanned the immediate area. "Is it necessary to tote antivenin into the rainforest? Is the threat that profound?"

Milton kicked his legs out in front of him, hands resting on his thighs. "No. That was why I asked."

"Aren't snakes a threat? Maybe he was just taking precautions."

"Yes, people are bit by snakes in the rainforest, but the most dangerous living species out here are things like the bullet ant, the Brazilian wandering spider which looks like a tarantula, various big cats, and the poison dart frog. On this venture, as we aren't going hundreds of miles into the rainforest, we won't encounter them. Snakes, yes, but most of their species won't bother us. Not out here."

Jake hadn't realized how stressed he'd become so quickly having not thought about the dangers of the rainforest. As a city boy with guides, he hadn't considered that possibility. These people did tours all the time. How much danger could there be?

"We have a small medical kit," Milton continued, "but antivenin isn't something that's normally added to it as you need specific kinds based on the certain snake that bites you."

"And my friend's vials were labeled as antivenin—"

"With the name of the snake beside each vial," Milton finished for him.

"You recognized the names of the snakes as creatures from this region of the rainforest?"

Milton nodded. "I did." He pushed off the ground and brushed off his butt. "Lunch is ready."

They ate under the shelter of trees, the sun's rays in search of them through cracks in the foliage. The canopy above was too thick for the sun to penetrate but the heat got through, thickening the air with humidity.

The chicken was magnificent and the soup, something seafood-like, filled him pleasantly and removed the final vestiges of the hangover.

Energized, revitalized, and ready to continue, they cleaned the area, repacked their bags, and started along the path, deeper into the rainforest. Several times Eduardo, moving at least ten feet ahead of them, would stop, inspect the ground, or examine leaves on a tree, then continue. At other times, he would turn to the right or left and forage a new path through the thickness. Jake took periodic sips of water from his bottles on a quest to stay hydrated, and listened to the macaws above, the creaking insects surrounding them, and the steady beat of their footfalls as the afternoon wore on. Eventually, the heat and humidity eased off as the sun began its descent.

"Not far now," Milton said from behind him.

Jake glanced over his shoulder. "Does Eduardo ever talk?"

"Of course. Just not so much when he's tracking."

"Tracking?"

"Yes."

"Why is he tracking? Aren't we going to a regular place where tour guides take their guests?"

"Your friend Luke—how close are you two?"

Jake slowed his pace, then stopped to face Milton. "Why do you ask?"

"You're not aware of the nature of his trip into the Amazon Rainforest?"

"Actually, I have no idea. Do you know what he was doing here?"

"We're not entirely sure ourselves, but he paid a lot of money to have the company I work for bring him out here and to have us"—he gestured at Eduardo and himself— "on stand-by in case you arrived."

Jake started walking again. "Is there anything specific about the area Luke chose to visit?"

"Not the area itself."

Jake stopped again. "Then what?"

Milton placed a hand against a tree and took a deep breath. "He wanted to be taken to the most populated area of the Bothrops Asper."

"What the hell is a Bothrops Asper?"

"One of the deadliest snakes alive. It's a venomous pit viper, sometimes called the *ultimate* pit viper."

"Now that makes sense. No wonder he had all that antivenin. My friend is a scientist." Jake shrugged. "He's probably here doing research on those pit vipers."

Milton motioned at the path. When Jake turned around, Eduardo had gone so far he couldn't see him anymore.

"We should be moving along," Milton said.

Jake started after Eduardo, the knot in his stomach increasing in size. The more he thought about what Luke was doing in the Amazon Rainforest, the more he wished his friend had never come down there.

CHAPTER SEVENTEEN

Jeffrey Harris surveyed his pencil art, placing the 6B pencil down on the easel's ledge after adding in the shadows behind his wife's face. The picture did the family justice. A certain splendor was given to the drawing, a glamorous appeal even. There was depth in his wife's eyes and promise in his son's. They were his and he was theirs.

He stepped away from the easel to wash his hands and prepare to clean his workspace. The early evening had lent itself to wine, drawing, and an easy release of his daily tensions. Nothing could be more pleasant than an evening with the family.

Back in the living room, he addressed his wife on the couch.

"One more glass of wine before we retire for the evening?"

She nodded.

"Very well. I'll pour." In the kitchen, he retrieved two wine glasses and stopped when the scrapbook caught his eye. A quick flip of the top revealed what his son had achieved. A lock of his son's hair placed strategically by a recent picture of himself gave Jeffrey chills.

"One day you'll be an artist like your father," Jeffrey gushed. "Maybe we'll paint together."

He closed the scrapbook and proceeded to pour the wine. As he entered the living room, the phone rang.

"I'll get it," he shouted.

He snatched the phone up on the third ring.

"Hello?"

"Bad news here."

"I'm listening."

"Detective Jake Wood has left the country. He's out of the picture now."

"Fair enough." Harris massaged his scrotum. Drawing naked allowed arousal moments, to do as he pleased. Especially when hearing such good news.

"We'll meet tomorrow. Go over what we have and what to do next."

"Fair enough," he repeated. "And Detective Aiken? How is he?"

"I just talked to him. He's fine."

Harris was actively stroking his member now. The news was a fillip to his arousal, which wouldn't be sated without another release. He raised the mouthpiece to keep it away from his short gasps of breath as he gripped himself.

"I'll call in the morning," the voice said. "Get some sleep. Say hi to the wife."

He lowered the phone to his mouth and held his breath for a brief second. "Will do, Detective Joslin."

CHAPTER EIGHTEEN

I t wasn't where they expected it to be. According to Milton, if they hadn't brought Eduardo along, they never would've found Luke's camp, but they came across it in the final light from the sun.

"The last place we recorded them by GPS was fifty meters from here." Milton rubbed his chin. "What brought them down to this area doesn't make sense."

Eduardo used his machete to cut a path for himself, then slipped between two trees and disappeared.

Jake turned to Milton. "Why not? What if those viper things were over here?"

Milton pointed back the way they'd come. "Basecamp is better suited up on that flat area we passed. Down here might be closer to the snakes but you don't want to sleep with them."

Jake scanned the immediate area in search of anything that slithered. "I see your point."

They were boxed in on all sides by thick shrubs, trees with a wider base than most of the ones he'd observed on the walk in. Luke's tent sat near the rim of the small rectangular clearing that was no larger than fifty by twenty feet. Several hammocks hung suspended between trees back up the small hill at the basecamp, but Luke had chosen to sleep down here in his tent.

Jake moved toward the tent, its canvas entrance peeled back, revealing an empty interior devoid of a human body. Thankful none of the men on Luke's tour had been found dead or incapacitated yet, he kept hope alive that they'd find them all safe soon enough. But why leave their belongings behind? What would cause them to run from their camp without any supplies to speak of?

Inside the tent was a single air mattress placed on the right side wall of the canvas. A silver flashlight sat by the base of a makeshift table by the mattress. As the remainder of the sun's light died out for another day, Jake studied the table. Several vials of green liquid sat capped and undisturbed. Luke had brought two cases with him. One was empty—no doubt the case that contained the vials of green liquid now sitting on the table. Another case revealed five large ampoules with syringes stashed in a recessed area near the bottom of the case. All the ampoules were neatly stored in a black foam casing. What concerned Jake was the empty spot where a sixth ampoule was supposed to be. Someone had already used whatever was inside Luke's case.

He gently lifted one of the ampoules out and raised it to his eyes, but there wasn't enough light to make out the wording. He exited the tent and read the small print in the fading light of dusk.

FER-DE-LANCE ANTIVENIN

"What the hell is Fer-de-lance?" he asked.

Milton was busy carving something with his knife again. He stopped what he was doing and moved closer. "That's just another name for the Bothrops Asper." As he stepped up to Jake, he asked, "What have you got there?"

"Looks like an ampoule of antivenin for one of those vipers we talked about earlier."

Milton nodded. "Resembles the vials I saw in his case." He started back to where he'd been carving. "Since they're not here and they left their supplies, I'm sure they'll be back."

"Not necessarily."

"Huh?"

Jake lowered the small container of antivenin. "They could be dead."

Milton shook his head in the last bit of light. "No. Eduardo would've been able to tell. Body or no body, he would've seen signs of a struggle. That's where he is now."

"Where?"

"Following the trail."

"What trail? And how can he see out here?"

"With Eduardo, there's always a trail."

A moment later, Milton clicked something, then clicked it again. A lighter caught, the flame casting an eerie glow on his face. He lowered it to the ground, and a glorious fire rose from the kindling. In moments, the fire rose several feet high, giving them light and warmth.

Jake reentered Luke's tent and returned the ampoule into the black foam cutout, then snapped the case closed. Underneath the case, he lifted what appeared to be a journal. Flipping through the handwritten pages, Jake wondered what he would discover about his friend. Would it be an invasion of Luke's privacy? If Luke was in danger, Jake needed to know everything.

Jake shoved the notebook under his arm and exited the tent.

CHAPTER NINETEEN

Eduardo had returned with a look of bewilderment, which communicated to Jake that he'd found nothing. There was no sign of Luke or his team. They would search more intensely in the morning.

Dinner was served and was quite filling. Milton fed the flames that he'd contained with a circular perimeter of rocks. He'd also piled another dozen strips of wood on the side to feed the fire well into the night.

"Jake." Milton leaned closer. "Eduardo and I are heading up to the basecamp where the hammocks are strung. That's the best place to sleep. We'd like you to join us."

Jake shook his head. "This was Luke's tent. When he returns, he'll come here. I'm staying right in there on that air mattress until he comes back."

"What if he doesn't come back? How long will you stay out here?"

That was a question he didn't have an answer for. "I'll give it a couple of days and decide from there."

"We thought you would decide to stay in the tent—that's why we prepared extra wood for the fire and your backpack has enough water. In one of the backpack's pockets you'll find an assortment of nuts and berries if you get hungry through the night."

"Thank you. I'll be fine."

Milton rummaged in a pocket, then produced a small cylindrical device. "Here, take this."

Jake took it. "What is it?"

"If there's trouble, blow on that. We'll hear it a mile away."

Jake inhaled deeply, then blew on the whistle. It shrieked a high-pitched call that startled him and quieted the sound of the evening's insects in the immediate area.

"Wow, that is loud."

"As I said. You need us, blow long and hard. We'll come running."

Jake nodded and slipped the whistle into his front pocket. "Go. Get some sleep. I'll be fine."

Milton rose to his feet and started toward Eduardo, who also got to his feet.

"Hey, Milton," Jake said.

Milton turned back. Eduardo stopped, too.

"Those viper snakes can't chew through canvas"—he gestured at the tent— "can they?"

Milton shook his head. "I doubt they will bother you tonight."

"Good. I'll zipper it closed when I'm asleep, too."

"You'll be fine, Jake. See you in the morning."

The guide and the tracker walked out of the light and disappeared into the blackness of the trees, Eduardo leading the way. Alone, Jake stretched out and opened Luke's journal. After several minutes of reading quotes from colleagues in the world of biology and cell structure, Jake threw more chunks of wood on the fire, then dragged the air mattress from the tent, and stretched out on it. The fire flickered on the page as Jake read on.

Luke Mercer had surmised that immortality was absolutely possible based on the Hydra, a genus of small fresh-water animals native to tropical areas. The Hydra experienced tissue regeneration when injured. It reminded Jake of high school biology and how he'd learned crabs could regenerate new pincers.

Jake read notes on a sidebar that quoted a man named Daniel Martinez, who had written in a scientific journal in 1998 that the Hydra were biologically immortal as they didn't age.

The fire intensified with the new wood. Jake shifted, easing back from its heat, and continued reading.

Since the Hydra had an unlimited lifespan, Fortech Industries entered into the science behind aging in their endeavor to create a Hydra Man. They had already increased the lifespan of aging mice by over thirty percent using something called DNA Methylation.

He flipped several pages ahead as the reading became heavier, more tedious, and stopped on a section called Telomeres. The *length* of a person's telomeres represented a human's biological clock. Two pages later, Jake read about a gene called Forehead Box 03, (FOX03) which was commonly found in humans living to the age of one hundred or older.

He glanced up as something disturbed the usual undulation of the night's insects. Jake stared at the wall of black at the limit of the fire's light. He held his breath and listened. After several moments, the crickets started up again and others followed. Within seconds, the usual din was back.

"Milton?" Jake whispered, his own voice startling him somewhat. "Was that you guys?"

When no answer came, he set Luke's journal on the ground and got to his feet. A quick examination of the rectangular clearing revealed nothing. Whatever had broken the evening's calm didn't seem to be predatory. Just to be safe, Jake pushed his way a couple of feet into the tree line and found a five-foot branch within minutes. After returning to the air mattress by the fire, he pulled a small knife from the backpack and carved the end of the stick into a point. Satisfied with his boy-scout skills, he placed the newly-fashioned spear in front of him and eased back onto the mattress.

After listening to the surrounding area and watching the fire for a few moments, he retrieved the journal and opened it to the final pages.

Instead of experimenting on mice, Fortech Industries had developed what they called the Immortal Gene, loosely based on their Hydra Man theory, and tested it on Adam, their first subject. Fortech was working outside FDA regulations by having the American-owned firm in Canada, north of Toronto. Some loophole, some form of diplomatic immunity afforded them carte blanche on all testing of any sort of drug on any subject they wanted, human included. According to Luke's notes, they were acting on their own in an illegal capacity and he wouldn't continue to be a part of it.

With Fortech's willing volunteers, Luke recorded half a dozen men who had taken the latest version of the Immortal Gene. As of his latest writing, the scientists at Fortech Industries weren't offering conclusive studies on the success or failure of the regeneration capacities, nor were they releasing any data on whether the Immortal Gene actually worked.

Jake rubbed his eyes and considered calling it a night. Eduardo and Milton would be up with the sun and would come to wake him.

He flipped to the last page in the journal, still trying to absorb what Luke was involved in. The ramifications for humanity were immense. The ability to arrest aging was a staggering feat. What happened if several hundred—no, thousands—of people were able to utilize this Immortal Gene? How would the earth sustain the perpetual lifespan of individual human beings? Would those injected be able to procreate? If so, would their offspring be gifted with the gene? People would soon be asking potential spouses if they would die one day or live forever. Couples would want to mate with only gene-related others. The ramifications were massive to the point where every road led Jake to conclude that death itself was necessary. If seven billion people on earth weren't dead in one hundred years, leaving room for another batch of people to populate it, the world would be overrun. In theory, the Immortal Gene was a wonderful scientific breakthrough. But in reality, humanity would die of starvation due to overpopulation.

On the last page of the journal, Luke had concluded exactly that. He had been sent to the Amazon Rainforest to test the Immortal Gene on a predator. They specifically wanted him to locate a bothrops asper and inject it with the Immortal Gene. On his trip, his companion, a professional snake handler, was to meet him in Manaus.

Jake closed the journal. He yawned, stretched his tired muscles, then rested his head as the fire slowly died.

If Luke had come out to this area to locate a snake, where was he now? What happened to his team, the snake handler?

Something moved in the bush again, startling Jake out of his thoughts. It was time to retire. He wasn't afraid of the bogeyman. He wasn't intimidated by things that went bump in the night. As a cop, Jake had seen only manmade horror. That didn't stop him from a fear of the unknown and the rainforest was an unknown.

Once on his feet, he kicked dirt onto the fire then stepped away to urinate in a nearby bush. At the opening of the tent, he dragged the air mattress back inside, crawled in after it, and then closed the tent's zipper. Once it was secure, Jake lay down by feel, then placed a hand behind his head. With the other hand, he felt his front pocket to make sure he still had the whistle.

He thought about Cindy and what she must be thinking. He hadn't gotten a hold of her since leaving Ontario. She had no idea where he was and neither did his partner. As soon as he was back in Manaus he'd contact them.

His mind turned back to Luke and what he must have been

dealing with at Fortech Industries, not to mention the ramifications of something like an Immortal Gene. Maybe the green liquid on the makeshift table was a sample of the Hydra Man Immortal Gene substance. Luke's research intentions of locating a dangerous viper explained why he had the antivenin with him, but it didn't explain why one of the ampoules was missing. That was probably why the basecamp had been deserted—they would've had to race back to their boat to take the bite victim to the hospital.

He sat up in the dark. That would explain the missing boat from the inlet. That had to be it. He snapped his fingers.

Something moved close to the tent in response to his snap. The sound of the rainforest's insects had stopped again. Absolute silence descended upon the area. The only sound Jake discerned was the beating of his own heart. Not sure what to expect, he eased the tiny whistle from his pocket and placed it in his mouth.

Then he waited.

Something moved again. Much closer than before—right outside the thin canvas wall of the tent.

What the fuck?

Should he blow the whistle? What would he tell the tour guys when they arrived and nothing was wrong? That he was afraid of things that go bump in the night?

While the night remained silent around him, he took a mental inventory of the tent. In his mind's eye he saw the air mattress. On the left, he saw the makeshift table with the glass containers filled with green liquids.

Whatever was outside moved again. It sounded like the thing was trying to be stealthy. Was it a predator? Would Milton and Eduardo leave him alone out here if the odds of attack were high? Didn't the Amazon Rainforest have jaguars and tigers? He regretted not researching what he was getting into. Although, on the other hand, if he'd known too much, maybe he would've avoided coming.

The flashlight.

It hit him like a wave smacking into a retainer wall. Why hadn't he thought of it before? Luke had left a flashlight at the base of the makeshift table.

Whatever was outside was close. His guts knotted. Jake rolled slowly and touched the floor of the tent. Leaning farther, he moved forward by feel, searching for the flashlight or a leg of the table.

The whistle firmly stuck between his teeth, he breathed in and out slowly, rolling off the mattress and onto the canvas floor.

Something touched his ankle and he nearly jumped out of his skin. A grunt escaped his lips and the whistle fell from his mouth, lost to the dark.

He kicked with his feet in a frantic gesture to dislodge whatever was in the tent with him, but nothing was there. Had he bumped himself? Was it only his imagination freaking him out?

He imagined the jokes his coworkers would have if they saw him now. They would never let him live it down.

Whatever touched his ankle had to be in his imagination. The zipper was secure. He was alone in the tent.

But it wasn't always secure.

"Shit," he muttered under his breath.

When he'd been reading Luke's journal, he'd left the zipper up, the tent wide open. Then he'd entered the tent in the dark.

His heartbeat doubled. Sweat broke out on his forehead. What if whatever had been tracking him was inside the tent with him?

Something moved. It was close. Too close.

He spun around and smacked the back of his hand into the base of the table. Lunging to the right, he knocked the cylindrical flashlight tube over.

Something touched his leg again. This time he was certain. The pressure was unmistakable.

In a panic, he snatched up the flashlight, thumbed the button halfway along its outer casing, and produced glorious light.

Something hissed in the half a second it took him to spin the flashlight toward his feet and the zippered door beyond.

The thick body of a coiled snake near the entrance to the tent stared back at him, its eyes reflecting the light.

Jake jerked away and bumped into the small table hard, its brittle wooden leg cracking in his ear. The table slanted downward, the bottles on top sliding toward him.

The snake shot forward, its powerful jaws snapping inches from Jake's chin.

"Fuck—" he yelled, but was cut off as the bottle of green liquid smashed into his chest.

The fluid shot into his face.

His eyes and mouth drenched, he gasped and began spitting, curling his body farther away from the snake near the door while he wiped at his eyes. The liquid stung like a wicked sunburn. Unable to avoid it, he swallowed several times to clear his mouth.

"What the fuck?" he gasped out loud.

The whistle.

His legs under him, he shone the flashlight at the floor and located the whistle by the pillow area of the air mattress.

One look at the snake, then back to the whistle was enough to determine he could reach it in time.

He shot forward, clutched the whistle, then jerked back as the snake made a feeble attempt to bite him again.

The damn thing had to be as afraid of him as he was of it. And the powerful flashlight in its face, blinding it, might be enough to stave off a serious attack. But if this was one of those ultimate pit viper snakes, he didn't know how long he had until it actually sank its teeth into him.

The whistle now back between his lips, Jake blew hard and

long. The whistle emitted a high-pitched shrill that startled the snake into lunging forward again. Jake snapped back until he was curled at the back wall of the tent.

Rip the canvas.

Why hadn't he thought of it before? He didn't have to use the door of the tent when he could cut an opening in the back. But with what? The knife was out by the remnants of the fire. He'd last used it to fashion a spear tip on his branch, which was also out by the diminished fire.

Distant thunder pounded toward him. Footsteps.

"Jake," Milton shouted. "You okay?"

Afraid to yell back and startle the snake, Jake waited. While he waited, his guides' footfalls drawing closer, something was happening to his skin where that liquid had landed on him. His mouth tasted like an old orange. The air smelled citrusy, like someone had recently applied cleaning products to a tile floor.

Milton stopped outside. "Jake?" He was panting. "You in there?"

"Yeah," Jake said. "Got a snake with me."

"There a reason you chose to try to sleep with a snake?"

"Funny."

"You bit?"

"Not yet."

"Okay, Eduardo is about to open the zipper. How close is the snake?"

"Right at the door."

"What kind of snake is it?"

"No idea. Don't know that sort of thing. I can tell you it's not a cobra, but that's it."

"Does it have a dark brown head and a pale yellow underside?"

Jake adjusted the flashlight to see it better. "Yes. Looks like it."

"Okay. That might be a pit viper."

111

"Oh shit. What are the odds, eh?"

"We're going to act like it is, okay?"

"Sure." Jake kept his voice even, slightly above a whisper. "Sounds great."

"They are an excitable breed, unpredictable when disturbed."

"Why is it in my tent?"

"These pit vipers are often found near human habitations. They're exactly the breed your friend was looking for, hence the vials of antivenin. So if you do get bit, we happen to be in luck."

"Glad you're feeling lucky."

"One more point," Milton said. "Before Eduardo opens the zipper, use something to cover yourself."

"I have nothing in here with me. Wait. Cover myself? Why?"

"Can you use the air mattress?"

"I'm half on it, half off. I move, it lunges at me. Why is that important?"

"Because the bothrops asper, if that's what it is, doesn't just bite. They're known for spitting their venom."

"*Spitting?*"

Milton and Eduardo moved outside the tent. Light shone through the walls. The snake turned to the left, then faced Jake again, fixing his eyes on him.

"They can eject venom over a distance of up to six feet," Milton added.

"*What?* Get me out of here. And kill that light. It's bothered by it."

The light outside the tent died. Jake aimed his flashlight at the snake's face. Its body moved, uncoiling slightly.

"It's doing something," Jake whispered.

"Hold on, Jake. We have an idea. Eduardo is going to slice the tent open at the back, on the opposite side of the zippered door."

"Do it. Now."

The sound of a knife entering the fabric was soft and smooth. Jake swallowed, the taste of oranges in his throat.

The snake grew more agitated as the knife worked its way down the wall.

"We still good in there?" Milton asked.

"Yeah. Just hurry."

The snake moved again. This time it raised its head to knee height. He had to be trying to see what was causing the new noise. Trapped as it was inside the tent, the snake was ready to attack, and more viciously than before. Its tongue flickered in and out rapidly, testing the air.

Jake begged the snake to wait a little longer.

"What's that smell, Jake?" Milton asked.

"I spilled a bottle of green liquid."

"Oh. Shit."

The knife stopped moving.

"Come on out, Jake. There's a door behind you now."

When he moved his foot an inch, the snake jolted.

Jake stopped moving. Then tried again.

"Shit."

"What?"

"I move. It moves."

"Can you just dive out?"

"I'm aimed at the hole, head first."

"Find a way, Jake. Just get out here."

"Working on it."

He moved ever so slowly until his legs were curled under him. After adjusting his weight onto his right side, he edged bodily away from the pit viper.

The snake had had enough. It decided to attack.

The small head shot forward with more force than before, trails of venom firing from its mouth. The viper's speed was incredible, the venom hitting Jake in the face before he had a chance to close his eyes or mouth. It hit the back of his throat and he gagged on reflex, swallowing.

Primal instinct kicked in. Jake scrambled out of the tent and launched himself into Milton before he realized what he was doing. Blinded by the venom, choking, Jake dropped to the dirt floor and tried to blink his eyes clear, then rubbed them vigorously. He saw snatches of stars above him as he focused on getting his breathing back under control.

Milton and Eduardo seemed busy with something else. He wanted to call out to them to finish what they were doing and help him, but couldn't. The pain started slowly. It rose in his throat, on his cheeks, in his eyes. Liquid—he hoped it was tears and not blood—leaked from his eyes. Something was moving beneath him, vibrating. Then he realized it was his own body, shuddering in the rising wave of torment. They were at least a six-hour walk to the boat and a two-hour boat ride back to Manaus. If the antivenin didn't work, he would probably die. As the pain increased to agony, his thoughts turned to Cindy and the missed opportunities.

Then Milton appeared above him, a syringe in his hand.

"Jake, you got venom in the face. Eduardo killed it and identified it. You can thank your friend Luke later. We're going to inject the antivenin into you now. You're going to be just fine."

Jake tried to nod, shuddering, then moaned as the shuddering turned to what felt like contortions.

"It'll subside soon," Milton said through the fog of pain. "The antivenin is in your bloodstream."

Something changed. The air, the atmosphere. His heart rate tripled. His lungs starved for air. Then his body began to shut down.

From far off, he thought he heard Milton say something like he had never seen that kind of reaction before.

On his last deep breath, he roared a primal scream. He was under attack from within. The pain was beyond intense and paralyzing as seizures started in what felt like his every muscle.

A flashlight crossed his vision. One of the men shouted something to him, but the lights for Jake Wood were dimming.

Then they turned off altogether.

PART TWO

THE SNAKE

CHAPTER TWENTY

Being cold had never felt like this. It was a comforting cold, like entering an air-conditioned clubhouse after a hot day of golf. He sensed, more than felt, the bedsheets on him, the room, a window emitting light to his right, the sun's heat on his skin. He took in the entire room without opening his eyes, remaining calm, breathing the room in.

Two people had come and gone recently. A woman. A man. The woman more frequently. He was unaware how he knew this. A sense, maybe? A feeling? Without an explanation, his mind wandered over the smells, the sensations of the room, enjoying the sun's warmth on his chilled body.

Rhythmic steps approached the room, vibrating minutely, muffled by a wall. As the person drew closer, the vibrations increased subtly. Until finally, the person—he deduced female by the softness of her footfalls—stopped at his door and turned the handle.

"Good morning, Mr. Wood," a pleasant voice whispered in an accent. "Ready for your morning exercises?"

Where am I?

The woman placed something on a table to his right and moved toward the window. The curtains were drawn shut, vastly reducing the light in the room as well as the direct heat of the sun.

He tried to say something to get her to open the curtains

again, but all that came out was a moan.

The woman jerked. Her gasp was cut short by her hand as it clamped over her mouth. Then, to Jake's consternation, the woman scampered from the room without reopening the curtains.

The room's temperature cooled quickly, and within minutes, Jake fell back to sleep. The commotion of people running toward the room was the last thing he detected before he lost consciousness.

CHAPTER TWENTY-ONE

Someone was in the room. A man. An old friend, maybe? They were close, sitting beside the bed.

Jake lay still and scanned the room with his newfound senses. He let his mouth fall open slightly, as if in a daze, to let the room in, the smells, the aromas. He tasted—felt—new flowers to his right. The blessed curtain was open again. Warm sunshine prickled his skin with life.

He opened his mouth wider, easing out his tongue, breathing deeply, taking in the scents, the feelings, the atmosphere. The woman from the other day had been there recently. Although something was different this time. He sensed she had a child, a little girl to be exact, who was sick. The woman carried a sick smell on her. Not her sick smell. Someone else's.

He wondered what could possibly have happened to him to cause an olfactory reaction which detected pheromones so well?

The man sat to his left. Without laying eyes on the man, Jake was pretty sure he was a doctor.

While Jake pondered the question of his whereabouts and why he was there, he recalled being a cop before whatever happened to him. A homicide detective.

Some of the past seeped in. Bits of information filtered through. Luke had called him for help. He'd flown to Manaus, Brazil, then traveled into the Amazon Rainforest. A snake had violated his tent, then sprayed him with venom.

He moaned and tried to move, to touch his face.

How long had he been there? Had they flown him home to Ontario, or was he still in Brazil? Maybe he needed special care, because he'd lost his memory.

He focused on the atmosphere outside the room. Perhaps his sense of smell could garner clues to where he was. His mouth open, Jake drew in deep and was able to isolate several different scents. The building was relatively small. A strong pine scent, like walking through the forest after a hard rain, came from outside the building's walls. They were surrounded by a dense set of trees. This area probably wasn't local to Toronto and it definitely wasn't Barrie as the highway was right outside the Barrie hospital's door.

So where was he? Orillia or Manaus?

In order to move him from the rainforest, where he was pretty sure the incident had taken place, he had to have been unconscious for a few days. Maybe even a week.

He remembered the sun on his skin. The curtains moved aside. The breeze meant a window somewhere close by was open. Which meant it wasn't winter. Manaus was hot most of the year. Could he still be in Brazil? If so, he needed to contact Cindy right away.

His heart rate increased to the point where he felt his pulse in his ears. How long had he been asleep? What really happened in the rainforest? Anger stirred. Who was doing this to him? To what end? Where was Luke? Had his guides, Milton and Eduardo, made it out of the rainforest?

He forced his head to turn toward the man in the room. He tried to open his eyes, but the lids wouldn't respond.

A moan escaped his throat.

The man started beside him, gasping.

"Sir?" the man said, his English sounding American-like. "Are you awake?"

Jake nodded, ever so slightly.

"I am your doctor. My name is Dr. Mark Sutton." The doctor touched his forehead with a damp cloth. "I'm an American doctor working here in Rio."

Rio? As in Rio de Janeiro?

Jake let his head come back to center as he listened, and smelled the air. The doctor stepped away, tapped on a keyboard, then hit some kind of buzzer. Somewhere along a corridor, someone rolled back a chair and began walking toward the room, their footfalls more discernible with each step. He had detected their presence before.

As a woman entered the room, the doctor said, "Sir?" He approached the side of the bed. "Can you hear me? Tap once with your hand if you can."

Jake lifted his right hand, then dropped it.

A level of elation vibrated the room, overwhelming him. Why was everyone so happy?

"How're you feeling? One tap for good, two for not so good."

Jake tapped once.

"Fantastic." Jake detected the doctor turning away from him. "Dim the lights," he said to the woman. "Close the curtains."

Jake tapped the bed two, three times.

"What is it?" The doctor's voice filled with concern.

He tapped again.

"Dim the lights?"

He tapped once.

"Close the curtains?"

He tapped violently.

"Okay, we'll leave the curtains open."

His breathing slowed at the mention of open curtains. He could detect the doctor surveying him, watching him. It was in the way the doctor's voice traveled to him. Sometimes the doctor spoke when looking at Jake's face, sometimes his legs or abdomen.

The woman moved to stand by the door.

"Do you know your name?" the doctor asked.

That's a weird question.

Jake tapped once.

"Can you tell us your name?"

He tapped.

After Jake didn't speak, the doctor said, "We have tape over your eyes. While you've been asleep we didn't want you opening them too suddenly, exposing them to light, so we kept them taped. Do you understand?"

He tapped once.

"Good. I'm going to remove the tape now, but please, keep your eyes closed until I can shield your head from the sun's rays. Do you understand?"

He tapped once. Then moaned.

"Don't worry. You'll be speaking again very soon. Everything will make sense to you. Let's just get you seeing again." The doctor leaned in close. The woman moved toward the window. Probably to close the curtains quickly if something went wrong.

"Okay." The doctor's fingers hesitated over his right eye. "You'll feel a slight tug, then the right eye will be clear. Ready?"

He moaned, tapped once.

Fingers gently touched his brow, then yanked hard, and what felt like the strip from a bandage peeled away.

"Let's do the other one now."

The procedure was repeated.

"Are you ready to open your eyes?"

Jake moaned.

"Do it slowly. Blink a lot. Take your time. Adjust for the light in the room. The overheads are dimmed. Whenever you're ready, sir."

Jake let his eyes flutter open to a slit. The light was so intense right away that it felt as if he was staring into the sun. He closed them, pushing his head backward into the pillow, waited a heartbeat, then tried again.

"It's okay. Your eyes will need time. They've been closed for a while."

Along with the increased heartbeat, his breathing had sped up. He clenched his hands and tried to lift them, but they were secured to the bed. When he tried to rise, a strap on his chest and forehead forbade movement.

The stirring of anger rose again. He clenched his jaw and pulled his right arm up. The strap on his right wrist snapped.

"What the ...?" the doctor whispered from the bedside.

"Sir, listen to me." The doctor scrambled around the bed and tried to restrain Jake's arm.

Something had happened to his muscles while he slept. They were stronger than he ever imagined.

"He shouldn't be able to do that," the doctor said. "His muscles atrophied."

Jake left his other arm strapped to the bed. The doctor seemed worried and since whatever had happened to him wasn't the doctor's fault, Jake eased back and relaxed. He moaned, let his right arm slip back onto the sheets, then forced his eyelids open even farther. Light filled his vision. He had to blink it away as his eyes adjusted.

"Good, good," the doctor said, his voice soft. "Take it easy. Go slow. There's no hurry."

The doctor edged away from the bedside. By the time Jake got his eyes open enough to see through slits, the two people in the room stood by the head of the bed.

After a few minutes of blinking, he finally was able to see.

Shapes took form. When he focused both eyes on one object, his vision zeroed in.

Had they put contact lenses on him?

He found the doctor's face and pushed his head into the pillow. The man looked like he could be Charlton Heston's brother. The tanned, rugged face with a strong jawline made him think he was looking at the Heston from the 1970s.

"Hello there," Dr. Sutton said. "Can you speak yet?"

Jake turned until he saw the nurse with the sick daughter, then fixed his gaze on the doctor again, who offered him a wide smile.

"It's so good to see you awake," the doctor said. "Let me tell you where you are. This is Ansel's Health Clinic just south of Rio De Janeiro in an area called Gávea. We're surrounded by lots of palm trees and greenery. The American University is a couple of miles away. Here, at this clinic, we've been taking good care of you around the clock and will continue to do so until you're up and at 'em."

How long? Jake moaned.

The doctor turned away. "Nurse, please get him some water."

Moments later, the nurse brought a cup to his mouth and bent a straw inward. He pulled on the straw, tasting the fluoridation immediately. He'd rather have the water without it. While he was asleep they must have cleaned and fixed his teeth, replacing two missing ones. He had a full set of teeth that seemed harder, more pronounced.

The nurse pulled the straw out of his mouth.

"Whoa, take it easy," she said, her accent clearly Portuguese. "Not too much."

The water hit his stomach and coalesced there, a cool blob of weight.

"Hhhooww llooongg?" he tried to ask.

"Take your time," the doctor said. "While you slept, your

body underwent subtle changes, one of them being your tongue. It thinned, as did most of your muscles from inaction."

He rolled his tongue. For the most part it felt the same, but getting it to help him talk seemed a challenge.

With great effort, he tried to speak each word slowly, finally getting *how* out and then *long*.

The doctor exchanged a cautious glance with his nurse. The nurse eased back from the bed as the doctor planted himself on the side.

"Sir," he said. "We're just glad to see you. Everything in its time. Can you tell us your name?"

Jake glared at him for not answering the question. Did Cindy know where he was? Had it been so long that they had caught the killer they had been hunting in Ontario? Had Luke ever been found?

Something in the doctor's pheromones explained a level of nervousness that didn't add up. There had been an accident. Venom. Milton had injected him with antivenin. Maybe he'd fallen into a coma. But he was okay now. Awake. A little physio and he'd be back on his feet. What was the big deal? Two weeks in the coma? A month? He needed to know how long.

"Hhooww llongg?" he asked, the words forming easier. The doctor's eyes clouded over. Jake frowned, then raised his eyebrows, expecting an answer. "Tell. Me."

"Sir, you've been in a coma for eighteen months. No one knows you're here because we don't know your name. All of our attempts to identify you failed. It's just a miracle that you're awake. That's what we want to focus on now. Rehabilitation. Maybe when you're stronger, we can reach out to relatives, let them know you're okay."

Eighteen months? Eighteen? Impossible. But yet, the doctor's tone told him it was true. He closed his eyes as questions assailed him. What had happened to Cindy? His job? What happened to his life? And how had he been able to afford medical care in Rio de Janeiro?

"Get some rest, sir," Dr. Sutton said. "We can talk more tomorrow."

The nurse shut the curtains, blocking the sun. Jake didn't protest this time. He wanted the sleep. He wanted to forget what he just heard. There was no way to process sleeping a year and a half of his life away. Not to mention his new teeth, new slimmer tongue, better sense of smell, and an innate ability to detect people approaching from a great distance by vibration alone.

No, it was better he took this lying down.

Just like how the transformation happened in the first place.

He'd slept for eighteen months.

He could sleep one more night.

CHAPTER TWENTY-TWO

Jake snapped awake, blinking in the light of the Brazilian sun as summer came on with the promise of warmth and light. The room's curtains were pulled wide and bound with a fancy cloth on each side. After Jake managed to eat breakfast on his own for the first time, he had the nurse elevate the bed following morning exercises.

In the ten days since he had awakened, Jake thought about how his coma would affect his life going forward. The answers to what had been happening with his career, his soon-to-be wife, and everything else would have to wait until Kirk and Cindy flew down to bring him home.

The positives were he hadn't died and he'd lost a lot of weight. Pre-coma weight had been 210 pounds. Post-coma weight was 160.

His teeth and vision were far better than before the accident. That would help with his job. His energy levels were at an all-time high, and it seemed no matter what he did, sleep had been elusive the past several nights.

The nurse had brought him a mirror. The changes to his face were minimal, other than aging and the color of his eyes. They'd turned a soft blue after being closed for the eighteen-month coma. Basically, he looked the same. The more drastic changes had been on the inside of his mouth. Dr. Sutton entered the room with a coffee in hand and took a seat by the window.

"Break time?" Jake asked.

"Chat time," the doctor said. "I'd like to discuss how you got here and what we've discovered since you arrived."

Jake folded the pillow into a ball under his head and angled himself to look at the doctor. "Then let's talk. Tell me about the changes in my physique. How are they possible?"

Speaking with the new shape of his tongue had taken practice, but now he was able to do it relatively easy, making mistakes only when excited. And all this without a speech therapist, which apparently most recovering coma patients needed.

"There were not many changes," Dr. Sutton said.

There was something about his tone that made Jake feel he was lying, but he decided not to press the issue. Cindy was due for a visit at any moment, and Jake planned to get his life back together as soon as possible.

The doctor sipped from his coffee. "I've heard from Kirk."

"And?"

"Kirk and Cindy arrived at the Rio airport a few hours ago. After they check into their hotel, they're coming here."

To see Cindy after a year and a half was going to be hard. And Kirk. What had his partner been up to all this time? There would be so much to catch up on.

The nurse entered the room and began tidying up in the corner by the window. She dusted a side table, then placed a vase of flowers atop a doily in the center. While dusting the windowsill, she checked her watch.

"How soon will they be here?" Jake asked.

"Supposed to be here within a half hour."

"Then help me into that wheelchair."

Jake had asked to be in the wheelchair for Cindy's first visit. Once he was comfortable in the chair and the nurse had gotten him a glass of water, he watched her work while the doctor sipped his coffee by the window.

"How's your daughter?" Jake asked her.

The nurse stopped what she was doing and slowly turned to him.

"My daughter?" she asked, her voice hesitant.

"She had a cold, right? Last week? She's okay now?"

She moved toward the door. "I don't recall telling you I have a daughter. Or that she had a cold."

"Is it your mother who came to visit you here at the clinic today? She brought you something. Your lunch? Am I right?"

She gasped and exited the room without answering. Last week, the nurse had reeked of her daughter's cold without having one herself, and earlier today she had entered his room to exercise and feed him smelling of Chanel No. 5, an old lady's perfume, one she didn't use.

He wheeled himself to the door to apologize, but someone was approaching his room.

Cindy Macmillan. His fiancée.

He offered a smile, then a gentle wave. Kirk followed Cindy. The doctor rose from his chair and moved toward the door.

Jake eased the wheelchair backward to let everyone in the room. Nervous as he was to see her, he reminded himself that he hadn't seen Cindy in only a few days in his reality. The horse allergy and hospital visit had happened. Then he'd driven to Toronto, flew to Manaus, and hiked into the Amazon Rainforest. Sure, he'd been in a long coma, but to him, he might have slept a couple of days. Mentally, nothing had changed.

But for Cindy, she'd had two Christmases and a long summer without him.

Cindy stopped at the door, her eyes welling with tears.

"It's a miracle, Jake." Cindy opened her arms and came across the room to him. "I'm so grateful you're alive."

"Me too," he mumbled into her shoulder as she embraced him. "Like how I look? They call it a coma diet."

She pulled back without responding and set her purse on the side table, wiping at her eyes. Kirk offered him a brotherly hug and pat on the shoulder, then leaned on the doorframe, shaking his head.

Jake saw the changes in Cindy immediately. The eighteen months had been good to her. She was thirty-one years old now, vibrant, and alive. Her hair had been recently done, and her curves were all still in the right places.

When Cindy grabbed several Kleenexes and stepped closer to the window, more truths about her hit him.

He *smelled* the truth on her and took it all in.

Kirk dropped a hand on his shoulder. "Hey bro. We thought you were dead. When we got the call ..." He stopped, emotion choking off the words. "Blew us away."

Jake nodded. "Dr. Sutton told me. I was a John Doe for eighteen months." He chanced a quick look at Cindy, his stomach knotting further, then shifted his gaze back to Kirk. "No hotel in Manaus had me registered, which makes sense. It was in Luke's name. The robbery in the hotel cleaned out all my ID. The hospital in Manaus found me on their sidewalk, near death, or so I'm told."

He glanced at the doctor, who nodded. "It took us days to discover the venom in his blood and that antivenin had already been administered. But with no ID, we couldn't learn his name until he woke up."

Cindy stayed by the window, wiping at her face.

"We're just so glad you're alive. How're you feeling?"

"Like heading to Boston," Jake said, trying to look around Kirk to see Cindy. "Maybe running the marathon."

"Thought so."

Sutton moved to stand by the bed. "Jake, there are a few things we need to discuss. Are you feeling up to it?"

Kirk moved aside. Jake kept his eyes on Cindy, who hadn't turned back to face him yet.

"Sure Doc, let's get this over with. How long before I can leave this place?"

"As soon as you're strong enough. That'll be up to you."

"Then I want to leave this week. While Kirk and Cindy are here. I want to fly home with them."

"Let's talk first." His tone grew firm along with his posture. Jake smelled it more than heard it. The doctor put out nervous vibes.

Something about Cindy's situation bothered him. He breathed in deeply, taking in more scents. His mouth dropped open, hair rising on his neck.

Another man had been with Cindy.

Cindy was pregnant.

In that one breath he understood everything and nothing. Tears leapt to his eyes and he raised a hand to wipe at them. Cindy finally turned toward him, but he swung the wheelchair in an arc to face the door and rolled into the sunlight, its warmth caressing his flesh.

"Jake …" Cindy managed to get out. "I'm so sorry."

She moved behind him. The taste in the air, the sense of movement, Kirk touching her arm, cautioning her to tread lightly in whispered tones, all came to Jake in a myriad of heightened senses. His vision had improved drastically in the coma, but it wasn't just his eyes that could see clearer now.

There would be another time, another day to deal with what was happening to him. Today he wanted to deal with what *had* happened to him.

"We didn't know you were alive," Cindy attempted to explain

herself. "*I* didn't know." Her voice cracked. "Oh Jake, I thought you were dead."

Allowing her to wallow in her explanation of a newfound love wasn't being fair. But it was only a few days ago—at least to Jake—that they had made love and he'd agonized over the second mortgage loan in order to give her the honeymoon of her dreams. Waking to learn she was no longer his woman shattered his heart like broken glass being rubbed into his stomach lining.

What else had changed? What other revelations were about to come?

"Jake," Cindy pleaded. "I need you to look at me."

He stared at the clinic door, the sun calming his limbs.

"Jake," Kirk said. "Hey man. It's not her fault. Dude, turn around."

Jake waited a few more breaths, then eased the chair back, and spun it around. He met Cindy's eyes.

"We were together a few days ago," Jake said, "as far as I'm concerned."

She nodded.

"Understand something for me. This feels like a betrayal."

She went to speak, but he shot up a hand for her to stop.

"For you, I was dead. I get it. But ..."

She looked at the floor.

"You were my woman. We were going to get married." He couldn't avoid the tears. "And now I have nothing." His voice broke. "No life, no Cindy, no job, no career, and probably no place to live when I leave here."

"Now, Jake." Dr. Sutton stepped closer. "Take things one step at a time. You're awake. You're alive. Rebuild as time goes on. Your life isn't over."

He glared at Sutton. "Who pays for this clinic?"

A quick glance at Cindy, then back to Jake. "An anonymous

donor," the doctor said.

"Anonymous donor? Really?"

The doctor set his coffee down and faced Jake, his hands clasped.

"After you slipped into a coma," he started, "the hospital in Manaus transferred you to us for care. Within days of you arriving, an anonymous donor set up a bank account for us to draw the money needed for your care. It never dried up."

"And no one investigated who this anonymous person was?"

"No one knew who you were." The doctor glanced at Kirk. "We sent Jake's picture to every major police force in the United States, but all correspondence came back as a dead end." He turned his attention back to Jake. "We had no idea you were from Canada. It just didn't come up."

Listening to the explanations, learning of Cindy's pregnancy, Jake's mood turned saturnine. A gloomy temperament overcame him as he thought about his future, alone. In his soul, he knew Detective Jake Wood would carry on in this world alone, not just because he'd lost Cindy to another man, but because the accident had changed him. He would spend the rest of his life like an ogre in the woods—one without his Fiona.

He turned to Cindy, looking daggers into her with the knowledge she wasn't his and would never be his again.

"You're pregnant," he said. "You're married. You're in love with another man. Why did you come to Brazil? Why not send Kirk with the news?"

She physically stooped lower, her posture crumbling. A wince crossed her face with each word. Her eyes puffy, she stared down at her hands, fumbling her fingers like an OCD patient examining them for dirt. Cindy sniffled, then wiped at her nose as the tension in the room thickened.

In a flat, monotone voice, that only broke once, Cindy said,

"I will sign the necessary papers to release me from being your power of attorney." She met his gaze, her face flushed, her eyes the same ones that once stared into his with love and respect. "I love you, Jake Wood. I will always love you." She moved toward the door. "Maybe one day you'll want to be in my life. Until then ..." She paused at the door. "I'll understand if you don't." She moved into the corridor and strode away.

Jake turned back toward the window and felt the vibration of her footsteps until they dimmed in the distance.

"That was harsh, man," Kirk said. He came to stand beside the wheelchair. "She fought for you for eighteen months, Jake. She set up a trust fund and flew to Manaus four times looking for you."

"That's enough for now," Dr. Sutton said, his tone firm again, authoritative.

"Think about what you just did, bro. I'll come back tomorrow. Maybe we'll talk shop for a while. I've got a few cases to tell you about. Shit like that."

Jake nodded and stared out the window.

Kirk patted Jake's shoulder then exited, leaving Dr. Sutton and Jake alone.

When Kirk was out of earshot, Jake asked, "What changed in me while I was in the coma, Sutton?"

"Now Jake, haven't we been through enough today?"

He spun the wheelchair around so fast, it tilted sideways and almost spilled him onto the clinic floor.

"No," he shouted. "What has happened to me?"

The doctor stepped back at the outburst. "Jake, take it easy. Small changes, things we haven't seen before."

"We?"

"The medical profession. But you're safe here. We've made sure of that."

"Safe?" he asked, using a calmer tone. "Safe from what?"

136

"Any sort of intrusion."

A thought occurred to him. "Who knows I'm here?"

The doctor hesitated, then crossed his arms. "No one other than Kirk and Cindy and that anonymous donor, plus my staff."

"Just as I figured." Fatigue swept over him. The sun's rays moved across the room. Soon he would need to sleep. "Is there something unique about my physical changes? Am I in some sort of hiding?"

The doctor shook his head. "It's not like that. You make it sound like a conspiracy."

"Then tell me, Sutton. What is this?"

The doctor fidgeted, uncrossed his arms, then opened his mouth to talk, but nothing came out. He blinked, tried again.

"Jake, your body changed because of what happened."

"What happened?" Even though fatigue was setting in, his anger rose. The doctor seemed to enjoy being evasive.

"A snake's venom was ingested with some sort of substance that we have not been able to identify as of yet."

"What substance?"

"I'm sorry, Jake, but we may never know. The changes your body went through during the coma were quite taxing." The doctor stood straighter, asserting a confident posture—back in doctor mode. "I'm sorry, Jake, but there's nothing we can do."

It dawned on him what the doctor was avoiding. Jake was dying.

"How long, Doc? How long have I got to live?"

"You won't live past the summer. Not with what's going on inside you. I'm sorry, Jake, but no human body could withstand what's happening to you and live through it. In fact, I'm amazed you're still alive."

CHAPTER TWENTY-THREE

Jeffrey Harris opened the door to the Tim Horton's donut shop and entered the line heading to the counter. The smell of donuts and muffins filled the cavernous store, making him yearn for something sweet. This particular Huntsville Timmy's was popular with the tourists as it had easy access off Highway 11 heading north to North Bay or south to Orillia, and Toronto beyond that. It was quiet on this particular Tuesday. A few seniors were having a discussion about the first year the young Justin Trudeau just had in office and all the Syrian refugees he brought over on the taxpayer's dime.

In another corner, two young men whispered in hushed tones, as if they were plotting some intense crime.

Two overweight men stood in line in front of Jeffrey, both looking as though they had spent the greater part of their day behind the wheel of a rather large vehicle.

When it was Jeffrey's turn at the counter, he ordered a large coffee and two toasted coconut donuts, which he took to a table where he could face the front of the store, but still be far enough away from the people discussing politics.

To his right, he had a full view of the parking lot. He didn't want to miss his future wife when she showed up. It had been almost two years since he'd taken Melissa Marcello and her son Jason to be his family.

It was time for another Gathering. Although the method of the Gathering was about to change.

He started in on one of the donuts, letting his coffee cool while he considered his surveillance methods. He had been stalking his new wife for two weeks now. He had learned her routines watching from afar, completely undetected.

In six weeks, on the first day of July, Canada Day would be celebrated with drinks, parties, and fireworks. It was also the day he would take on his new family.

Canada Day. A lovely day for a Gathering.

His new wife had three daughters. They would make a warm, welcoming family atmosphere in his Toronto home. Jeffrey just knew they would love their time with him in Toronto, and in July, they would all move in with him. As before, his scrapbook was ready to receive their locks of hair and he was prepared to sketch their likenesses in a vivid display of his love for them.

He had met Megan Radcliffe months before at his job in Toronto. She had recently lost her mother and was in Toronto for the funeral. On the day of the funeral, Megan had brought her daughters, Lindsay, Erica, and Tracy with her. Terry Radcliffe, her husband, was out of the country on business, she'd explained. Terry would be back late June, just in time for their annual Canada Day party, and Jeffrey was invited if he could make it up to Huntsville.

How nice of them. To invite the future man of the house to his own party.

He wouldn't miss it for the world.

The timing couldn't have been better. His son, Jason Marcello, had moved out and his wife, Melissa Marcello, had recently left him because of it. Jeffrey had removed the wedding ring and left it in Toronto. He'd collected the family pictures and placed them in storage. It was time to remarry. Time to take on a new family. July would mark over twenty months since his last family Gathering and he was ready for another one. This one would be easier. There would be revelers, partiers, drinking, and noise. After the commotion of the party wound down, he would deal with the youngest of the daughters first.

Eight-year-old Tracy would be asleep earliest that night. Then twelve-year-old Erica and finally, fourteen-year-old Lindsay. Once their parents were too drunk to know what was happening, he would restrain Terry and deal with Megan, gather the rings, the locks of hair, and the family pictures. He would then take his family to Toronto to be happy once again as a married man.

Textbook. Routine. Nothing to it.

He would leave no trace for the bumbling amateur local cops to trip over.

Jeffrey wiped his mouth and opened the lid to his coffee. The first sip washed down pieces of toasted coconut. He took another and enjoyed the taste known only from a Timmy's cup.

It was after lunch. Megan was due any time. As a full-time mother of three in her forties, she drove into Huntsville in the early afternoons on Tuesdays to do her grocery shopping. In the two weeks he'd been observing her, this was routinely her first stop. A coffee and a muffin for the road. His surveillance had revealed a lot about Megan. Most of it he liked, even the yoga classes she attended four times a week.

He checked his watch.

1:12 p.m.

He looked out into the parking lot. No movement.

The interior of the coffee shop reminded him of the one where his stepfather had given him his first lesson in the Gathering when he was ten years old. Wally—Jeffrey never called him Dad—had taken Jeffrey's homework away that night. Wally had explained that he needed his new son to be taught what it was to be a man.

He'd driven him out to an all-night coffee shop and lectured him on women and what kind of breed of animal they were. Talked about the Taming and the Gathering of the species.

At first, Jeffrey had been lost. It hadn't made any sense to him. The feelings he had for several girls at school were childish and unnecessary, according to Wally.

Jeffrey could see that now. Wally had been right. But what Wally didn't understand was once he taught Jeffrey everything, the next natural step in the process was to take Wally and Cynthia—Jeffrey's mother—out of the equation.

A secret that three people knew was only a secret if two of them were dead.

He scanned the counter, the chairs, reminiscing on that night. Jeffrey saw the chair he'd sat in as he listened to his stepfather talk about taking a woman, owning her, and the pleasure exacted from it. No nagging, no whining, no reasoning, and no cost. Wally's father had told him when he was young that every woman came with a price. The woman you stayed with only meant that she was the price you were willing to live with. In other words, you had to settle for the low-cost vehicle.

"Well, fuck that," Wally had exclaimed that night as the clock passed one in the morning. "I ain't never pay for no damn woman. They're here for us, man. They need to pay us. Don't you get it?"

Jeffrey had nodded enthusiastically, hoping to please his stepfather. He remembered being in awe of Wally's presence. He had been a captivating man, energetic. No wonder Jeffrey's mother had fallen for Wally.

Later that night, with Jeffrey scrunched down in the backseat of Wally's car, Wally had driven through downtown Toronto, cruising the hookers until he saw one he wanted. He had picked her up and driven to a quiet parking lot near one of the beaches on Lake Ontario.

Wally had ordered Jeffrey out of the car while he and the hooker did their thing, whatever that was. The back window fogged up while Jeffrey waited on a patch of sand in front of the car. When his father was done, he'd called Jeffrey back to the car.

The hooker had appeared to be sleeping. Wally later said she was unconscious. She couldn't handle a real man. She'd wake up in the morning, he'd said. Maybe later.

It was the blood that Jeffrey remembered the most at that tender age. And not the blood seeping from her mouth, ears and right eye socket. He'd never forget that and how the open eye bulged in a grotesque manner. It was the blood from under her skirt that shocked him. Wally had hauled the hooker's body from the back of the car and dragged her onto the sand of the dark empty beach. With a small flashlight, he'd lifted her skirt, proud of his work, and showed his ten-year-old stepson Jeffrey both female openings and how much blood had oozed from them. Jeffrey remembered thinking about her bathroom visits and how awful that would be tomorrow.

That was his stepfather's first lesson in relationships and Jeffrey never forgot it.

Two days later, Jeffrey had seen that girl again. She was on the front page of the newspaper with a caption about a dead woman found on Cherry Beach.

Jeffrey had beamed all day, knowing that was Wally's handiwork. The female species was one less. They had to pay a price, according to Wally.

Jeffrey endeavored to learn everything he could from Wally to make sure he never paid a single piece of currency for a woman, ever. So far, he never had and with due diligence, he never would. Yet he'd had more sex and intimacy times with women than anyone he knew. He had even been married five times now.

Megan Radcliffe would be his sixth wife.

To his right, the two seniors still discussing Trudeau had devolved to name calling. The young prime minister was now a cow-sucking, mule-fucking, cesspool of goat shit. Oh, and an asswipe. That almost made Jeffrey laugh, but he held it in. Wouldn't be prudent to get noticed by strangers too often, to stand out.

Movement in the parking lot caught his eye. He drank his coffee, the donuts not settling well in his stomach, then set the cup down slowly. With measured ease, as natural as possible, he looked out at the parking lot. With his index fingers, he pushed his glasses up his nose.

Megan Radcliffe was getting out of her car. She slammed her door and started for the entrance to the donut shop. The sunshine enhanced her lovely features. Her long, auburn hair, pretty smile, and lush lips were easy to see from his seat. With each step, her hips swayed to an inner soundtrack that displayed the toned legs of a mother who worked out. A disciplined mother who worked hard to take care of her family and herself.

Megan Radcliffe would make a fine wife. Too fine. For a moment, Jeffrey allowed himself to get excited and even considered taking his new family earlier than July. As fast as the idea hit him, he nixed it, knowing he had to wait for Terry Radcliffe to come back before any Gathering could take place. They could never be Jeffrey's family without the Blood Eagle, without the father's submission of power to be the head of the family.

He watched her a moment longer, then averted his eyes. After she entered the Timmy's, he waited until she was in line, then rose from his chair, the garbage from his donuts in his one hand, coffee in the other.

At the counter, he tossed the garbage away, turned and almost bumped into her.

"Oh, sorry—" he stopped. "Wait, Megan?" He pushed up his glasses.

She drew her head back, a hand flying to her chest, mouth open. "Jeffrey? Jeffrey Harris? Oh my goodness. How have you been?"

"Megan. Wow, long time. It's been a couple of months. How are you feeling now?"

"Ma'am?" one of the female clerks beckoned to them. "This till is open."

"One sec, Jeff. Let me order."

He nodded. "Of course," he said, then he backed off and headed to his table. A quick swipe of his hand through his short hair kept it off his face. When he sat, he fixed his glasses and waited for his bride to come to him.

Megan ordered a large tea, bag in, paid and joined him.

Not the usual coffee and muffin?

"What brings you up here?" she asked.

"Looking for a cottage. Thought I'd come up and see what Huntsville was all about." He gestured at the empty seat. "Please, have a seat. Join me for a quick minute, unless you're in a hurry."

"Well." She checked her watch. "I guess I have a minute."

Megan set her tea down and eased in across from him, her lithe body slipping into the chair with a liquidity only afforded to tight, fitness-bound bodies. Her breasts offered a subtle jiggle, pulling on his eyes to lower, but he refused the temptation.

No woman has power over me.

"What's it like living up here?" Jeffrey asked, reaching habitually for his glasses to ease them higher on the bridge of his nose.

She leaned forward and rested on her forearms. "Quiet, slow, calm. Think retired life. Lots of trees, wildlife. Beautiful really. Deerhurst Resort is close by. You've heard of it?"

"It's one of the reasons I'm here." This conversation couldn't last too long. Being seen in public too often by too many people increased risk later on. Although, this visit, six weeks before the Gathering, shouldn't register on anyone's internal radar. He checked his watch. "I was just heading out when we bumped into each other," he said. "Appointment with a realtor."

"Well, don't let me keep you." She started out of her chair.

"It's nice to talk to someone local, though. I wanted to get a feel for what cottaging up here would be like and eventually, I was thinking of retiring up here."

In an exaggerated fashion, she swung her arm in an arc and said, "Oh, this is the best place to retire. Living in nature with good people. You'll love it."

They started for the door together. "How are the winters this far north of Toronto?"

"They're okay. A bit of a problem, but they're doable. Hire some local kid to do the driveway and stay indoors on those real cold days. Otherwise, they're not bad and worth it to get to experience the summer around here."

He opened the door for her and followed her out of the Timmy's and across the parking lot to her car.

"Wow, it's been nice talking to you," he said. "Thanks again."

"No problem, Jeff. Anytime." She opened her car door. "See ya." She dropped into her seat.

He started away, then pivoted back around and raised a hand. "Wait. Megan."

Before the car was in gear, she lowered her window.

"Megan, I almost forgot. Aren't you guys having your annual Canada Day party this year?"

"Of course," she said, smiling wide at the thought. "I invited you the last time I saw you. Bring your wife. What a great way to welcome you to the neighborhood."

With the invite now official, something stirred in his loins as he stared at Megan's gorgeous countenance. He imagined all the things he was going to do to her during the night of the party and how she would make a fabulous wife.

"Oh, you're too kind." He waved at her. "Let's stay in touch and that way I can get directions."

They exchanged cell numbers and email addresses, and Jeffrey Harris was set. He watched his future wife drive out of the Tim Horton's parking lot, a smile playing across his lips. He hadn't had such a fit wife before. Maybe things needed to be different this time. He had over a month until the party to create a new plan.

By the time he got behind the wheel of his car, he had decided. Why treat women like his stepfather had? Why use them once and discard their physical body? The memory only lasted so long.

Megan Radcliffe would be the first wife that he would keep. Alive. In his home. With him. There would be no picture of her. No pencil drawing. No framed facsimile placed on the wall. Always a willing partner in their bedroom. Always ready. As a wife should be.

If there was ever a price to pay, it was Megan who would pay it. As his mother had. Rightly so. And all the women Wally had dealt with before Jeffrey had killed him.

The father would lose his soul and the three daughters would be dispatched, their locks of hair secured for the scrapbooks. But he would keep Megan as his souvenir this time.

The only thing he needed to do in the meantime was figure out how he could keep Megan drugged until he got her to Toronto and into the basement. He would drive her down right after the party, arriving at his home before six in the morning. He would wake her just enough so she could walk under her own steam. Once inside, the basement would be prepared with enough restraints to keep her there as long as he wanted. And with access to several debilitating drugs, Jeffrey would have his new wife live with him until he bored with her.

THE IMMORTAL GENE

The modus operandi was about to change and Jeffrey Harris was ready for it. It was time for a change. What he'd done before was child's play. It was time to raise his game. Elevate the stakes. He wasn't getting any younger. Women wouldn't find him as attractive in a few years. It was definitely time to take on a new wife and keep her where he would always have her available.

And when he was bored with her, Megan Radcliffe would be disposed of in the way only Jeffrey knew how.

Acid.

No physical traces.

Nothing to lead back to him.

Wash cycle. Rinse. Repeat.

He grinned to himself in the rearview mirror as he rubbed his beard. Life had been good to him. And now it was time to be good for someone else, to *do* good for someone else. Taking Megan and offering her this chance of a lifetime was a blessing in disguise. She could shirk her mundane existence and be his wife.

If this was a lottery, Megan had just hit the jackpot.

If only she knew how good things would be in her near future, she would turn her car around and pull back into the donut shop's parking lot to beg him to take her now.

With his erection at full mast, he left the parking lot, his mind full of the possibilities, dreaming of each and every one of Megan's orifices and all the best and worst of what he was going to do to her.

"Oh, such joy," he whispered to himself as he entered Highway 11 heading south. "What bliss."

He pushed his glasses up his nose with his index finger and drove south to Toronto, his previous wife far from his thoughts.

CHAPTER TWENTY-FOUR

Kirk didn't show up the next day. Or the day after. Dr. Sutton brought in a scribbled message from Kirk on a small yellow piece of paper explaining that he was sending Cindy home and would return in a couple of days to take Jake back to Ontario.

The doctor had supplied him with a laptop and a briefcase of papers to sign. Once the formalities were done, a tidy sum in the hundreds of thousands in a trust fund was transferred to Jake. Some of the money came from the sale of his house and his personal belongings, the rest from the anonymous donor.

Jake got on the Internet and began looking for a new home. He wanted something farther north, away from Cindy and Kirk, away from his old life. Something secluded, remote. If, according to the doctor, he really was going to die sooner than later, he wanted peace and quiet in his final months.

At noon, the nurse brought his lunch and disappeared quickly without a word.

Jake had sent one email to inquire about a quiet-looking home on Boundary Road in Novar, Ontario, and two homes near Emsdale and Burk's Falls. Once he was back in Ontario, he would rent a car and drive up to tour the houses.

Dr. Sutton knocked on his door mid-afternoon and said he was there to take Jake's empty lunch dishes.

"The plates are over there." Jake pointed at the side table by the window.

The doctor hesitated by the window a moment. "Jake, I was wondering if we could have a final chat."

Jake looked up from the screen. "I thought you'd never ask," he said, his tone more sarcastic than he intended. He closed the laptop.

Dr. Sutton pulled up a chair and sat a few feet from Jake.

"What happened to Milton and Eduardo, my guides?" Jake asked. He reached for his cup of water, trying to appear nonchalant, but knowing hard truths were coming. "Now that everyone knows who I am and how I came to be in Manaus, have they been located?"

"They were never found. Both men are still listed as missing persons, presumed dead." Sutton arched one eyebrow as he studied Jake's face. "When I first saw your test results, I knew something was wrong."

"Wrong? How?"

"Things had changed." Sutton fidgeted with something under the nail of his ring finger. "With your heart."

Jake raised his water glass, but stopped. "What? My heart?" He set the glass down. "How does someone's heart change?"

"It has become encased in a sac—"

"A what?" Jake snapped, not sure he heard Sutton correctly.

Sutton nodded. "A sac. When you first got here, things were fine with it. But then your body began to change." Sutton stared out the window now, lost in his thoughts.

Jake lowered his voice. "Change, as in plural? Like multiple changes?"

Sutton turned back to him, then after a few seconds, rose from his chair and walked to the window.

"You lost the use of your left lung. After a while, the left lung deflated and began to wilt. Through x-rays, we've found it had edged in and around the right lung. Your kidneys have changed, too. Eyesight has become acute, almost binocular-like, and, over time, you might experience trouble closing your eyes."

"What does all that mean?" Jake asked. "What the hell could've happened to me?"

Sutton faced Jake, his arms crossed. "Your teeth got stronger, similar to a snake's teeth. Snakes are polyphyodont, which means they continuously replace their teeth, unlike us. We are born with two sets. Lose them and it's false teeth until the end. Not so with snakes."

Jake blinked several times, trying to grasp where the doctor was going with this. The teeth in the back of his mouth had been replaced. Also, there was a texture change to his skin he'd been meaning to ask the doctor about.

What could it all mean? Could he be turning into a snake because of the venom? But that was impossible. Utterly and virtually impossible.

"Is there more?" Jake asked, worried there was.

Sutton plopped down in the chair in the corner, looking physically spent.

"There's more." Sutton coughed into his hand.

Jake waited, taking the break to drink from his water glass again, suddenly parched.

"You can smell better, can't you?" He met Jake's gaze. "You can detect people approaching. The curtains"—he gestured behind him— "you need the sun's rays, its warmth, or you tire easily."

As Sutton talked, Jake sensed a feeling akin to violation.

"How do you know all this?" Jake asked.

"When the nurse closed the curtains in those weeks you were slowly coming out of your coma, you'd sleep. When she opened them, you'd stir awake. When we learned this, we raised the temperature in the room to get it to thirty degrees Celsius, which is the temperature that an ectothermic needs to digest their food while dormant. Haven't you noticed everyone sweating in here when they come to visit you?"

The words hit him like knives, each one stabbing his consciousness, his reality. Was the doctor telling him that the change in him was happening or had happened? Was he part snake now? Was that why he only had months to live?

Sutton continued, "Several doctors came calling. I've seen things change with you over the past year, but even I kept it confidential."

Jake looked away, the doctor's words weighing on him. His strength had returned double what it was. His eyesight was incredible. To never lose a tooth again was good news. It didn't matter that he needed it warmer wherever he was. It just meant winters would be a bitch. What he needed to know now was the downside.

Oh right, I'm terminal.

"What happens when the changes go wrong for me?"

"Your heart will give out. Massive coronary."

Another thought occurred to Jake. "You said you knew my sense of smell got better. How?"

"The nurse. You knew about her mother coming over. You knew her daughter was ill. The fact that you even knew about the daughter was because you *smelled* her on the nurse." Sutton leaned back. "Tell me I'm wrong."

Jake rolled his hand. "Anything else? Tell me everything. Full disclosure, Doc."

Sutton got up and moved to the window again. "We have yet to learn why you were in a coma."

"Doesn't a snake's venom contain a neurotoxin?" Jake asked.

"Yes. It causes paralysis. Certain snakes carry a mix of neurotoxins, pro-coagulates and myotoxins that paralyze muscles, inhibit breathing and can cause hemorrhaging in blood vessels and tissues, ultimately damaging muscles." Sutton glanced at Jake over his shoulder. "In some cases, death comes within hours without treatment, but you were successfully given the exact antivenin needed within minutes, so it's utterly confusing in medical terms."

"I was in the hospital a day or so before the incident. Could they have given me an anti-histamine that fucked me up somehow?"

The doctor slowly spun to face him. "An anti-histamine? What did they claim you were allergic to?"

"Horses. I had some kind of reaction to horses at a crime scene ..." Jake stopped when he saw the color leave the doctor's face.

"Oh my." Sutton clutched the window sill, then dropped into the chair.

"What is it, Doctor? How's that relevant?"

Sutton's eyes were wide, staring at nothing. "It's the antivenin," the doctor said, his voice soft now, subdued. "I should've seen that. I should've known."

"What about the antivenin?"

"Horse blood."

Now it was Jake's turn to be surprised. "Horse blood? What about horse blood?"

Sutton placed a hand on his forehead, dabbing gently. He eased back in the chair. "Antivenin is made using horse blood. I've researched antivenin. I know."

"*What?* How?" Jake tightened his hands into fists, his nails digging into his palms.

"Snake venom is injected into a horse until the horse is immunized. Blood is then extracted from the immunized horse and the serum is separated and further purified. Because of this, people allergic to horses are likely to suffer an allergic reaction to antivenin, which is what must have happened to you. Were you unconscious at any point during your allergic reaction at that crime scene you mentioned?"

Stunned, he wondered how he was still alive. "Yes. Unconscious. Yes."

"Understand something, Jake. The venom from a bothrops asper would've killed you. The antivenin was necessary. Without it, you would've died for sure. But then you were faced with an extreme allergic reaction to the antivenin that knocked you into a comatose state, or as it's called in the ophidian world, dormancy or brumation. It's a miracle you're alive at all."

"Yeah, great. Alive long enough to learn my life back home is over and I'm about to die soon, anyway." Jake inhaled deeply. "Wait a second, brumation?"

"To brumate is to hibernate. Happens in late fall, as it did with you. A brumation period can last up to eight months, but it's triggered by lack of heat and daylight, like wintertime. As a human being, you needed more heat than a snake would. That's why your coma lasted more than double the norm. And that coincides with you waking as soon as we raised the room's temperature." Sutton clapped his hands. "It's all making sense, now."

Jake stifled a laugh but couldn't restrain the grin. "Are you suggesting I'm no longer a man? That I'm part snake now? Or am I *all* snake? Tell me, Doc, how is it? What's your official diagnosis?"

"Go ahead, laugh about this, but it's your life. Many of these changes have occurred. There's no denying what you were and what you've become. What we need to look at now is moving forward, learning to live with it as long as you can."

"Tell me about the sac around my heart."

"We all have a sac around our hearts called the pericardial sac. I haven't opened you up, but I can tell you it's harder to hear your heartbeat through your chest, as if it's encased in something much thicker than the pericardial."

Jake took a deep breath, then exhaled. "My lungs? Are they cool? They feel fine."

"Listening to your chest while you slept can only be done effectively on your right side. Sounds on the left side are almost non-existent. But your body seems to be managing just fine."

"Okay, humor me. I have two more questions." Jake wrapped his hand around the water glass and gripped it tight. "How do you know so much about snakes? Were you a veterinarian before this clinic business?"

"After you were placed here, I researched the snake that spit venom at you, then snakes in general. Everything I've witnessed with you was either human-like or snake-like, so I've continued studying them for over a year."

"Second question. If what you say is true, and I have taken on some of the attributes of a snake, then why doesn't this happen to everyone who gets bitten by a snake? Why just me?"

"Firstly, you weren't bitten. Secondly, there's that mysterious substance they found on your clothing and in your hair. It has yet to be identified. I saw trace elements of it in your mouth. You certainly ingested it, along with the venom."

"What mysterious—"

He recalled knocking the makeshift table over in Luke's tent. The green liquid had splashed onto his face.

He explained what he could remember to the doctor.

"It had a citrusy taste. I swallowed reflexively."

"Any idea what it was?"

Jake shrugged. "Just something Luke had in his tent. I have no idea." He stared at the floor for a moment. "What does all this mean for me?"

"I have no idea. You will live or die with what you've become or will still become yet."

"You think I'm going to start slithering around the

neighborhood or something? Shed my skin?"

Sutton headed for the door. Once there, he stopped without turning around. "Before you leave, we can run some tests. Get better informed." He glanced over his shoulder. "In the meantime, don't bite anyone."

"What's that supposed to mean?"

"I tested your saliva. The liquid closest to your gums. I found traces of modified saliva, similar to a predigestant found in snake venom."

"Predigestant? What the fuck, Doc? Do you mean like when a housefly goes to eat something, it vomits on it first to make it easier to digest?"

Sutton kept talking as if Jake hadn't asked a question. "Your particular saliva has a neurotoxin that doesn't seem to affect you in any way. You're safe from your own teeth, just don't bite anyone else."

"Hey, thanks, Doc. Was thinking about heading to the beaches of Rio for an evening of fun, dancing, wine, and a little biting."

Sutton's footfalls echoed down the corridor.

The water glass in Jake's hand cracked. He glanced down at it as he squeezed tighter. A moment later, it broke into several pieces. Blood seeped from two spots where the glass had cut him. The pain curbed his anger and the blood had a calming effect, reminding him he was still human after all.

What he needed was an exit plan. He needed away from lunatic doctors with conspiracy theories. He needed time away from people in general.

After opening the laptop, he checked his email inbox.

Nothing.

He'd find a house soon. Maybe before that he'd get an apartment for a month or two. He just needed out. To get away.

Before he lost his mind or hurt someone.

If what the doctor said was true and he had taken on snake-like attributes over the previous eighteen months, then he needed to remove himself from society before he hurt someone.

Sutton had told him that it was quite common for people waking from a coma to have unexplained swells of anger. It seemed everything made him angry. Someone wanting to visit. Someone talking. The Internet page not changing fast enough. The temperature too cold. The food not tasting just right.

He Googled Fortech Industries and came up empty. He Googled Luke Mercer and came up empty—the man had never been found. He needed to learn everything he could about Fortech. Maybe they had a cure. It was their liquid that Luke had had in that tent.

Jake had nothing to lose. His Cindy was gone. He was on disability at work and would never be allowed out in the field with a doctor convinced he was part snake.

Athina, his dog, had died during his coma. There was nothing left for Jake but the trust fund money and a terminal case of snake-itis.

The phone rang.

Jake snatched it up, blood covering the receiver.

"What?" he snapped into the phone.

"Holy shit, dude," Kirk said. "Lighten up. This isn't the Jake I used to know."

"Just had a talk with the doctor. Pissed me off."

"Oh, sorry man. Okay, one quick question then I'll let you go and be pissed off on your own. Cool?"

"Shoot."

"I need your help as a consultant on a case."

"Me? No way. I'm still in a wheelchair."

"I know. Listen. You remember Detective Keri Joslin?"

"Yeah. Wasn't she working the Blood Eagle killer case?"

"The one. She was reassigned a few months after you disappeared. Something about evidence going missing, fingerprints smudged. In other words, she screwed up at the worst time. We probably would've caught the guy."

"And now you have the case?"

"Yup. Transferred down after I was lonely in Orillia without you. I'm back in the Toronto office and working the case. There's been nothing new since the Marcello family where you got your horse allergy shit. But our killer is due. It's been over a year and a half. This asshole will strike soon. I'm under pressure to come up with something. Just thought you'd want to come in on this. Be useful. Read all the files. Offer up some thoughts. I know, I know, you're on disability leave. But reading files and making notes could be done in a wheelchair. So, how about it, man? Once I get you settled back in Ontario, are you up for it?"

"No."

Jake hung up, smashing the phone down so hard he cracked the cradle.

An email dinged on his computer. He opened it. A realtor. A meeting. The house in Novar could be viewed in two days and was available immediately.

It was the first news that had made him genuinely smile all day. It was also the first time his mood lightened in recent memory.

Once he was in his own home, he could do whatever he wanted, unseen. Even if that meant hunting, eating his meat uncooked, or rubbing at the skin that peeled on his shoulders.

His last thought as the sun set outside on another day was how Dr. Sutton would probably say the peeling skin was a form of molting or shedding like snakes do with their skin. And who knows, maybe it was.

Maybe Jake Wood was a snake in man's clothing after all.

If so, he was okay with it because it was a snake that would find Fortech Industries. And it was a snake that would find the Blood Eagle killer. Investigating with Kirk meant Jake would have to follow the rules the police were bound by, and that was precisely why he'd said no.

Doing it alone would allow him to hunt the Blood Eagle killer and see for the first time what a Jake Wood bite would do to a man. Jake had wanted the case before he'd fallen into a coma and he still wanted the case. Who better to test his modified saliva on than a serial killer?

His hand had stopped bleeding. He wiped it clean and examined the cuts in his flesh.

There weren't any.

The skin had closed, leaving only blood behind. Not a single blemish could be detected anywhere. It had been cut and bleeding and now looked clean and healthy.

How could his hand heal in less than two minutes without a mark?

What the fuck's going on?

CHAPTER TWENTY-FIVE

W ith the use of a cane, Jake entered his new home on Boundary Road in Novar three weeks later, the real estate agent on his heels. Outside, it was sunny and warm, but the first thing he did was raise the heat to get the house to at least thirty degrees Celsius.

He set his laptop on the dining room table and looked around the new home.

The house sat back off the road with a hundred-yard-long driveway. He'd gotten it for a steal as the bank had repossessed it from the previous, delinquent owner. No moving truck was needed as he didn't own anything anymore. One of the many perks of leaving a relationship via coma.

Cindy had boxed up his personal items after Jake had disappeared, not sure if he would ever surface again. By the time his birthday came around in April, he'd been gone for six months and Cindy placed his things in storage. When she met Derrick, her husband and the father of her child, Cindy had removed the rest of the reminders of Jake, a relationship lost by misadventure.

By Christmas—six months ago—Jake's house had been sold and his portion of the money was added to the trust fund.

All memory of their union, their marriage to be, was removed in that one act. He couldn't even visit his old house that he had shared with Cindy. A new family with three kids lived there now.

To start fresh in Novar, Jake hired a maid service to clean the house and ordered furniture to be delivered prior to moving in. Having done all this online, walking through the house now marked the first time he'd seen his living room and bedroom suite in the flesh, all clean and ready for him.

After the walk through, the realtor bid him adieu and left with a pep in his step, bounding out to his car to either deal with another client or distance himself from Jake.

The kitchen hadn't been dealt with yet. He needed forks, knives, spoons, plates, and cooking utensils. Not only that, the fridge was empty.

His new car, a 2017 Mustang Cobra, wouldn't be delivered to the Huntsville dealership until the next day. It was an expensive model, but he had the money and what the hell, a snake had ruined his life, so why not drive a Cobra? There was no telling how much time he had left according to Dr. Sutton. What was important wasn't when he would lose his life, but what he was going to do with it in the meantime.

He limped out of the house, locked the front door, and headed to the small grocery store near the highway.

Once inside, without his hips bothering him too much after the thirty-minute walk, he headed for the meat section. T-Bones, pork chops, and chicken breasts filled his cart. As he meandered the store, local folks nodded at him. He nodded back to be polite, but he hadn't come to Novar for the company. This was about seclusion, privacy. Yet there was still a certain amount of the old Jake inside him that made him even smile at a four-year-old that smelled of syrup. By the time the mother walked by, her small boy in tow, Jake deduced the boy had spilled his breakfast pancakes into his lap within the last hour.

The boy touched the area, then brought his finger to his mouth and smiled at Jake. Jake smiled back, understanding this connection for what it was. Two naughty boys who would partake in getting in a little trouble for the greater good.

At the till, he realized he had no way of getting the load home.

"Excuse me," he said to the cashier. "Is it possible to wheel this shopping cart to my house? I'll bring it back when I return for groceries in a day or two."

"Oh, I don't know," the young woman said as she looked around for someone. She faced him again. "I can't let you take the cart off store property, but my manager might say it's okay. If you ask her, I'm sure—"

"You know what, don't worry about it. Just call me a cab."

"I'm sorry," she said. "I can't call from here." She gestured behind Jake, then in a lowered voice, said, "I've got customers. But there's a payphone just outside. The taxi company's number is on the wall beside it."

His lips tight, forcing his reply down, he paid his bill and used the phone for a cab. It came within five minutes and drove him to his house. When he got his car tomorrow, this problem would be solved.

He placed all the bags on the driveway, paid the driver, and waited until it backed down and out onto the road.

Hand on the cane, the grocery bags at his feet rustling in the soft breeze that came through the trees, he detected something was off. He closed his eyes, opened his mouth, and focused.

A smell. Something in the air that hadn't been there when he'd left for the grocery store.

Perspiration.

Fear.

Several different people close by. The smell of anxious men.

He stared up at the house. Nothing moved. The sun forced itself through the trees, warming his face. He took in the air, assessed direction, then got down on one knee and placed his hands flat on the cement driveway where he waited for a location based on the vibrations in the ground.

The scent weakened by the second. Four males. On Jake's property within the last five minutes. The ground moved so subtly that he barely felt their footfalls in the trees to his right.

Four men in their early twenties had been here and were now running parallel to Boundary Road, headed toward Long Lake Road through the trees.

Why?

Perspiration. Fear.

They had done something wrong here.

Jake opened his eyes and stared at the house again. His detective skills honed in on what might be different in the hour since he'd been there.

Ignoring the groceries on the driveway, he limped closer to the house. Along the side, to the left of the front door, broken glass reflected the blue sky.

He had been vandalized and broken into on day one.

Without losing time, he unlocked the front door to see what they had done. Jake gave himself one minute to scour the house so he wouldn't lose their scent before they got too far away.

Forcing his anger down, he entered the kitchen. Cupboards were left open and in disarray. In the living room, the couch had been pulled away from the wall. Ascending the stairs with his cane, fueled by the anger of being violated, he ran into his bedroom. The new dresser was left with all its drawers yanked open. Whatever they had been looking for they hadn't found because Jake had no valuables stashed in the house yet. Other than the furniture, there was no cash or jewelry for the taking.

Back in the living room, the dining table was empty.

The laptop Dr. Sutton had given him was gone.

A shriek escaped his lips, heat rising to his face. Like an angry golfer after a horrible shot, Jake threw the cane across the room, where it smashed into the wall and dropped out of sight behind the couch.

In two easy lunges, he was back outside. He jumped over the bags of groceries still sitting in the driveway, ignoring the pain in his weaker leg, and ran for the trees, his limp barely evident with the rage propelling him.

He was on his first hunt as a new man and it felt good. Ever since he'd awoken from the coma, there had been an anger inside him that didn't make sense. The doctor said it was natural.

But this was different. His anger flowed with his blood, pumping him into a coiled mass, waiting to snap at the smallest provocation. The human side of him understood that to deny this new impulse was to go mad. It was a part of him now. The new Jake Wood.

Modified saliva and all.

When he broke through the first set of branches and picked up their scent again, he promised himself he wouldn't kill any of them. He was a good man. He was a cop on disability. He wouldn't even hurt any of them. Not too bad at least.

He just wanted to ask them—in the strongest way possible—why they'd stolen his laptop.

Why would they break into his house? Why today?

With another guttural cry that resembled a howl, Jake ran through the trees faster than he had run in years.

When he realized how fast he was going, he knew the truth. He was a new and improved Jake Wood. He had found the fountain of youth in a snake bite.

The man that resembled Jake ran through the forest hunting four men like a cheetah after a gazelle.

CHAPTER TWENTY-SIX

Renovation construction on Jeffrey's basement started earlier than expected. After meeting Megan in Tim Horton's and making his decision to follow in his father's footsteps, he needed to get to work right away. Stalking the Radcliffes wasn't needed after all. That one visit cemented his presence at the Canada Day party. That was all he needed.

His wife couldn't make it to the party, he'd tell them. She had recently left him. Walked out on him. His story would dispel any awkwardness they might feel having a man show up at the party by himself. That and the wine he would supply.

With the party arrangements secure, he realized on the drive back to Toronto that he needed to get his home ready for his new wife.

Safe Roomz Inc. came out right away and gave him a quote. Base model of four walls and a strong door—$5,000. High-tech model with cameras, monitors, generators, and sustainability for a family of four—$500,000. Basically the kind of panic room seen in the Jodie Foster movie.

Jeffrey went with a $25,000 model.

Today marked the last day of workers being in his basement. He'd been busy at work lately and needed these guys out of his house. The first of July, Canada Day, was one week away. He had taken the day off work before the party and had requested vacation time for the week after. They didn't expect him back to work until the eighth of July.

Jeffrey followed Steve, his Safe Roomz representative, through the safe room as he pointed out the features Jeffrey had ordered and how they worked.

"You know, these things are popular in Mexico," Steve was saying.

"Really?"

"Yeah." Steve nodded dramatically. "What with all the kidnappings down there. Also in London. Israel too. Rich guys, worried about burglaries. You just never know."

"What's this?" Jeffrey asked to get Steve back on track.

"That's where you store your non-perishables."

"Oh. Right. Okay." Jeffrey headed toward the thick door.

"You know," Steve went on, "any lock is only as good as what surrounds it."

"Agreed."

"That's why we have multiple locks and a reinforced frame." Steve bent over and pointed at the locks, one by maddening one. "This electronic door can withstand the pressure of a three-hundred-pound man pounding on it incessantly. And it's not just bulletproof. It's machine-gun proof, too."

"Wow." Jeffrey minded his sarcasm. He needed to be just another customer and not someone Steve would readily remember. Not too much irksome behavior, but also not too much praise.

Steve snatched the work order off the table just outside the safe room door and scanned it.

"We didn't add a phone and dedicated line as per your request," he said. "But we put a power supply over there and a cellphone on charge. Cell coverage works with everything closed down."

Jeffrey nodded and bounced from one foot to the other.

Steve set the tip of the pen in his mouth as he continued down the page. "No shatterproof glass because no windows," he said, almost as if he was talking to himself. "Alarms, cameras, monitoring is all turned off at this point." He looked up. "But you can turn that on at any time once you're inside if you ever need to use this room."

Jeffrey clenched his fists out of Steve's field of vision.

"If you'll follow me into the basement, we'll perform the last task, sign this and I'll be off."

Jeffrey gladly followed and allowed Steve to close the safe room door. In this part of the basement, Jeffrey had a large TV and two reclining chairs. On each side were two well-stocked bookcases. The door to the soundproof safe room lay behind the bookcase on the right wall. When it was shut, it was virtually impossible to know a panic room existed behind it. Jeffrey's safe room was impenetrable. It simply looked like a bookcase.

Once Megan was inside, he could sleep in one of his recliners while she hammered at the door and screamed her head off and not a single sound would escape the room four feet from his chair.

Steve walked him through the codes to enter the safe room, closed and opened the door twice, then had Jeffrey sign the contract. After Steve left, Jeffrey shut the front door. Alone again. At the front window, he pulled the curtain back far enough to watch Steve trot out to his truck and drive away.

A silence fell over the house. Jeffrey smiled to himself. He had done it. His father would be proud.

He headed back down to the basement and opened the safe room door, stepped inside and held the door ajar, careful not to let it shut and lock himself in.

He started to work immediately, removing any sharp objects and placing a small table and chairs against the side wall. He moved the twin mattress to the far corner and made sure he hadn't overlooked a single thing. Once Megan became a permanent resident of this room, he couldn't allow her to injure herself in any way.

That was his job. Only he would do the maiming.

Satisfied that she would be comfortable and there was a place to tie her up by the bed, he exited the room but stopped short of closing the door. There was something he'd forgotten.

After a moment of staring into the safe room, it hit him.

The cellphone plugged into the charger.

He couldn't leave that inside there.

Once the cellphone was removed, he closed the door without latching it. Next week he would want the door partly open, waiting for his wife. When she got inside, it would be absolutely impossible for anyone to ever know she was there. No amount of screaming, banging, or violence would ever alert a single neighbor.

Once Megan entered his home, she would be safe from the outside world in Jeffrey's *safe* room.

Jeffrey's safe room.

There was something about the way that sounded. A certain ring to it. He shrugged as he headed back upstairs.

Perhaps it was the irony of the statement.

CHAPTER TWENTY-SEVEN

Behind the houses on Florence Street, an old quarry had come and gone. Left behind was a mass of sand covering the terrain where piles of it had been knocked down when the developers had packed up and left.

When Jake came over the small hill of shrubbery, the scent grew stronger. They were close. The four thieves were in catching distance now. For some reason, they had slowed down.

How charged was his computer? Had they stopped to see what was on the hard drive? If so, they would find a list of searches for furniture, real estate, and all the orders for everything from the new car to the new couch.

What would they do with that information? Order something for their own house? That would be stupid and reckless as it would lead the authorities to their address. His credit card and banking information was protected by passwords, so unless one of their crew was a hacker of any worth, there was nothing valuable in the laptop.

Except the information.

Jake had been looking up Fortech Industries and their involvement in the accident a year and a half ago. So far, the information was spotty to nonexistent. He had used a VPN, which made anyone who looked up his IP address think he was in Alabama. This changed daily, giving him anonymity on several

Internet pathways.

If they were local kids, they would know the house had been empty. But today the new owner had moved in. Theft on day one wouldn't amount to much. Let the guy settle in, bring valuables to the house before trying to steal anything. As in this case, the house only had furniture in it. Jake hadn't even bought any new clothes yet.

The crime was most likely a random hit. It was unlikely they had targeted him. It could be that the kids were from out of town and didn't know he had just moved in, but Jake didn't think so. If they were from out of town, they wouldn't have known to run back here. They wouldn't have known how to get to the sand behind Florence St. that led to several different escape routes.

Jake eased up to the edge of the foliage where the shrubs met the sand and pulled back a branch. Four men of various builds talked in a huddle-like formation. The smallest one appeared skittish, glancing over his shoulder twice in the minute Jake watched them.

Each man was early twenties, with maybe one in their late teens. None of the four held his laptop. Had they tossed it?

He stepped out of the bushes and felt the light breeze on his sweat-covered skin. The sun was still high enough to offer the kind of warmth he needed. He strode toward them, covering the distance quickly before they detected him.

"Yo," the biggest one said. "Hey, what the fuck, man? You got a problem old man?"

Jake picked up his pace toward the biggest guy. The small, skittish one backed up two steps. The other two fanned out.

"I axed you a question," Big Guy shouted.

In two strides, Jake reached Big Guy, stepped into him even as the guy took a swipe at him, and drove his fist into the guy's stomach.

Big Guy jackknifed at the waist, the air in his lungs dispelled. He wavered on his feet as Jake stepped back, then fell over, trying to catch a breath.

How hard had he hit him? Was it too hard? Internal injuries? He had to remember he was much stronger since the coma.

The guy on Jake's left moved, as did the other one on his right. Someone leapt on his back as a fist slammed into Jake's mouth. He lost his balance and stumbled backward, emitting a small growl. The guy on his back dug in, wrapping an arm around Jake's neck, severing his air intake. Without thinking, Jake let himself stumble with the added weight, then threw himself backward.

Another fist missed his face as he dropped, the guy still on his back. He landed hard, sandwiching the guy between himself and the ground. The impact crunched something in the guy's abdomen. He sucked in air and tasted blood.

With a scream of rage, the third guy dove on him, but Jake lifted both fists, his right connecting with the guy's shoulder, the left fist, the guy's forehead.

As the kid's shoulder popped out, he screamed, then rolled over and writhed on the sand, his free hand clambering at his injury.

The fourth guy, the smallest one, had stumbled farther back and was now twenty yards away. When Jake got to his feet, the fourth guy turned and split like the proverbial bat had come out of Hell and was just now on his tail, chasing him.

Jake let him go. One of these three would explain their actions.

Big Guy was collecting his breath, up on his knees now, a hand over his stomach.

Shoulder guy still writhed, shouting in pain.

Jake leaned down to the one who had climbed on his back. He backhanded him across the face.

"Make your friend with the fucked up shoulder shut his

mouth so I can think, or I will break his bones until he passes out."

The guy rolled away from Jake and crawled to his friend.

The taste of blood filled Jake's mouth. He used his tongue to feel around his teeth. The canine tooth on the left had been knocked out when he'd gotten a fist in the face. It was gone, having dropped from his mouth when the other guy's arm was wrapped around his throat.

I'll just grow another one.

The screaming became incessant, maddening. No matter what the friend did, the guy with the dislocated shoulder only grew louder.

Big Guy still clutched his stomach, rasping breaths in and out, but Jake couldn't hear him too well over the shouting.

The small guy had made it to the highway in the distance. He waved his arms, attempting to flag down a car. This was devolving fast without a single question answered yet. He had thought that if he put down the biggest guy of their group, the rest would've listened, but instead they'd attacked.

He recalled something the doctor had told him.

Neurotoxic saliva.

Calms people, puts them out, immobilizes them. But how would it handle the pain of a dislocated shoulder?

He didn't have time to think about it. Shut the guy up or knock him out. He needed answers from the Big Guy and concerned citizens would be involved very soon.

Jake dropped down beside the guy who still thrashed on the sand, clutching the guy's injured shoulder.

"Hey, what are you doing?" his friend shouted. "I'm trying to shut him up. It fucking hurts, though, man."

Jake opened his mouth, blood seeping out over his lips, and bit the screaming young man on the forearm hard enough to puncture the skin.

The wounded man tried to squirm away from Jake, panic in his eyes. The friend got up and stepped back from Jake like he was a vampire.

"You're crazy, man," he said loud enough to be heard. "Fuckin' insane."

The wounded man didn't make it more than a few feet before he slowed and stopped squirming altogether. He released his shoulder, his free hand descending in a slow arc. On his back, he became motionless but for his eyes, which darted back and forth in a frantic bid to find Jake.

"What'd'ya do to him?" the friend yelled. "Huh? What the fuck just happened?"

Jake had an idea, but he didn't explain it. The human, caring part of his mind hoped he hadn't permanently hurt the guy. The new, reptilian, part of Jake's brain wanted to bite him again. And then again.

"Go," Jake vociferated loudly. "Leave here." He pointed at the immobilized man on the sand. "Or be paralyzed like him."

To the friend's credit, he knew when the getting was good as he turned for the highway in the distance and bolted. Jake watched him run, then scanned the road in the distance. The skittish one had gotten a black SUV to pull over for him. Two men had exited and were talking to him near the front of the vehicle.

He lowered his gaze to the Big Guy still on his knees in the sand.

"Where's my laptop?" Jake asked.

Big Guy dropped his hand from his stomach until he was on all fours, then pushed up and rose to his feet, his face red with the exertion.

Jake stepped closer. Big Guy retreated a step.

"We were hired," Big Guy rasped out.

"Who?"

"Some guys. Didn't get a name."

"You live around here?"

Big Guy shook his head.

"How much they pay you?"

"Thousand bucks—"

"A thousand bucks?" Jake snapped, taken by surprise. "And you didn't think that suspicious? Why pay you that kind of money to steal a used computer?"

Over Big Guy's shoulder, Jake watched as the friend made it to the young guy at the highway. The men from the SUV ushered them in the back.

"Where's the laptop?" Jake asked again.

"Gave it to the guys in the SUV when we crossed the road to come up here."

"And the money?"

"Already paid. We were about to split it up when you arrived." Big Guy looked over Jake's shoulder. "What'd you do to Bobby?"

"Nothing. A paralyzing move I learned years ago in Ninjutsu."

Big Guy stared back at him with disbelief written all over his face.

"Ninja shit," Big Guy said. "Yeah right. Isn't that illegal?"

"Where's the money? I want a new computer."

"They have it." He pointed at the SUV on the highway.

The two men in business suits stood with their arms crossed, watching Jake as he watched them. Who were they and what did they want with his computer? There was no point in heading their way. By the time he got halfway, they could get inside their SUV and disappear.

"You got a name for me?" Jake asked, figuring it was useless to ask but asked anyway.

"I'm not telling you my name," Big Guy said, his voice improving already.

"Not yours. Theirs." Jake pointed. "The guys who hired you."

"They didn't say."

Some of Big Guy's bravado was coming back. He had taken a fist to the gut and didn't seem willing to let that be enough. The sense of the fight in him oozed off his flesh. Jake felt the change in Big Guy before he saw evidence.

It started to make sense to Jake. Every situation had a smell, a mood. Simply by letting that sense in, he could detect intentions before they became actions.

The guy behind Jake moaned. Evidently the paralysis was wearing off. One bite had given Jake a few minutes of submission.

"That leaves us in a quandary," Jake said. "You broke into my house, stole my computer. For that, I need you to come with me to the police station and offer a sketch of the men in that SUV. I'll recommend they go easy on you if you help identify those guys over there—"

"How did you find us?" Big Guy cut in.

"Tracked you."

"What? How?"

"By smell."

That caught Big Guy off balance. A blank expression crossed his face.

"Like an animal?" he asked.

"Something like that." Jake smiled, revealing his missing canine which didn't seem to hurt as much as it should. Had his pain tolerance increased, too?

Jake watched the guys by the SUV and wondered if they were with Fortech Industries. If they were, he wanted to talk to them but couldn't come up with a way to do that right now. If it was them, they would be back. They evidently had an interest in him. They would want to meet.

Jake would be waiting.

But before then, he wanted to leave them with a little demonstration.

With Jake's attention temporarily on the SUV, Big Guy withdrew a long blade from his pants pocket, flicked it open, and lunged at Jake's stomach.

Jake dropped, lowered his center of gravity, and snapped his hand upward at the exact moment the blade passed over it. He wrapped his fingers around Big Guy's wrist, ceasing his arm's forward momentum just as the tip of the blade touched his shirt, pricking it.

Jake squeezed, not thinking about how much strength to use. He just tightened his grip.

Big Guy howled as his knees buckled and he dropped to the sand in front of Jake. There was something oddly satisfying about that howl. Something that spoke to the loss and anger Jake had been feeling since he'd awakened from the coma.

And now he had enemies. Enemies that were hunting him, stealing from him.

He held up Big Guy's knife hand until the offending blade slipped from his grasp. The men on the highway could easily see what he was doing as he turned Big Guy's arm to show them its full length. An image of a boxing ring where the referee held up the arm of the winner flashed through his mind.

Jake squeezed tighter, like the talons of an eagle clutching its prey. Big Guy cried out with the renewed pain. Jake waited a moment longer, clenched as tight as he could, indenting the man's flesh like he held a balloon. Then, with a sudden flick of the wrist, snapped Big Guy's forearm bones in two, the break vibrating up Jake's wrist.

When he let go, Big Guy dropped to the sand and stared at his deformed arm where it was bent at an odd angle. His eyes wide and rimmed in red, an aching moan escaped his lips.

To be merciful, Jake grabbed the broken arm and bit down near the broken bone until the skin split, allowing some of his saliva into Big Guy's blood stream. Big Guy shouted something unintelligible and collapsed on the sand.

The screaming died a few moments later. Big Guy lay on his back in the sand, eyes darting back and forth like his friend with the dislocated shoulder had.

A quiet calm descended over Jake. The blood in his mouth had ceased flowing. There was virtually no pain from the missing tooth.

He studied the men by the SUV in the distance for another minute as they studied him. Then he turned and headed back to his house.

He would call to have the window fixed by tomorrow. A security company would set up an alarm system on his house. Cameras, internal and external, wouldn't be a problem. Motion detectors, monitors, battery backup, the whole enchilada, wouldn't be too much for Jake. He had the money to waste.

What he had no time for were unknown enemies. And when they came for him, he would be waiting. He would be ready.

There wouldn't just be broken bones and people getting neurotoxic saliva. Break into his home again and he would dole out severe punishments. Under threat of extreme pain, whoever came for him next would explain everything Jake wanted to know. Jake had just tested his strength and understood just how powerful he was. If he could snap a large man's forearm with the grip of one hand, who knew what he could do in anger to a man's whole body?

There was a side of Jake that wanted to find out.

As soon as they came for him.

The scent on the breeze told him it would be very soon.

He smiled to himself as he walked back to his house remembering how he had left the grocery bags sitting in his driveway.

CHAPTER TWENTY-EIGHT

The house was ready. Most importantly, Jeffrey was ready. The party was days away. He planned on being in Huntsville the day before. Stay in a hotel for the last day as a single man. He was simply too antsy to remain in his quiet house, alone, staring into the yawning opening of the safe room's maw.

The old clock upstairs in the living room made the familiar dings to signify midnight. After a long day at work, he'd poured himself a Scotch and sat, staring into the void of the safe room. The fun he would soon have. The wife, in the soundproof room, would be his to offer comfort and joy at will. And for her to offer duties as a wife to a husband. Oh, the fun they would soon have was unbearable to think about.

He loved the name Jeffrey. The name his stepfather had given him. His real name, his legal name was Edwin Gavin. Detective Joslin always called him Dr. Gavin. He had grown to like that.

Edwin.

Gavin.

He thought of Wally. Wally's women. No wonder his stepfather had done it this way. How come Jeffrey/Edwin hadn't thought of it before? Probably because of the mistakes his father had made. Stupid old man. You can't take a woman and possess her without precautions in place. His father had been sloppy. Wally the sloppy.

Edwin grinned. He sipped from his Scotch, felt it calm his insides.

Wally had been reckless. The only real woman he'd tamed was Edwin's mother, Cynthia. He had tamed her so well, she'd even gotten to the point where she helped him with Wally's Gatherings. Complacent, understanding of her husband's needs, Cynthia had often led the random women into Wally's trap.

Karla Homolka and that fiend Paul Bernardo came to mind when Edwin thought of his parents. Just like Karla leading her own sister to slaughter, Cynthia had led countless women to Wally. And just like Bernardo, Wally had kept the women for days, sometimes weeks, sexually torturing them until there was nothing left of their sex organs. Wally didn't film any of it like Bernardo, though. Wally was smarter. He'd tortured and murdered at least a dozen women before the police had come looking for Wally when Edwin was only twelve.

He remembered that night like it was yesterday. His dad had kept calling him Jeffrey, the son his father had lost too early.

Edwin still used the name Jeffrey in honor of his father's memory. He still wore the glasses and grew the beard, just as Jeffrey would. To be Wally's son was to be a part of Wally. And to be like him was to take on his mannerisms, his understanding of women and their place as a separate species among men. The feminized world didn't understand it, so laws were enacted to reduce the amount of sexual violation. Laws were passed to make people accountable and humiliate them in public when they were simply doing what testosterone-filled DNA called for. Wally had natural impulses. They weren't alien. They were human.

And Edwin had impulses. Real men had these notions, these ideas of how to deal with the opposite sex. It had been society that had forced men to be more afraid of the consequences of acting out, so they didn't.

Although, once they secured themselves a girlfriend or a wife, those same men *role played* and acted out their desires where the law didn't intrude in their private lives.

Look at how popular *Fifty Shades of Grey* was. There's the answer right there.

Edwin was smart. He'd studied medicine. He'd studied law. He'd devoted his time to learning what CSI crews found and what evidence they convicted criminals on. The Bernardo case had fascinated him when he was in his early twenties, watching it unfold before his eyes.

Once he'd gotten his degree, he became a mortician to start. Then a medical examiner and coroner. As luck would have it, he'd gotten so good at his chosen field—passionately good—he had been pegged to head up the investigation into the Blood Eagle Killer—dubbed BEK—after his second gathering.

Basically, he was supposed to find himself.

A laughable matter.

And after a series of mistakes, he'd even got Detective Joslin released from the case.

The last family, the Marcellos, came as close as he had ever come to being caught. One of the crime scene individuals had found his fingerprint on the bottle of red wine he'd brought as a present. Usually something like that would be retrieved before he left the house, but he'd stupidly forgotten it. He wouldn't make a mistake like that again.

Detective Joslin had been delighted that they were finally making headway. Then Edwin had destroyed the evidence against him and set the case back to square one. The accident had taken place in the lab, after hours. Edwin explained his whereabouts and was never even criticized for his work. It was Detective Joslin who had lost her position as lead in the case. She was the fall guy when everyone from local mayors all the way up to the premier of the

Province of Ontario wanted the BEK unsub found and incarcerated so families across the province could rest easy.

Detective Kirk Aiken took over the case after a transfer to Toronto and began working with Edwin. It kept him close to what evidence came out of the Marcello farmhouse.

What a sad thing that happened to Kirk's partner. Horse allergy. Jake disappeared. Got attacked by a snake, then in a coma for almost two years.

Edwin shook his head at the unfairness of life. He sipped the rest of his Scotch, then got up to pour more. Once he was back in his chair, he thought of his first kill and remembered how honored he'd felt about it.

The night the police linked his father to the murder of some seventeen-year-old girl they'd found by the Don River, Wally had come home in a frantic state. He'd pulled Edwin aside and told him to put on his thinking cap. He needed an escape plan. A foolproof idea that enabled him to leave the house and go somewhere, anywhere, to avoid being taken to jail. The court system would take years and it would be a constant humiliation and reminder of what he had done. There was no way Wally was going to spend a single day being judged for what was a righteous action. If God didn't want men to *take* a woman, to *take* a family, then why engineer men with those impulses, those urges? Not that it was God's fault, Wally had said that night. He thanked God every day for the delight women offered him. Just that there might have been some foresight needed if he wasn't supposed to do it.

"There's not much I can say," Edwin had mumbled, afraid of the knock on the door coming at any second.

"I can't make it to the States in time. That's almost a two-hour drive. They'll watch for me at the border and you're still too young to drive." Wally paced the floor, walking back and forth rapidly. He slapped his forehead. "Think, dammit."

"Hide 'n' Seek, Dad."

He snapped his head to the left briefly, glared at him, then resumed watching the carpet as he paced.

"That might work, Jeffrey. That might work."

"Go hide in someone's basement. I'll bring food. Mom can help. In a while, go somewhere else."

"You're smart, little Jeffrey. But where? Whose basement? My list of friends is somewhat limited at the moment."

Wally snatched a pack of cigarettes off a side table, lit one and puffed twice, then resumed pacing, drawing on the cigarette every third step. It was interesting how Wally wasn't a smoker, but when he was nervous, he smoked two or three.

"I'm out of options," Wally seethed. "They'll be here any moment."

Edwin's mother came bounding down the stairs. "Wally, I'm not leaving my home in police custody," she screamed. "Come upstairs. We'll leave together. Leave this place forever."

Wally stopped pacing so suddenly, Edwin thought he'd fall over. He cast a quick glance at Edwin, drew on the cigarette, then looked at his wife on the stairs.

"Come here a moment, darling," Wally said in the soft, alluring voice he used on his subjects.

"We haven't got time, Wally," Cynthia said as she started toward him anyway. Edwin's mother knew better than to defy him.

Wally braced himself. Edwin had seen the pose before, heard that voice before. When he'd picked up the hooker and left her on the beach, the same look had come over Wally's face. He puffed on the cigarette, letting the smoke encircle his face, most likely in an effort to hide his thoughts as his wife might be able to read him, too.

Cynthia stopped a few feet away. Edwin moved backward until he bumped into the wood-paneled wall of the basement.

"Cynthia, I've come up with a plan and I think you're going to love it."

"Okay, Wally, but we have to leave right away—"

He raised an index finger. Cynthia quieted. He drew on the smoke once more, then placed it in an ashtray to his right.

"We are going to leave. Together," he said. "No one will *ever* take us. I promise you dear, you will never see the inside of a courtroom."

"Okay," Cynthia muttered, then looked sideways at Edwin. "What about him? Do we leave him or take him?"

"He stays," Wally said, his tone as dry as stale bread.

Cynthia didn't react to the knowledge that her son was not going with her. That was either a mark against her and her maternal instinct, or it was a sad mark of how much abuse she had endured over the years of living with Wally. Who was she now? Who had she become?

At the age of twelve, Edwin had been fascinated with his father and the stories of his adventures. Hearing his mother didn't care one way or the other whether she left him or not hit him in the solar plexus. It was probably more out of shock that his mother would be like that than from a place of actual pain.

So, when Wally had punched her in the face and blood shot from her nose upon the first impact, Edwin had actually cheered him on. What a show that was. Wally punched and punched and punched until Cynthia's lifeless body only moved because it was being pummeled.

When Wally rolled off his bloodied wife's body, Edwin pushed off the wall and came to stand above her. Cynthia's face had caved in, a brown jelly-like liquid oozed upward and out of her eye sockets. Edwin concluded that it had to be her brains. He almost smiled as the saying *beat her brains in* echoed through his head. Blood was everywhere, but he couldn't see her eyes anymore.

Cynthia's hair was matted with dark blood that seemed more black than red.

Wally moaned on the floor beside his wife. He held his hands up and showed them to Edwin.

"Looks like I really did it this time, eh, Jeffrey?"

"What, Daddy?"

"My hands. I got so angry that I split my knuckles and I think I broke my finger on her eye socket."

Edwin stepped over his mother's corpse and knelt by his father. He was so proud of the man that was his dad that he beamed with delight, water seeping from his eyes.

"Why are you crying, boy?" Wally shouted.

"I just ..." Edwin's voice choked off in his throat with emotion.

"Just what?" Wally bellowed.

"I just love what you did. Mom needed to know how you felt about her."

Wally lowered his head to the basement floor, a smile playing across his lips.

"You're a good boy, Jeffrey Harris. I'll always remember that about you."

"I love you so much, Dad. You've taught me so much and made me so happy."

Someone knocked on the door upstairs.

"Shit. They're here."

A man shouted something from outside. Flashlights scanned the basement windows on the other side by the stairs.

"Run upstairs. Go to the kitchen. Get the butcher knife out of the cupboard."

"For what?"

"Just do as I tell you, boy."

Edwin hadn't needed coaxing. He would do anything for his

father. In under a minute, he'd made it back downstairs with the large chopping knife in his hand. The police had knocked two more times on the door, yelled to identify themselves and ask someone to open up, but Edwin ignored them.

"You have to do something for me, boy. You listening?"

Edwin knelt beside his father and nodded.

"Run the knife across my throat. Run it deep. If it doesn't work the first time, go back and forth like you're cutting one of your peanut butter and jam sandwiches. Can you do that for me?"

The thought made Edwin sick.

"But that'll hurt you, Daddy." He started to cry. "That'll hurt you bad."

"Listen to me, boy," Wally shouted. The knock upstairs on the front door grew louder, more insistent. "I'm not going to no courtroom. I've saved your mother from that. Now you save me. Then all you got to do is scream and scream. They'll come find you and take you to a new family and your life will begin. Take a family. Perform your own Gatherings one day as men are supposed to do. Follow in my footsteps. Just don't make the same mistakes I made."

Something smashed the front door upstairs.

"Do it now, boy. I'll even hold the knife with you so it looks like I did it to myself. Don't talk to them. Don't admit nothing"— another bang upstairs— "just do this one last thing for me and then go and take all the women you want for the rest of your life and stay smart about it. You hear me, boy?"

Through tears, Edwin nodded at his father.

"And take our wedding rings. They're yours. Take them as a memory, but also as a trophy of what happened here today. Remember boy, always take a trophy."

Edwin nodded, then took the knife and guided his father's hand on the blade. It hovered above his father's flesh for a brief second.

"Thank you," Wally whispered. "Thank you, son. Release me."

His eyes softened, filled with an inner glow, as an expression of contentment covered his face. He looked heavenward briefly, then closed his eyes.

Edwin applied pressure and began to slice downward, nearly severing Wally's head clean off with the first plunge of the sharp blade. Edwin hadn't known how easy flesh opened up until that day when he had almost decapitated his father.

By the time the police barged in upstairs, Wally was dead, the large knife still in his hand. His body had stopped convulsing seconds before the police bounded down the stairs, guns drawn, to find Edwin curled up in a corner, covered in blood, crying, their wedding bands safely secured in his pocket.

They ushered him out of the basement as fast as they could. On the stairs, Edwin blew a kiss to his father and swore to himself that his father's legacy would be continued. But unlike his father, Edwin would be smart. He would be patient. Not only would he learn all the tells a CSI agent looked for. He would learn how to cover them up, too. In addition, Edwin would do everything possible to be close to the investigations on himself, or even be a part of them.

Wouldn't his father be proud of him now? After all these years, and having taken five families without any consequences, Wally would have slapped him on the back and told him that Jeffrey was the man he had expected him to grow up to be. The man Wally had always strived to be.

Edwin held his glass in the air to toast the memory of his father, then drank the last of the Scotch. It was time to turn in for the night. He would be busy before the party and then he would bring his new wife to her new home where she would be safe.

He was doing her a favor by enriching her life with him as Wally had for the women he'd taken all those years before.

It was time for a little family Gathering and Edwin was ready. Jeffrey was ready.

More than ready.

CHAPTER TWENTY-NINE

J ake turned up his driveway. The grocery bags were gone. *What now?*

He moved to the side of the cement and edged closer to the house, going tree to tree, listening, smelling the air. A deer or some other large animal roamed to his right about forty yards away. Small animal scents like raccoons and squirrels wafted to him. How he could tell the difference in direction, size and shape, he had no idea. That was just the way it was now. Other than animals, he detected the smell of expended gasoline, oil from a car engine, and a radiator close by that was leaking coolant.

He dropped to his knees and placed both palms on the ground in search of vibrations, but nothing was remotely close. A truck of some kind going over the train tracks half a mile up the road was all that came to him.

So where had his groceries gone?

Anger seeped back into his consciousness. After the fight in the sand pits, his energy had waned, the adrenaline had worn off, and he was tired, hoping to come home, call a window company, and nap until they arrived.

But someone had absconded with his food.

He advanced on the house, moving slowly in case the thief was still close, waiting Jake out, up wind. At the front door, he eased it open to find the grocery bags on his kitchen table.

He frowned as he let the screen door close softly.

"Hey," a voice snapped behind him.

Jake spun around, reflexively raising his hands and dropping into a defensive gesture. His old partner sat on his chair beside the couch.

"Thought you might want your food put in the fridge," Kirk said. "That was a lot of meat. Thinking about having the town over for a BBQ?"

Jake lowered his hands and stood up straighter. "What are you doing here?" he asked.

Kirk sat with his elbows on the armrests of the chair. "Haven't chatted in a year and a half until you wake up in that clinic in Rio. Only see you sporadically because you're so fucking angry all the time. Doc says it'll pass. I tell him, I don't know. Jake's actually a nice guy. So, here I am. Coming to visit my old partner, my best friend. And all I get is, *What are you doing here?*"

Jake entered the kitchen and grabbed a glass of water. He drank it back, washing the rest of the blood from inside and outside his mouth, then set the empty glass down and returned to the living room.

"What happened to you?" Kirk asked.

"I was in a coma."

"No, just now. Why run off like that through the trees? Then come back with a missing tooth. You fight someone?"

Jake studied Kirk's face. He knew the man, loved the man like a brother. But he felt something different now. The new Jake didn't dislike Kirk, just couldn't figure a place for him in his new life. There wasn't an easy explanation for it—it was just the way it was. Like a puzzle with defective pieces that didn't fit.

"You don't want to talk about it?" Kirk asked. He tilted his head to the side. "Did someone break in?"

Jake gasped and offered Kirk a dazed look.

"I'm a detective, Jake. I detect things. There's broken glass on the side of the house. Inside, there are ransacked drawers, furniture moved out from the walls. You running into the woods, groceries left on the driveway. Have you forgotten how this shit is done?" Kirk got to his feet and approached Jake. "So, tell me. Did you catch them?"

Jake nodded.

"And beat them up? Teach them a lesson?"

Jake turned away and headed to the freezer. "Why are you here?" he asked.

"I need your help."

"I already told you my answer. It stands."

The freezer was packed with meat that hadn't had the chance to freeze yet. Jake began taking it all out and placing it in the fridge. Everything would be eaten within the next day or two. There was no need to freeze it.

"Jake. Reconsider. Come back as a consultant."

"I can't. I'm on disability."

"Your cane is over there behind the couch. You aren't walking with a limp. You're fine."

Jake tossed a packet of T-bones on the counter and turned to Kirk.

"They want to reinstate me? Is that it?"

"No. Not yet. There's tests, evaluations. You know how it is."

"I don't have long to live, Kirk."

Kirk's expression changed. A tentative smile crossed his face as if Jake was kidding. His smile built with anticipation of a punchline, then sank.

"What?" Kirk stammered. "Who told you that?"

"Dr. Sutton."

"Why? You just woke up. You're not going anywhere. You're healing very fast. Shit man, I just saw you run through those trees like you were eighteen again."

"Without tests, Sutton says there's no way to tell how long I've got."

Kirk shook his head. "Oh, shit man, you got it all wrong. See brother, you gotta listen to me now." Kirk backed up and plopped down on the couch. "Sutton doesn't know shit. You're in better shape than I've ever seen you." He steepled his hands. "Those men in that black SUV, though, the guys in business suits. We have to chat with them."

"Men in business suits?"

"The first few months you were missing, someone was following me. I talked to Cindy, watched over her. They were following her, too."

"Any leads?"

"None. But I think I know who they are. Luke's people. Fortech Industries."

Black SUV? Suits? Before he could stop himself, he dropped his mouth open in surprise. He had just seen two men in suits standing by an SUV. Men who had hired punk thugs to rob him of his laptop. If they were watching Kirk and Cindy, it was likely they were after him, too. Now that he was awake and researching them, looking up anything and everything he could learn about Fortech Industries, they were coming for him. It had to be Fortech's men.

An idea occurred to Jake as he headed back into the kitchen.

"Hey, what'd I say?" Kirk yelled after him.

Jake opened the T-bone's packaging, lifted the red meat and bit into it. Instantly, he felt his stomach yearn for more. He bit again, feeling no pain where his missing tooth used to be. It was incredible really, a miracle, but he didn't waste any time thinking about why he didn't have pain. To be grateful was enough.

"Holy shit, man. That's certainly blue rare. Ain't you gonna cook that shit?"

"I have an offer for you," Jake said, his mouth full.

Kirk stepped back, watching Jake devour the T-bone.

"Okay," he said. "I'm listening."

"I'll look at the Blood Eagle Killer case as you've requested—"

"B.E.K." Kirk shrugged. "That's what we're calling him now."

Jake nodded and tore off another piece of meat. "I'll look at what you have and see if I can help—consult—on the case. In exchange, you help me."

"With what?"

"The guys in the SUV."

A slow smile built on Kirk's lips as he crossed his arms, studying Jake's face.

"You want me to help you find the guys responsible for Luke's disappearance?" Kirk asked. "The ones watching all of us?"

Jake nodded, his mouth full. The meat tasted so much better raw. He wondered how come he hadn't eaten it this way before. Barbecues were so overrated.

"They were here. Hired some punks to break in. Stole my laptop."

Kirk frowned. "You saw the men just now? The SUV?"

Jake swallowed a thick piece. "On the highway. Maybe thirty minutes ago."

"Which way were they headed?" Kirk asked as he retrieved his cell phone from his back pocket.

"Put that away," Jake said. "They're long gone now. But they'll be back. Until then, help me learn everything I can about Fortech Industries."

Kirk slipped his phone away, then slapped Jake on the shoulder. "You have a deal, my friend. Back in business. Partners." He extended a hand to shake.

Jake grabbed it, pumped twice, then headed into the living

room, what was left of the T-bone in his hand. He detected Kirk wiping the blood from the handshake off on a kitchen towel before following him.

"But we need to leave now," Kirk said.

"Leave? Why?"

"The unsub will be striking again soon. It's in the MO timeline to kill again. I want you to come to the Toronto office and review everything I've gathered on all the cases. We need fresh eyes on this. Maybe you'll see something we've missed that ties the families together."

Jake shook his head. "I remember this killer. He's peripatetic without reason. No one knows where he'll strike next. He could be a wanderer, a nomad for all we know. At least that's what I remember about the cases around southern Ontario. It didn't make sense to Joslin. It won't make sense to you or me."

"Still, I need you to come to Toronto with me. Get involved. Keep busy with it. You'll be able to see things differently than me. And I can watch your back in Toronto. Those Fortech fuckers come, we'll both be ready."

"No." Jake shook his head. "Forget about it."

"What?" Kirk asked, eyes wide, hands out at his sides, open-palmed. "We just shook on it."

"I'll help. Forget about me coming to Toronto, though. Bring the stuff here. I'll review it here."

There was no way he was leaving his home with the men in the SUV close by. They would come for him and he wouldn't need Kirk's help when they did. But if they didn't come, having a homicide detective on his side was the next best option.

Kirk seemed to consider his options a moment. "Okay. It's the long weekend coming up."

"What's the holiday?"

"Canada's birthday, dickhead."

Jake looked at him, unused to the humor.

"Sorry, but man this is killing me," Kirk said. "You used to be so much fun."

"I can be fun again." Jake gnawed on the bone. "Give me time."

"Fair enough. It's Canada Day coming up. The long weekend. I'll bring everything I've got on Saturday. We'll spend the weekend here going over it. Cool?"

Jake nodded.

"Hey," Kirk said. He wiped at his forehead. "I gotta ask, though. Why is it so fucking hot in here?"

"I like it that way."

"Okay. I'll bring beer. Like the old days." Kirk headed for the door. "I'll probably have to work in my skivvies if it's going to be this hot in here."

Jake needed more meat. And a nap.

Kirk stepped outside the screen door. "Don't get up. I'll let myself out."

"Kirk. Wait."

Kirk stuck his head back in.

"You parked up the road. Didn't use my driveway."

Kirk nodded. "Yeah. So? Didn't know what to expect. How angry you'd be. You know. What the doc said and all. Thought I'd saunter up the driveway, holler your name."

"You have a hole in the radiator. Smelled the antifreeze leaking from here. Fix it before you drive up from Toronto or it'll overheat."

Kirk frowned, then nodded and pulled back, letting the screen door close.

"You're stranger than I remembered," Kirk said.

"Thanks, dickhead," Jake said.

As Kirk walked the length of his driveway, Jake headed into the kitchen for more meat.

PART THREE
CANADA DAY

CHAPTER THIRTY

Kirk arrived earlier than Jake expected. He pulled into his driveway and parked beside Jake's new Cobra before ten in the morning. The drive from Toronto was almost three hours, two and a half if Kirk had broken speed limits. With this being a Saturday morning—Canada Day—the traffic would've been the worst coming out of Toronto the previous night. On a Saturday morning, it would've still been pretty thick.

"When did you leave Toronto?" Jake asked as he stood on the top stair holding his screen door open, a steaming cup of coffee in his hand.

Kirk was standing by his open trunk. "Stayed in Orillia last night." He lifted a box of files out of the trunk of his car, set it on the ground, and smiled up at Jake. "Didn't want to deal with the traffic. Left the house Thursday afternoon, early." He disappeared behind the trunk of his unmarked police car to heft more boxes. "You wanna help?"

"Sure," Jake said. "After I finish my coffee." He turned and retreated into the house.

"Gee. Thanks," Kirk said behind him as the screen door slammed shut.

Ten minutes later, Kirk had five boxes piled by Jake's front door. Jake helped him bring them inside where they set them by the dining room table. That would act as a desk. Each man could take either end, giving them lots of room to spread out.

"I have to thank you," Kirk said when he set the last box on the floor by Jake's chair.

"For what?"

"The radiator. It's fixed. Had to fix it in Huntsville before heading home when I was up here last." Kirk plunked down on a chair. "How did you know?"

Jake shrugged. "Smelled it. Haven't you ever walked by a car and smelled leaking antifreeze?"

"Yeah, but how close did you get to my car to smell it?"

"Does it matter?"

Jake opened the box marked *Boyd Family.*

"It's a box for each family. The Boyd Family in 2006, then Reilly, 2008, the Hapsteads in 2010, Lucas in 2013, and finally the Marcello clan, 2015." Kirk hefted one more box. "This box contains miscellaneous material, sketches, witness accounts and so on. But it's only half full."

"What about autopsy reports? Cause of death?"

"In each family's box. It's all there."

Jake opened the Boyd box and set the files in piles in front of him. He stopped moving and looked up at Kirk.

"What? You're staring at me."

"The tooth. How is that possible?"

"What tooth?" As soon as he asked the question, he understood what Kirk was talking about. The canine tooth he'd lost in the fight with the punks who broke into his house had grown back. It was whiter than the rest of his teeth and seemed a little stronger. It was also tapered with a small pointy tip.

"When I was here a few days ago, you were missing a tooth. Now it's back. How is that possible?" he repeated. "Unless it's a fake."

"No fake." Jake opened his mouth and tapped the tip of the

tooth with his tongue. "I have no idea why it grew back so fast. Just did."

"Have you told Sutton about it?"

"No. Not going to either." Jake gave Kirk a stern look. "And neither are you."

For the next five minutes, both of them worked in silence, Kirk wiping his brow as he perspired.

"It's July, Jake," Kirk said.

"I know."

"Then why is the heat on?"

"Need it that way."

"Why?"

Jake stopped rustling papers and met Kirk's eyes. "We're here to work. Let's just do that."

Kirk shook his head slowly. "We'll work. We'll figure things out and move forward, but first, you have to be honest with me."

"About what?" Jake gave him a troubled expression as if this line of questioning irritated him.

"Level with me. What happened to you? How have you changed since the coma?"

"I had a reaction to the antivenin. Woke up eighteen months later and blasted through physio. Nothing to it." He smiled. "You should try it sometime."

"No one grows teeth like that," Kirk said, ignoring Jake's attempt at humor. "The doctor isn't talking to me. You're not talking to me—"

"What is it—"

"I want answers!" Kirk shouted over Jake's interruption. "I've lost my partner, my best friend, and Cindy lost you, too."

Jake considered Kirk, how he looked at the moment, his expression. He contemplated telling him everything. Then chose not to. If Jake wasn't living proof of the changes, there was no way he'd believe his own account of what was happening to him.

"Look, I appreciate your concern, but there's nothing to tell you because I don't know anything. I'm here. I'm awake. I get cold easier than before. Something might have happened to my brain, my body, that makes things different, but I'm not entirely sure what. Just know that I'm the same on the inside. I'm still Jake."

Kirk watched him a moment longer. "Okay. For now, that's good enough." He cleared his throat. "But in the future if something comes up, tell me first. Don't talk to Sutton or anybody else. I can help. They can't."

Jake found that comment strange.

Kirk got up and headed for the door. "I said I would bring beer. I didn't buy any." He slipped on his shoes. "So I'm driving into town to pick some up."

"I'll come," Jake said. "Just like old times."

Kirk smiled. It was the first genuine smile he'd seen on Kirk's face since before the coma.

"Good. I'll meet you in the car."

Kirk stepped outside and let the screen door slam behind him. In his familiar tone, Kirk sang a rhyme made up on the spot as he trudged to the car.

"Heading out with my friend Jake, to buy beer and maybe a steak, and I'm making up funky rhymes, just like the good old times."

Jake put on his shoes and followed Kirk outside, locking the door behind him.

Every situation had a smell, a distinctive odor that told Jake what had happened recently, what was happening, and most importantly, what was going to happen.

As he walked to Kirk's unmarked cruiser, all he could smell was the pine off the trees, the oil of the machine under the vehicle's hood, and the stupid Axe underarm deodorant Kirk always wore, thinking he was a ladies' man.

Nothing else bothered Jake. No one sat watching his house. No scent of nervous sweat wafted to him. No breeze carried distinct odors of predators coming his way.

So he dropped in the passenger side, cranked the car's heater, and rested his eyes on the way to Huntsville in search of alcohol.

CHAPTER THIRTY-ONE

Edwin Gavin rented a hotel room on the north side of Huntsville, near the highway. Easy access, good restaurants, with no need to be in town. He wasn't staying the night to enjoy Huntsville. He had a purpose and that purpose was Megan Radcliffe.

Before checking out of the hotel, he performed one more routine check of his supplies, which eased his nerves. Nerves were evident at times, but mostly because of the anticipation of a new wife. Any extra anxiety he experienced this time was because of the change in routine.

It was a break from routine that had gotten his stepfather under the police microscope.

He had met Megan during the regular course of his job as chief medical examiner in Toronto. She knew him as Jeffrey Harris even though he went by his other name—his legal name—at work. The instant he'd seen her, he'd known she had to be his. Introducing himself as Jeffrey was an instantaneous response. No one he worked with saw them talking briefly, therefore no one heard her address him as Jeffrey.

This was also the first time he would perform a Gathering with all his hair intact. Shaving his head wasn't needed this time. As a friend, he had been invited to the party. A party where someone would disappear. The idea that someone could attribute any of the crimes that were about to take place at the Radcliffes to him was preposterous.

This Gathering would make the rounds with homicide and everyone would be upset that the BEK killer had struck again. Detective Aiken would do what Detective Joslin had done before him. He would come to the scene of the crime, gather evidence and have photos taken and make another file for the Radcliffe family. Edwin Gavin would perform the postmortem examinations on the Radcliffe family bodies and a hunt would be underway for the location of the missing mother, Megan Radcliffe.

Textbook. It was all textbook. And Jeffrey Harris had written this particular textbook.

In order to be the good guest he wanted to be at the Canada Day party, he would need to BYOB. *Bring Your Own Booze.*

Edwin grabbed his bag and exited the hotel room, leaving the key inside the room. He tossed the bag in the trunk of his car and drove to the liquor store in Huntsville.

He wiped his forehead. It was already getting hot this first day of July. A flick of the air switch on his dash had blessed coolness blowing on him, keeping his underarms from leaving wet spots.

It wasn't until he was downtown and pulling into the liquor store that he realized he had been smiling the entire ride in.

"It's going to be a fine day," he muttered.

He parked and exited his vehicle.

"Edwin!" a man shouted. "Hey, what are you doing up here?"

CHAPTER THIRTY-TWO

Kirk drove the fifteen kilometers south to Huntsville and pulled off the highway on an exit ramp without saying a word about the heat. When he finally did speak, it startled Jake, who had drifted off.

"You want a coffee at Timmy's?"

"No," Jake grunted.

"What? Coma do something to your brain? We always grabbed a Timmy's when we were on the road."

"Not this time. Not for me," Jake said, keeping his eyes closed.

"Fine."

Kirk did drive-thru and got them to downtown Huntsville without delay. Jake ruminated on the case. He'd make notes on the Blood Eagle Killer's methods so he'd be able to match them up to the other files. He would make timelines and a mind map of the family, their jobs, schools, and religion to see if the victims had something in common. If there was a pattern anywhere and it emerged, he was in the best position to see it.

The cruiser slowed and turned into the liquor store parking lot.

Jake opened his eyes and sat up.

"We're here, sleepyhead." Kirk turned off the car and faced him. "Coming in?"

Jake took in the building, the parking lot. It didn't look too busy.

"Sure. Why not?"

Outside the car, Kirk used the key fob to lock the doors, then turned to a man walking by.

"Edwin!" he shouted. "Hey, what are you doing up here?"

Jake edged around the hood to stand close, but not close enough to be involved in the conversation.

Edwin, obviously a colleague of Kirk's, seemed surprised to see him.

"What brings you up here?" Edwin asked.

A memory surfaced for Jake. The Marcello farmhouse. Wasn't Edwin Detective Joslin's medical examiner?

"We're going over files on the case," Kirk replied, slapping Edwin on the arm. Kirk turned and gestured toward Jake. "You remember Detective Jake Wood?"

"I do." Edwin moved closer, his hand extended.

Without wanting to, Jake shook it. Edwin's sweat made the inside of his palm moist and cool. Jake sniffed the air, his mouth hanging open slightly. An odd collection of pheromones emanated off Edwin. Anxiety, nervousness, mixed with apprehension and excitement. It was as if he was going to get drunk but feared the hangover.

"How're you feeling?" Edwin asked. "Terrible thing that happened to you. We all thought you were dead."

Jake nodded, then turned to Kirk. "I'll be inside."

This was why he didn't want back on the force. He didn't need the money and didn't want to be as busy as he used to be. But it was the questions, the probing intellects that saw him as a story or a punchline. Edwin's concern was a mask. He didn't care about Jake. The scent gave him away. Edwin was all about himself. Even the handshake hadn't been genuine. When Edwin had said *terrible thing,* he could have been asking Jake if he wanted cotton candy. It meant nothing, and in the end, Jake didn't care.

"Um, okay Jake," Kirk fumbled his words, probably feeling awkward for having introduced them. "I'll meet you inside."

Before Jake got two steps toward the front doors of the liquor store, an RCMP police cruiser stopped four feet from him.

Jake made a face at Kirk as he gestured at the vehicle. "More friends?"

The driver double-parked the cruiser and opened his door. On the passenger side, his female partner got out, too.

Jake backed up so Kirk could handle them. This was steadily becoming too much interaction for one day. A simple alcohol run didn't have to be so busy.

Before the male officer—the driver—spoke his first words, Jake's attention was drawn to Edwin. His scent had changed. Drastically. He smelled just nervous. Jake raised his head slightly to enjoy the full warmth of the summer sun, but kept his eyes on Edwin.

Edwin's hand twitched, then he rubbed the back of his neck. He blinked rapidly a few times as his pupils seemed to dilate. He cleared his throat as if he was about to say something, but instead eased back a few steps to stand behind Kirk.

"Jake Wood?" the RCMP officer asked.

Jake nodded. Kirk eased forward, flipped out his OPP ID badge.

"Homicide. Name's Detective Kirk Aiken. What can we do for you?"

Edwin eased back another step again.

What the fuck is it with this guy? Jake took in a strong scent of fear. He frowned in confusion. Had Edwin done something to make him fear the police? His behavior seemed irrational.

"I'm Officer Manks and my partner is Officer Duncan." The female passenger in uniform nodded. "We were headed out to

Jake's house on Boundary Road in Novar to talk to him about an incident that happened recently. Duncan here saw you get out of the car. So we pulled in."

"An incident?" Kirk asked. "What kind of incident?"

"Mr. Wood, please step over here for me."

"Hold up," Kirk said. "Tell me what this is all about first."

When Manks looked at Jake, he nodded. "Tell him, Manks," Jake said. "It'll go a lot easier."

"Four men laid a complaint against Jake." He focused on Jake's face. "Said you attacked them. One of the complainants left the hospital with a broken forearm. Two of them were..." He stopped and glanced at his partner, then back to Kirk. "Two of them were bitten."

Kirk barked a short laugh, then covered his mouth with his hand. "Bitten? Are you serious? And you think Jake did it?"

Manks nodded. "The complainants admitted breaking into Jake's house but said he was too rough as they weren't on the premises when Jake attacked them. According to their statement, Mr. Wood *hunted* them and beat them and bit them."

Edwin peeked at Jake sidelong. Jake felt his glare momentarily, then it was gone.

Kirk stood straighter. "Detective Jake Wood is my partner. He was in a coma for eighteen months and in the last week relocated to this area. Sure, his house was broken into, but if he *hunted* anybody, he would have to be a fast runner with his cane. Only just the other day, Jake stopped using his cane to walk." Kirk leaned his upper body backward as if he was disgusted with something. "And to think, a man in his weakened state, able to take on four men at once and come out unscathed. Really? Not to mention that he's a cop. C'mon guys, find someone else to harass."

"It's easy to solve. The report stated that their attacker lost a tooth and bled from the wound." Manks stared at Jake. "Open your mouth. Show me your teeth. Then we'll talk about what might be possible and what might not be possible."

Jake smiled, showing his white teeth, not a single one missing. He used his thumb along the bottom of the teeth to try to shake them loose. Each remained rigid in his mouth.

Manks exchanged a glance with Duncan.

"I guess that about sums it up. I'll have to recheck their statement." His tone turned serious. "But let me ask you something, Detective. Why didn't you report the break in?"

"I'm a detective. Kirk here and I are dealing with it."

That seemed to satisfy Manks. He nodded at Kirk as he stepped back to the cruiser.

"You might want to look for two well-dressed men in a black SUV," Jake said. "I think it's a Suburban. Whatever those boys said in their statement, it's coming from the SUV guys."

Manks frowned as if that didn't make any sense. Jake didn't care. The more people who knew about the black SUV, the better. Manks and Duncan nodded, slipped back in their cruiser, and started away.

Edwin's nervousness had calmed in the time Jake and Kirk had handled the police, but his scent still rankled Jake. Something was wrong with the guy. Or maybe it was because he worked with dead bodies all day and the thought of dealing with too many live ones freaked him out.

Kirk and Edwin chatted a few moments more after the two RCMP officers pulled out, then said their goodbyes and entered the liquor store, Edwin going his own way down another aisle. Kirk was itching to ask Jake something, he could tell, but before he said anything, Jake had a question.

"What's the burnout rate for morticians and medical examiners? Guys like Edwin?"

Kirk scratched his chin. "Don't know. I think it's something like five years. Maybe a little longer."

"How long has Edwin been doing it?"

"Too long."

"That's what I figured."

CHAPTER THIRTY-THREE

Edwin stood in the section where various kinds of rum covered the shelves. He stood alone, breathing slowly in an attempt to calm his racing heart. If he'd believed in signs, that had been a sign to back off the Radcliffes tonight. But he didn't believe in new age bullshit like that. A man was in control of his destiny and things got fucked up if the man fucked them up. That wasn't fate. That was reality.

Whatever happened had nothing to do with a chance meeting with two detectives and two police officers from different detachments in the course of minutes in the parking lot of a liquor store three hours from his house.

And after the Gathering, the police would never think to suspect him. Edwin would be back in Toronto by tomorrow morning with his new wife. The modus operandi will have changed so they may not even attribute this to the BEK killer. Sure, the blood eagle would have to be performed on the father, and the three daughters had to die, but the BEK killer had never kidnapped the mother. Also, once the blood eagle was done on Mr. Radcliffe, Edwin had considered dismemberment. He wanted Mr. Radcliffe's body spread about the house. This crime scene would resemble a copycat killer doing his best to look like the real BEK killer. Edwin would do his best to achieve this.

He placed a hand on his chest and waited another moment

before grabbing a bottle of Kraken rum. After snatching up some wine, he started down the aisle toward the whiskey.

At the party, he would tell partygoers that he was leaving early to make it home at a decent hour. Being seen at the party was also a new development. No way would the BEK killer do that. In other words, the situation was completely changed and there was no way the authorities would ever look at him. Ever.

He wasn't just sure of it, he knew it.

In the whiskey section, he grabbed a cheap bottle of Grants and headed to the cashiers. At the till, he paid for the six bottles of wine, rum, and whiskey, and started for his car. Kirk's cruiser was gone.

See, he told himself. *It was nothing.*

The chance meeting was just that. A coincidence and fuck Carl Jung if he thought there were no coincidences, only synchronicity.

Synchronize this.

He got behind the wheel, started the car. It wasn't until he pulled out of the parking lot that he noticed a minor tremor in his hands.

It was that Jake Wood guy. Intense and mysterious. The way he'd watched Edwin from the side. The way he'd scrutinized him. What the hell did Jake want anyway? What was his problem?

Maybe when he was back to work, he would sit Kirk down and ask about his old partner. Find out what the hell had actually happened to the guy.

Who knows, perhaps something in Jake's brain had slipped off its track and that's what had caused the coma that lasted eighteen months.

Or maybe Jake was just fucked.

Edwin smiled to himself as he headed to East Side Mario's for a veal parmigiana lunch.

Yeah, Jake Wood was fucked. That had to be it.

Nothing else to it.

CHAPTER THIRTY-FOUR

"**Y**ou want to tell me what the hell that was all about?" Kirk asked.

He had remained quiet in the liquor store. Said nothing as they drove out of Huntsville and just now had asked his first question. He'd already slapped the steering wheel twice.

"You're a fucking detective with the OPP on disability and local cops want to talk to you about putting guys in the hospital." He snapped his head sideways to glare at Jake. "And don't deny it. I saw the fucking missing tooth in your mouth."

Jake shrugged and stared down at his hands in his lap. "What's there to say? Four guys. I was outnumbered. They attacked me. I defended myself. One was untouched. One got a little roughed up. The other guy accidentally got his shoulder dislocated—"

"What!" Kirk shouted. "Dislocated? And the other guy got a broken arm. Holy fuck, man. What the hell happened?"

"The dislocated shoulder guy busted out my tooth. Broken arm guy pulled a blade. Blocked it too fast. Must've snapped something in his arm." He put his head back and watched the white lines on the road race by the vehicle, trying to temper the rising anger. He didn't want to go off on Kirk. He was the closest thing to a friend Jake had and he wanted to keep it that way.

Kirk didn't say anything for a few kilometers. He watched his mirrors, giving the appearance that he was busy driving but Jake knew different. He had things he wanted to say, things he wanted to know, but was lost on how to extract them from Jake. The truth was Kirk wanted to handle Jake with kid gloves.

"What is it?" Jake asked. "Go ahead. Ask away. Don't be nice because of what I've been through. I don't want sympathy or pity."

Kirk looked his way briefly.

"How did the tooth grow back so fast?" Kirk asked.

"No idea." Jake noticed Kirk's grip tighten on the steering wheel. "Really, I don't know. I didn't allow the tests Sutton wanted to perform on me."

"Sutton told me something," Kirk said. "Apparently coma patients often come out of their coma with anger issues. Once they're grounded, visited by the people they love, basically get reoriented back into their old lives, the anger abates. Why didn't that happen with you? I can feel your anger sometimes. A sense of rage that oozes off you. That's not the Jake I know."

Jake studied a red Camaro as it passed them, following it up the highway.

"Don't know. I just feel angry. But maybe it has something to do with that orientation thing you just mentioned. I didn't get the people I love back. I've lost Cindy to another man. I even lost my fuckin' dog. So what, I'm not supposed to be pissed about it?"

Kirk ran a hand through his hair. "Fair enough. You're right. I'd be pissed at the world, too."

"Will I have a job when they deem me not disabled?" Jake asked. "Do I need one? Do I *want* one? I get broken into on day one in my new home. I just want to be left alone." He watched the trees zip by on his side of the cruiser. "What does this world want from me? Take my life, take my woman, take everything away, then wake me almost two years later to keep fucking with me. Yeah, I'm angry. That's why I need time away. That's why I'm up here, convalescing." He checked, but Kirk's eyes were still on the road and not looking at him. "So let's work on the Blood Eagle asshole and find Fortech Industries and then leave me be." Knowing the cold months were only twelve weeks away, he added, "I want to hibernate for the winter, take it easy. Stock up the house and just veg until spring."

"Got it. I understand." He hit the signal to take the exit ramp. "Let's stick to the job, get it done, and I'll leave you alone." He smacked Jake's leg. "For what it's worth, I understand you better now. I'm cool with it. Just promise me you'll take it easy on the bad guys if they come around the house again."

"Can't promise that."

Kirk jabbed him in the shoulder like he had in the early days. "C'mon, man."

"What I can promise is state-of-the-art security, twenty-four hours a day monitoring. That'll keep them out. Sirens going off. They'll scram before I even get downstairs. No one gets hurt."

It was Kirk's turn to shrug. "I guess if that's the best I can get out of you, then fine."

They drove in silence until Kirk killed the engine in Jake's driveway.

"You know Cindy is beating herself up over this."

Jake grabbed the door handle and waited. "Tell her I'm sorry. I wish it wasn't like this. But it is what it is."

"It's not that easy."

"Sure it is."

"She's having trouble with her marriage now. Nothing she can't fix, but you can imagine how hard it must be. She loved you, man. Hardcore. For you to be found alive after waking from a coma just to treat her the way you did."

Jake snapped his head toward Kirk, who raised his hands in surrender.

"I know," Kirk said. "Anger issues. Waking from the coma

and shit. Take it easy. Don't bite my head off. Just telling you the way things are."

"The way things are is she got married. There isn't a day goes by that I don't think about her and what could've been. Not a single day goes by that I don't think about the baby she's carrying and wish it were mine." He punctuated his words by jamming an index finger in the air. "Now, we have a serial killer to catch and a company that is getting away with murder. Deal with that and we'll talk about me making reparations to the way I treated Cindy."

He pushed the door open and exited the car.

He was inside the house before Kirk got out, leaving him to grab the booze.

There were case files to read, patterns to study, a killer to catch.

Jake had no interest in dealing with the past right now.

Maybe never.

CHAPTER THIRTY-FIVE

The house was in rural Huntsville with no sidewalks. The lawn ran the length of the house and stopped at the shoulder of the road. The shoulder was littered with at least a dozen cars, but that didn't bother Edwin. He parked on the far end by an access area to the forest. Once he had Megan sedated, he would guide her outside the back of the house under the cover of night and lead her through the woods until they came out at the opening by his vehicle. He had hoped for such an opening and was overjoyed to find it.

Chance favors the prepared mind.

Well, if so, then so be it. But fate wasn't real. Neither was God. Or the Devil. There was dust, air, fire, man, animal, and a rotating Earth circling a star and that was it. And what people did with the time they had on planet Earth was up to them. Edwin thought of himself as an entrepreneur in the flesh. He chose his family and he chose them well. He enjoyed what he did, as his father had. This is what they were made to do. Wally had taught him that. His stepfather had stolen so many lives, little Edwin could never count the times he saw dead bodies in the basement. Sometimes, before Wally had disposed of a decaying woman, he would bring another one home and violate her for days while the other corpse was bound to a chair. It was to obtain obedience from his new victim. And Wally had let Edwin observe it all from the stairs.

Learning about sex in such a way at twelve years old had given him core values, an understanding of what women were here for, and all the tools he would need to make Megan's life better than any woman Wally had taken. Because Edwin was better at it than Wally, he would keep Megan alive for at least a year. Or until he tired of her. Even when he performed his fetishes and fantasies on her, hurt her in ways that would make it hard for her to perform her wifely duties, Edwin would allow her time to heal. He would provide ointment, oil, gauze, bandages. He would also offer lubrication for the tighter spots. This wasn't about Megan's suffering as much as it was about Edwin's pleasure.

"I mean," Edwin whispered as he turned off the car, "what's a wife for if not to pleasure her man?"

He checked his mirrors, saw nothing untoward, then exited the Honda. Under one arm, he held the small box of wine and in the other, the bottle of rum and the whiskey.

At the front door, the bass from the music sounded as if someone was knocking on the inside to a rhythmic beat. The sun was setting, the sky a mix of purple and pink. He admired the pink, making him think of his new wife.

"Tonight, baby. Tonight."

Edwin rang the doorbell.

CHAPTER THIRTY-SIX

Jake had read through three case files, three separate boxes and wrote so many notes that a bump had formed on his writing finger. Kirk had been reading case files as well, but had stopped half an hour ago to open a bottle of wine. Kirk seemed to be handling the heat better, but Jake could tell it was making him sleepy.

Jake got up to make coffee. Wine would put him out. He grabbed the beans from the freezer, ground them and poured hot water over them in a French press. He leaned on the counter and crossed his arms to wait.

"Tell me about Edwin the mortician," Jake said.

Kirk looked up from his work, set down his pen, and lifted his wine glass to his lips. He sipped, rolled the wine around in his mouth, then swallowed, and set the glass back down.

"What's there to tell? He's our chief medical examiner. When bodies pile up, he's the one who deals with it without protest. He's also the go-to guy for the Blood Eagle Killer. Edwin works late nights, all the time, does an awesome job according to the lawyers he ends up working with. He excludes or implicates suspects based on fact. Lawyers love him. Why do you ask?"

"Nothing really. Just got an odd feeling about him when those cops showed up at the liquor store."

Kirk took another sip of wine, his eyes on Jake. "Did you sense something?" Kirk asked. Then in a lower voice, "Or smell something?"

Jake's eyes narrowed. Kirk had to suspect something was different about Jake, something physical, but was likely waiting until Jake brought it up. The longer Jake left Kirk out of the loop, the further he would push the boundaries of their friendship.

"Edwin physically stepped back when the cops showed up." Jake shrugged, ignoring the other comment. "It just seemed to me that he was afraid of them." He turned around and poured his steeped coffee into a cup. "Have you ever checked the guy out? Is he on the up and up?" He started back to the dining room table, coffee in hand.

"Edwin worked with Detective Joslin. If there was something fishy about Edwin, she would've rooted it out long ago. No doubt in my mind."

"And where is she now?"

Kirk leaned back in his chair. "No idea. Working homicide in Kingston or somewhere. Why?"

"That's my point. She was all about control. The cases she worked were about her. I'm not sure she put solving the case as her priority, otherwise she might have had a chance at solving this one. Evidently, she was pulled from the case and it was given to you. And look what you're doing with it. If she was as good as we all thought she was *and* lost the lead on this case, who's to say she didn't miss things about the people she worked with?"

"Wow, you're really on Edwin's case. Did he piss you off or something?"

"You're missing my point. His behavior among colleagues was unbecoming. I'm simply asking a few questions, maybe raising some. Look into it. Think about it. Or leave it alone. It's up to you. But one thing is for sure. He acted off and if I could smell him, he emitted the scent of fear when those officers pulled up."

Kirk seemed to consider things a moment longer. Then he nodded slightly.

"Point taken. How's everything going with those files? Patterns emerging? Getting anywhere? One of the biggest dilemmas we've had with this case is how he picks the families. If we could nail that down, we could begin to track him geographically and pinpoint with a certain level of accuracy a probable location for the next time and then work from there."

"I can tell you that the blood eagle shit is obfuscating. He's doing it to confuse, to be unclear with his motives. We see what he leaves behind. But what he's really doing is murdering families and raping the wife. In the end, his motive is to steal a family—the soul of a family—like what probably happened to him when he was younger. Your unsub will have bounced from foster home to foster home. He would've been a problem child who lost his parents before he was a teenager."

"How can you tell when he lost his parents?" Kirk asked, going for more wine.

"He was old enough to know them, to love and be loved by them, to have felt their loss when they were either incarcerated or killed. Family is something that he takes. It's not something you work on, nourish. If he believed in the traditional family, he wouldn't be destroying them."

Kirk seemed to think about what Jake was saying. He stared off for a moment, blinked, then turned back to Jake.

"Tell me something else, Jake."

Jake gestured with his hand to go on, then drank more coffee, swallowing it hot.

"I finally got a hold of Dr. Sutton down in Brazil. He faxed me a couple of medical files. Figured you'd be angry, but what the hell? You gonna fly back down there to punch the guy?" He paused, studying Jake's face. "I read the files. Did Sutton share everything with you?"

Jake shook his head and sipped from his mug. He didn't like where this was going.

"So you don't know what happened to yourself? What happened to your body?"

"Sutton mentioned a few things, but I didn't pay much attention."

Whether it was the sun setting or what he surmised Kirk was about to ask him, Jake felt a chill go through him as if a thick icicle had rubbed along the enamel of his teeth.

"Your body has mutated. Yet you seem to be living a normal life. Above normal, actually."

"Okay," Jake said in a cautious voice. "Why do I care?"

"Because it could affect your life span. Or the quality of your life going forward."

"Fair enough. I'm not a doctor and I haven't self-diagnosed myself. So, end of discussion?" He made the last part sound like a question.

"But those cops said you *hunted* those perps," Kirk went on as if he was talking to himself. "I saw you run through those woods like a cheetah. I saw your tooth—your adult tooth—replace itself." Kirk stared at Jake, his head tilted to the side. "A fight against four guys? In your condition? And yet you are unscathed and a few of them are hospitalized? You need the house to be thirty degrees. You eat raw meat now. And when I saw you return to the house after fighting those four guys, you came up the road, turned down the driveway and paused before you entered the house. But two things got me and I haven't been able to figure them out yet."

Jake held his mug with both hands. How had he ever thought he could hide from a seasoned detective like Kirk? He'd been fooling himself. Now, since Jake hadn't been forthcoming and honest, Kirk had decided to draw it out of him. It probably didn't hurt that Kirk needed a drink or two first, but here it came nonetheless.

"I watched you stop and sniff the air, your mouth open. Then you advanced on the house, cautiously. It was as if you could smell me and knew I was in the house. Secondly, I parked a hundred yards away, toward the highway, the opposite way you came. That meant you picked up the scent of my radiator leaking from a great distance and it wasn't windy or some shit, so don't try explaining it away." Kirk drank the last of his wine, grabbed the bottle, filled his glass, and sat back in his chair, looking accomplished. "Anything you want to say?"

Jake contemplated maintaining silence. He considered the ramifications of honesty and the loss of his friend, really the only one he had in this new world of his. If he was going to die in a month or two, or even live another year, wouldn't he want Kirk in his life? He'd lost so much and to keep Kirk meant he had to be honest.

That decided, how would Kirk respond to the news?

"Let me start from the moment of consciousness in the clinic," Jake said, looking down at his hands. "There was this nurse. She has a daughter."

Jake talked about the vibrations, the scents, knowing when people came and went. How he'd known Cindy was pregnant, how he'd detected fear on Edwin, and how he'd hunted those thieves through the woods. Yes, he'd broken the kid's arm with one hand. Yes, he'd lost a tooth and it had regrown in less than a day. He had no idea what had happened to him because of the snake bite and during the subsequent coma, but he was determined to find out.

Jake studied Kirk's pensive face. "I told you everything because you gave me your word you'd help discover who Fortech Industries is. In order to do that, you might need to know what happened to me because of their fucking green liquid shit that I ingested in Luke's tent."

Kirk had listened with rapt attention. His wine glass was empty again, but he didn't reach for the bottle. Jake figured what he had told his friend had sobered him up pretty fast.

"I'm so sorry, Jake." Kirk shook his head. "For everything."

"I'm not. Not now. I'm alive and feel one hundred percent. I just want to know what happened to me."

"We'll do it together. We'll find out and nail those bastards."

Jake nodded, his lips pursed, a sense of determination overwhelming him. He sipped from his coffee, then spit the cold liquid back in his cup. "I hate cold coffee."

"I'll make some more," Kirk said, getting up from the table. "I could use some myself." He stopped beside Jake and placed a hand on his shoulder. "We'll get through this, bro."

"I know, but I don't have much time." He faced Kirk. "Sutton said I'm dying. My left lung is not working right. My heart formed some kind of protective sac around it. I have neurotoxins in my saliva. I think my blood is even chemically altered. My eyes changed color. A lot has happened to me that the human body isn't supposed to endure."

"How much time did he give you?"

"He wasn't definite, but he said I could go any time. A month, maybe two. Could be as long as six months."

Kirk's eyes welled up. "Dude, I couldn't lose you again. Not so soon."

Jake got to his feet and stood in front of his partner, feeling closer to him now.

"Then help me find the guys in the SUV and make them reverse what their liquid did before it's too late."

Jake stuck out his hand.

Kirk ignored the proffered hand and instead pulled Jake in and hugged him tight.

"We'll do it together, man," Kirk said into his ear. "We'll do it together if it's the last thing we do on this planet. We'll find Fortech Industries and make them pay for what they did."

"We won't have to look too hard. They know where I am. They've been watching me." He pulled back and looked Kirk in the eye. "It's only a matter of time before they make their move. They aim to kill me, but I have a surprise for them. We'll see who's the better hunter, the better killer."

They hugged again.

"It's only a matter of time, brother," Jake said. "Then I'll die in peace."

CHAPTER THIRTY-SEVEN

The Canada Day party was in full swing early with Terry, Megan's soon-to-be-former husband, cooking burgers and hotdogs for the guests on the backyard BBQ.

Edwin had been nursing the same glass of wine for the last hour, pretending to drink as he chatted with several guests, being overly pleasant on purpose, but keeping a close eye on Megan's children.

One of the biggest changes to his MO was that he was going to be at the scene of the crime before it happened, where he could be recognized and named as a guest at the party. During previous Gatherings, Edwin befriended his prey, shaved his body hair, then dealt with the family, mindful of leaving no chemical trace of himself behind. And if he made a mistake, he was in a position as the chief medical examiner to clean up his own mess.

Up until now it had worked absolutely.

Tonight, he was a part of the action *before* the crime. He would be seen. The fact that the crime was going to be different and the chief medical examiner for the BEK killer was at the party where Megan Radcliffe was abducted, would never lead the authorities to suspect him. He was so sure of it that he'd staked his freedom on it. In fact, he wouldn't be at this party if he was even slightly nervous about being caught.

Bumping into Detective Aiken and coma man at the liquor

store in town earlier today had been a freak accident. When those RCMP officers pulled into the parking lot, he was sure they were backup, arriving to arrest him.

What he'd realized from that incident was that he really didn't like coma guy, Jake Wood. There was something about him, something about the way he stared at Edwin. Like he could see right through him. Like he saw Edwin's will, his belief systems, and everything else about him. Even the wonderful stuff.

Jake Wood creeped the hell out of Edwin.

Across the room, Megan excused herself from a conversation to meander through a throng of guys discussing a golf game, on her way to Edwin.

"Jeffrey, so glad you could make it." Megan raised her glass in a toast to Edwin, then sipped from it. "And your wife?" Megan made an effort to scan the crowd. "I haven't seen her."

Edwin bowed his head and looked longingly at his beverage.

"She left me a few days ago." He shrugged as if there was nothing that could've been done.

"Oh, I'm so sorry." Megan clutched at her chest. Her faux sympathy came across devoid of feeling.

"It's okay," he said. "I guess she traded up for a younger, better model. But that's why I'm here. I needed to get out. Be around people."

"Of course. I completely understand. Good for you. You have to be strong. Have you gotten enough to drink?" Megan didn't pause for an answer. "If not, there's more on the table over there." She pointed at the table where Edwin had placed the wine he'd brought. "Make yourself at home. Mingle. Get to meet people." She edged away. "I'm sure we'll see each other again later. Gonna go check on the husband. I'll talk to you soon."

Megan stepped outside onto the back patio and disappeared behind a wall of people waiting for hotdogs.

That would cost her. A wife shouldn't treat her new husband that way. She deserved a beating. The kind of destructive beating that took a week to heal. To treat *him* like that when she'd invited *him* to the party was unconscionable.

"You're supposed to treat your invited guests a little better than that, wifey," he muttered under his breath.

Edwin checked the kitchen for the children, but they weren't there. Megan's three girls had slipped out when he wasn't paying attention. In the living room, he caught sight of Tracy, the eight-year-old daughter, talking to a young woman. Tracy's sisters, Lindsay and Erica, sat to her left. The smiles on their faces, the joy in their voices, almost made him think they knew their fate. Their new father was across the room watching them and they were mingling like little adults in an attempt to impress him.

How lovely.

A man in a Molson Canadian T-shirt waddled up to Edwin, an extra beer in his hand.

"Got one for ya," the guy said.

He was either from Australia or Newfoundland. Edwin could never tell the difference.

"Thanks." Edwin set his wine glass down on a cabinet-hutch unit and took the beer.

"And you are?" the Aussie asked.

"Jeffrey Harris. You?"

"Chris Manks. Pleased to meet you."

They clinked the necks of their bottles together, then ceremoniously drank a sip.

"Manks?" Edwin said. "Isn't your brother a cop?"

"That's the one." Chris smiled, then frowned as a thought hit him. "Wait a sec. How do you know Dwayne? You're not in trouble with the law, are you?" He laughed to make the question come across as a joke.

"I'm a medical examiner. That's how I met Megan's family. I work with the police all the time."

From the corner of his eye, Edwin saw the three girls headed for the front door. Tracy giggled. Then Erica bolted outside, followed by Lindsay. Tracy followed her sisters a moment later.

Shit. I have to watch my daughters. The sun has gone down.

"Oh wow, that is so interesting. Medical examiner." Chris looked over his shoulder and turned back to Edwin, leaning in conspiratorially. "There's two empty chairs out on the front lawn. I've always wanted to talk to a *medical examiner.*" He said the last two words in that heavy Aussie accent, then grabbed Edwin's arm and pulled him toward the front. "C'mon, mate. Talk to me. I'm bored at this party. Need to get out and hear about all the dead bodies you have to deal with."

Edwin allowed himself to be pulled forward. His daughters had slipped out the front door so that was exactly where he wanted to go. He had another two hours to kill before people began to leave so talking to Chris would help pass the time.

Outside, the daughters were running around on the vast front lawn, playing some version of London Bridge is Falling Down.

Edwin angled his lawn chair to face Chris, but also to keep an eye on his daughters.

"What do you want to know about dead bodies?" Edwin asked in an eerie voice, a fake smile pasted to his lips.

"First, tell me about autopsies. What's that like, cutting into dead flesh?"

"It's a job. You get used to it over time."

"What's that like, though?"

"The room I work in smells of Pine-Sol and bleach and overripe camembert."

"Ewww." Chris leaned back in his chair, miming a reaction as if he could smell the autopsy room at that very moment.

Edwin nodded. "That's better than smelling the bodies, let me tell you."

Megan's three daughters ran in circles until Tracy fell and the other two descended to the lawn in a fit of giggles.

Chris agreed as if he had intimate knowledge of what Edwin was talking about.

"Go on," Chris pleaded, eyes widened by either the alcohol he'd drank or genuine interest. "Tell me details. Gruesome ones."

Edwin glanced once more at the girls and thought about coming back up here tomorrow to collect their bodies from the crime scene. It will be fun to open them up, see what was inside. A child autopsy was always difficult for his colleagues, but not for him.

Wally taught him well.

"When a body sits for any length of time, did you know the skin mottles where the blood has settled?"

Chris jerked his beer bottle in his mouth, drank back a large gulp, then refocused on Edwin with a nod.

In his peripheral vision, Edwin watched his daughters. Soon they would go to bed and before anyone knew what hit them, those three lovely girls would be on his autopsy table.

"The exact time of death is very difficult to determine," Edwin continued. "It's practically unknowable. But investigators need the time of death to be as accurate as possible. It can mean the difference between a conviction or an acquittal."

"Interesting. The average person doesn't think about this stuff." Chris leaned in and lowered his voice. "What's it like, you know, the bodies? Tell me about the kind of bodies you work on, the state they're in." He leaned back. "I mean, if you don't mind."

The daughters still played. To waste time like this, while watching the girls, was magical. It had to be a coincidence that Chris wanted to talk in this exact spot where Edwin could watch the girls. It was supposed to be this way. If that's what they called fate, then so be it. Because if it wasn't supposed to be this way, Edwin Gavin—AKA Jeffrey Harris—would've been arrested or killed years ago.

"I wear glasses. A Tyvek suit."

Chris nodded enthusiastically.

"I start with the head. It's the most sterile part of the body, far from areas that are streaming with bugs and filled with gases. Autopsy technicians determine the interval between a person's last breath and the discovery of the body by three ways. Temperature, what we call *algor mortis*. Stiffness, known as *rigor mortis*. And the settling of the blood, *livor mortis*."

"Who knows all this stuff?" Chris said. "Fascinating. Must've taken a lot of school."

The girls ran to the other side of the lawn. Edwin kept a sharp eye on them but didn't want to stop talking to Chris Manks. It felt good to be appreciated for all the work he did, all his education. Without that he wouldn't be the man he was, the man he'd always wanted to be.

"Did you know that bacteria infiltrate the liver within twenty hours of death and spread to the heart, among other organs, in less than fifty-eight hours?"

Chris was shaking his head, his eyes losing focus.

"Because we know this, microbes function as timekeepers to establish time of death. We all have two biological clocks. Death only stops one of them."

Chris's eyes swam in their sockets. How he hadn't detected how drunk Mr. Manks was earlier, he didn't know.

"Are you okay, Chris?"

The man across from him nodded, his balance wavering. However drunk Chris might be, discussing dead body dissection probably wasn't helping.

"Come on," Edwin said. "You need to go inside for another drink. But water this time. And lots of it."

He helped Chris to his feet. Once inside the front door, he aimed Chris toward the kitchen and went back out front. He needed to keep an eye on his kids. They meant everything to him.

His father had taken women for his selfish needs. Not Edwin, though. Edwin took whole families. And it wasn't about satiating a personal need. This was love in its finest hour.

On the front lawn again, he searched the grounds, but the young girls were gone. All three daughters had vanished. His fatherly duties were lacking and would need a refresher. How could he let them get away like that?

He tossed his half-empty beer bottle into the bushes by the front door and strode toward the driveway and the recessed garage to his right. A man and a woman passed him on the walkway. They said something to him, but he ignored their bullshit. He had kids missing. Kids who needed their father.

At the corner, he stopped so abruptly that he had to take another step for balance.

Tracy, Lindsay, and Erica were getting into a van out on the road and Megan was there, letting them leave.

She can't do that!

"Megan," he called and started after her. "Wait."

Megan turned to him as the van's side door slid shut.

"Don't let them leave," Edwin pleaded.

From twenty yards away, he saw her frown.

The van pulled away, all three girls in the window, waving at their mother. Megan turned to the van and waved back, slipping something into her pocket.

Edwin reached her when the van was already too far to get back. He would make Megan call the driver, return his kids. This had gone too far. They were his family. The Gathering was supposed to happen tonight. How could she let this get so unraveled?

"What have you done?" he asked, his tone harder than he intended.

"Excuse me," Megan took a step back. Even in the streetlight's dim glow, Megan's face had reddened. She looked outraged. "What are you talking about?" She lowered her head, her gaze steady. "Jeffrey, how much have you had to drink?"

The rage at what she had done settled to his core. She had potentially just thwarted the entire Gathering. If not for her, he would have his daughters and autopsy them too, but not now. He was too angry to get them back.

"Call the driver," he ordered, his jaw clenched. "Bring my girls back to me. Right. Now."

Megan stepped back, her hands coming up. "I think you need to leave, Jeffrey." She snuck a glance at the house.

"Bring them back!" he shouted.

Coming undone had never been something one should enjoy, but with anger came power and right now with Megan easing away from him, afraid, he lost all his cool.

He stepped up to her and threw a punch. Megan's head snapped sideways with the blow. She emitted a small cry of pain, but it was silenced with the next punch.

Megan fell to the pavement before she had a chance to know what hit her. A sickening crack denoted the skull taking a bad bump on the ground. Megan's eyes fluttered, then stopped moving.

Two people were still on the lawn, talking, drinking.

He had planned to wait until the party had died down, but he couldn't do that now. Megan had fucked everything up. The daughters were gone to who knew where and his new wife was unconscious. He couldn't let her wake up. Not until she was in the safe room in his basement. Then he'd wake her with a beating of Biblical proportions—Old Testament shit—and bring her to an inch of her life.

She would learn to serve her husband.

He wrenched her up off the ground, leaned in to her stomach, then hefted her weight onto his shoulder. The road was somewhat sheltered from the house by a row of trees and cars, with the streetlights spaced out enough that as long as no one drove by in the next minute, he'd make it to his car unseen.

If anyone did see them, Megan had simply drunk too much.

The two people on the front lawn laughed about something and entered the house.

Perfect timing.

The front of the house had been deserted. He trudged up the road, Megan's weight an easy chore. Three cars away, two cars.

When Edwin was one vehicle away from his car, Terry, Megan's old husband, stepped out on the front porch, scanning the yard and the driveway.

"Megan?" Terry called. "You coming back in, baby? We're starting a fucked up Canadian version of charades before the fireworks at midnight." He waited a moment, then stepped off the porch and walked toward the garage. "Megan? Come on."

Edwin popped the trunk with his key fob and dropped Megan inside. She stirred, moaning something before Edwin closed the lid.

He slipped behind the wheel and started the car.

There was no way he could stay now. The police would arrive. Cars might even be checked.

That meant no daughters. That meant no blood eagle. Terry would live.

Edwin glanced at the bag of tools in the passenger seat footwell and felt another surge of rage. In that brief moment, he wanted to kill her, decapitate her, pop her eyes out and piss in her skull. But he wouldn't.

Megan was his new play toy and with his knowledge and experience with the human body, he would be able to keep her alive for as long as he wanted while he slowly drove her mad as penance for what she did tonight.

He turned on the car and eased out onto the road, headlights off.

A thump came from the back.

Megan was awake.

He needed to get clear of this area. Stop somewhere. Knock her back out. If she alerted anyone he would have to kill them, too, and this situation would quickly devolve.

Maybe he shouldn't have switched course. His MO should have stayed the same. He was the Blood Eagle Killer, after all. Why hadn't he stuck to that method?

As he idled past the driveway, the lights off, he glanced to the right.

Terry Radcliffe was walking up the driveway, concern written all over his face.

Their eyes met briefly with the little light afforded them.

Then Edwin was gone, easing past the driveway.

Terry shouted something.

A thunk banged the back of the rear seats in the car.

Edwin hit the gas.

CHAPTER THIRTY-EIGHT

Ten kilometers from Megan's house, Edwin found a darkened side road. He turned up it and parked on the shoulder far enough away from the highway to remain unseen. Feeling the tang of panic in his chest, he exited the car so fast he stumbled and caught himself before falling flat on his face.

He got two steps toward the trunk before he stopped and listened. Someone was talking. Were they in the trees or down the road? Could there be a house nearby?

The voice came again.

It was Megan. She was talking to someone.

Blood pressure pounded his inner ear as he fumbled with the keys to the trunk. When he got it open, the trunk's interior light gave her away. She hadn't been able to hide her cell phone fast enough and simply gave up.

"Jeffrey," Megan said his name in a non-threatening, soft tone. "Please. What are you doing? Where are we going? Jeffrey Harris, I'd like to know what we're doing here. Where are we?"

Using his name. Asking for the location. All while the person on the other end of her cell phone listened in.

How could his new wife betray him so horribly? He should have stuck to the original routine. There would be no cell phone, no Terry Radcliffe looking for Megan and no way Terry would've seen Edwin driving away from their property.

235

He stuck his hand out for the cell phone, controlling his breath, controlling his anger.

Megan glanced at his hand, then back to his face, the dim light inside the trunk giving her a blanched look. After a moment, she shook her head.

He made a fist, pulled it back, and dropped it like a hammer's business end across Megan's cheek. Her head bounced off the tire iron nestled in the corner of the trunk, then settled, her eyes fluttering again. Blood seeped from where the jab had split her cheek. She moaned and reached for her face in a daze, rubbing the back of her head with her other hand. Maybe the tire iron had smacked the spot where she'd hit her head on the pavement.

Edwin retrieved the cell phone and raised it to his ear. At first, there was only breathing.

Then, "Megan," the teary-sounding voice of the former husband whispered in Edwin's ear. "What's he doing now? Are there any indications of where you might be? Megan, help me," he pleaded. "I need to find you."

Edwin cleared his throat. "You will never find her," he growled. "She's mine and she's dead to you."

"You son of a bitch," Terry screamed. "I'll kill you if you lay a hand on her."

"Here. Listen."

Edwin lowered the phone. Megan had regained some of her composure. She looked up at him.

"Megan, your former husband wants to hear from you."

Then he punched her in the cheek and jaw repeatedly, earning grunts and groans of pain until she passed out. His hand bloody now, the cell phone emitting shrieks of anger, Edwin brought the phone to his mouth and whispered, "She's dead to you."

He switched off the phone, silencing the wail. He shoved Megan's bloodied head aside and withdrew the tire iron. He set the phone on the road by his feet and with one swift stroke, smashed it into pieces. He hit it again to make sure, then kicked the pieces off the road and into the foliage by the shoulder.

"That doesn't bode well for you, eh mate?"

Edwin pivoted so fast, he had to grab for the trunk to keep his balance. Without processing where the voice came from, he slammed the trunk closed and scanned the darkness behind the car.

"Easy does it," the Australian voice said.

Chris Manks from the party? Could he have followed him here? No way, Chris had been too drunk.

"Who's there?" Edwin asked.

Car wheels, crunching gravel, eased closer near the front of the car. When Edwin turned, the silhouette of a large SUV stopped at his bumper. He ducked as if his car would offer him shelter from whoever was coming for him.

More gravel crunched behind him. Another SUV crept closer from the highway side. It stopped two feet from him, the thick bumper level with his thighs. Neither SUV had used their headlights and no one got out.

"Who's there?" he called.

"Stranded on the side of the road. Looks like you need help."

"I'm fine."

"Car trouble?" the voice called.

"Felt sick. Thought I'd throw up. Fine now."

Edwin edged along the side of his car. He needed to get back inside, drive away and figure out how to deal with Terry Radcliffe. Terry had seen Edwin leave. Megan would've told him that Jeffrey Harris had kidnapped her. The same Jeffrey Harris who was a medical examiner in Toronto and had worked on her mother's death.

Terry knew enough to have Edwin picked up and arrested by the morning. Which meant he didn't have time to deal with whoever was blocking him in.

With an arm resting on the roof and the other on the open door frame, he stared at the silhouette in front of him.

"Hey," he called out. "You wanna move your vehicle so I can get by."

"We want to help you, Edwin."

He turned at the voice directly behind him. They knew his name? How could they know his name?

"Sounds like you know me, but I still don't know who I'm talking to. It's too dark out here to see faces." His anger rose along with his frustration.

The SUV's headlights turned on, blinding him at first. Three men in dark suits, two in overcoats, stood in a triangle formation by the SUV. In the black, inky darkness, he hadn't seen any of them exit their vehicle.

Chris Manks sat behind the wheel, his white teeth shining as he smiled at Edwin, a cell phone pasted to his ear.

"So what's this?" Edwin asked. "You're going to arrest me?"

The man not wearing the overcoat stepped closer.

"No, Edwin, we're not here to arrest you. We're here to help you."

"Help me? How?"

"Terry Radcliffe."

"Terry?" He had to be dreaming. What could this guy be talking about?

"Chris is on the phone with him right now. Directing him to this location."

The pit in Edwin's stomach grew to a lead ball, then dropped to his bowels.

"And how will that help me?" he asked.

"We know you, Edwin. We're okay with it. We have other fish to fry, as they say."

238

If anyone *knew* Edwin, they wouldn't be having this conversation with him, let alone helping him achieve his goals.

"I don't believe you."

"We didn't think so. That's why a demonstration is in order."

"A what?"

A car screeched to a halt on the highway. Then it made the turn and started up the side road toward them.

"Here comes Mr. Radcliffe now," the man said in a maddeningly casual voice, his timbre even, monotone.

The urge to drop into his car and squeal away overwhelmed Edwin, but he couldn't. These men were a mystery and without knowing their intentions, he was stuck.

The truth was, he desperately needed to deal with Terry Radcliffe as soon as possible. To have him lured here allowed Edwin that chance.

But why? Who were they and why help him kidnap Megan? Nothing added up.

Terry's car raced up to them and skidded to a halt beside the SUV. Before the car had fully stopped, the driver's side door swung open, spilling Terry out too fast. He dropped to one knee, pushed up off the ground and lunged toward Edwin.

Before he made it to Edwin, two men, one on either side of Terry, ceased his forward motion by wrapping arms up and around his shoulders. They lifted him up, Terry's legs pin wheeling several times before they set him down. He grunted and struggled to get by them, reminding Edwin of the game called British Bull Dog that he'd played as a youngster back in grade school.

The man without the overcoat moved closer to Edwin.

"We're not that dissimilar."

"How so?" Edwin asked.

"You take specimens. Isn't that what she is?" The man pointed at Edwin's closed trunk lid. "A specimen? For your lab?"

Edwin shot a glance at Terry who was strangely quiet. One of the men had jammed what looked like a tennis ball in Terry's mouth. A quick look at the man beside him, then the trunk, and Edwin nodded.

"Yes. A specimen."

The man stuck his hand out.

How odd? Why so formal? Edwin took the proffered hand and shook it.

"Call me Adam," the man said. "Always address me as Adam." Suddenly, his other hand came out of his pocket holding a cell phone. "Use this. Call me only on this. One number is programmed. When you have what we want arranged, call me. You'll have twenty-four hours to achieve our goal. Do we have a deal?"

Edwin had zero idea what he was agreeing to. Adam had told him nothing.

Edwin released Adam's hand and took the cell phone.

"I'll call," Edwin said, his voice cracking. He cleared his throat and tried again. "But you're going to have to tell me what the hell we're doing here. I have no idea what you're talking about."

Adam stepped away to stand directly between Edwin and Terry. The headlights of Terry's car cast a strange light on Adam's face. He appeared more sinister than a moment before.

"We aren't very different than you, Mr. Gavin. You collect specimens and do experiments. Your experiments are more depraved than ours, but we won't split hairs. We don't judge." He turned his full attention to Edwin. "I collect things and use them in experiments. If certain souls knew what I do, those people would call me Lucifer, or God, depending on who I'm talking to. Having said that, I am willing to offer you a trade."

"What trade?" Edwin asked.

Terry grunted from somewhere deep in his throat. A large

truck drove by down on the highway, breaking some of the surrounding silence the night offered. "What could you possibly have that I would want?"

"Your freedom."

Edwin thought about that a moment. He looked up at Chris Manks, who was staring back.

"Option number one. We release Terry Radcliffe here and help him break your legs. Chris Manks then calls his brother and explains that Megan Radcliffe was kidnapped and that the perpetrator was captured by Megan's husband, Terry here."

Terry grunted deep, struggled with redoubled strength. Edwin felt sick. Was there a way out, an escape route? Could he make the bushes by the car and hide out in the woods overnight? But to what end? Where would he go? Home was out of the question. Using bank cards would lead the authorities to wherever he was.

Edwin wasn't the kind of man that could live a life on the run. He knew nothing about that. All he'd ever wanted was to follow in his father's footsteps and be a better man about it. To have families. To perform Gatherings. He didn't want this trouble. There was no way he could've foreseen Adam and his crew of seven to eight men in professional attire. This was like some science-fiction novel or a movie, like Neo and Morpheus in *The Matrix*, about to make a deal with the Agents, well dressed, besuited men with deadpan voices and lackluster expressions.

"Option number two. You take Megan with you—" Adam stopped talking as Terry growled and lunged hard to the right, causing one of the men to momentarily lose balance. The man on the left yanked something from his jacket pocket and aimed it at Terry just as he broke free.

A clicking, like an electrical unit shorting out, filled the quiet evening and Terry danced where he stood. The Taser did its job with unfailing accuracy and without mercy, bringing Terry first to his knees, then the ground, where he vibrated a moment longer. The electrical snapping stopped and Terry stilled.

Adam faced Edwin again. "As I was saying. Megan is yours. We will deal with Terry. No one saw a thing and we never have to see each other again. You're free to go. But I need Jake Wood and you are the one person who can bring him to me."

"The coma man?" Edwin asked, confused.

What would Adam want with Jake Wood?

"The one. You work on the BEK killer case. Your contact with that case is the lead detective, Kirk Aiken, Jake's old partner. Arrange within twenty-four hours to have Kirk and Jake come to your office. Call me once that meeting is set. My men will apprehend Jake Wood and your obligation to me is over." Adam moved back toward Edwin as Terry tried to get up. "What will it be? Option one, where you're arrested and hospitalized? Or option two where you keep Megan?"

Edwin didn't have to think about it. This was a no-brainer.

"What about trust?" Edwin asked. "I deliver Jake, then what? How do I know this won't come back to bite me?"

For a brief moment, it almost looked like Adam cracked a smile, but then it was gone.

"Tell me if we have a deal or not."

Edwin frowned. This guy seemed odd. How would he secure anything?

"Number two," Edwin said. "I take Megan. I will arrange a meeting. You get Jake Wood. Now, secure it for me."

Adam pivoted to face Terry. A wounded man, exhausted with the struggle, urged on by loyalty, love, fighting against odds he couldn't win, surrounded by men stronger than him and armed with Tasers. Terry raised his head. Adam pulled something out of the inside of his pocket. The SUV's headlights shone on the gun's shiny surface, looking to Edwin like the weapon had just been polished.

They were going to deal with his Terry problem for him. Right there and then. He could take Megan and move on. It was a deal after all. A pact. An arrangement. And Adam was prepared to seal the deal on the spot.

The gun roared in Adam's hand, recoiling twice. Terry's head jerked back as two neat holes formed in his forehead. Slowly, like he was in a yoga pose on his knees, he leaned back, farther, farther, until he was at an impossible angle, then fell to the cement. A small amount of blood was visible in the car's headlights as he died.

Edwin felt nothing. If he had done it like he'd done it countless times, he would've been the one taking Terry's life. The man's back would have been ripped open, his lungs fluttering outside the ribcage. Terry should thank whatever God he believed in when they met up shortly.

Two bullets were better than a bird in the cage.

Adam handed the gun to one of his men. Several of them moved out of the light coming from Terry's car and hopped back inside the SUV. Their impromptu meeting was coming to a close.

"Edwin, I've secured our end of the deal. Terry Radcliffe has been dispatched. He will be found dead by his car right where it stands. His wife will have disappeared. No one will be the wiser. I will get Jake Wood and Kirk Aiken tomorrow from your lab as agreed. Use that phone. Call me. Give me the time. Is there anything left unsaid? Do you understand your role?"

Edwin nodded.

"I need to hear your compliance."

"Agreed. I will call. Tomorrow. And you can have Jake. Kirk too."

Adam backed away. Before entering the idling SUV, he stopped and looked back.

"Don't break our arrangement. If you know the story of Adam

and Eve, I'm the serpent in the grass. I will rise and strike without warning and the tree of knowledge you eat from will cause great pain and enormous suffering for eternity if you betray my confidence."

Adam disappeared inside the vehicle and slammed the door.

Simultaneously, both SUVs backed away and disappeared on the highway within a minute.

Edwin glanced down at Terry's body. It was Jake Wood he was thinking about. How creepy that man was. How he had watched him. And how these men were going to deal with him.

He pitied Jake. Whatever Jake had done to piss these guys off would cost him dearly.

Edwin felt the weight of the phone in his hand. He looked at it. One meeting, one call. That was all it took to finish this chapter in his life. Then he would never deviate from the plan again. He would return in a year or so as the Blood Eagle Killer and offer a Gathering to another deserving family. One that didn't throw parties and one that was less visible. They were all over the country, just waiting for his arrival.

Eager with anticipation, he needed to drive home and secure Megan in his safe room. There was still so much to do.

In the morning he would call Detective Aiken and set up a meeting.

It would all work out. The people who were supposed to die would die. The woman in his trunk would serve her purpose. Life just went back to normal in one quick moment.

He was on the right path in life. If there was a God, this intervention would have been the end for Edwin. But as before, he didn't believe in such silliness. He couldn't imagine following a man who was born from a virgin. A man whose blood and body are eaten as wine, or juice, with crackers in large churches where donations pay to employ child-molesting priests. Accept him in your heart as Lord because a woman, borne from a man's rib bone, was conned into eating fruit from a forbidden tree, deceived by a talking snake who was possessed by an egotistical angel. And this was the largest religion driving humanity.

And they thought Edwin was crazy.

Edwin Gavin was a rapist-murderer and humans were his prey and nothing would ever stop him because he was supposed to be here. He was supposed to be as good as he was.

He was the living proof that there was no God.

And soon Megan Radcliffe would know why God hadn't saved her or Terry.

Elated beyond his wildest dreams, he dropped behind the wheel of his car, performed a U-turn, and headed for the highway. It was time for a beating. It was time to hurt Megan for the trouble she had caused.

And when he woke her from her stupor in a week, he would thank her.

Edwin smiled as he drove, a Duchenne smile, maintaining the speed limit all the way to Toronto with his prize in the trunk.

CHAPTER THIRTY-NINE

Jake woke to the sound of Kirk blabbering on his cell phone in the living room. He got up and sat on the edge of the bed to rub his face.

Kirk's voice grew more agitated. Jake stared at the closed bedroom door for a moment, then got up and got dressed. Whatever was bothering his old partner could be worked out with coffee.

Once in the kitchen, Jake put on a pot of hot water and waited patiently until Kirk hung up. During the call, he had overheard snippets. Something about a crime scene and how it had nothing to do with Kirk but they wanted him to attend anyway.

Kirk entered the kitchen and nodded at the water about to boil.

"Good," he said. "Need that." He plopped down at the kitchen table.

Jake pulled two large mugs out of the cupboard.

"What was that all about?"

"Kidnapping a few kilometers from here."

Jake turned to him. "Kidnapping? Since when do they call Homicide for a kidnapping?"

Kirk drummed his fingers on the table. "Murder too. Husband shot twice in the forehead. Car left on the side of the road." He continued drumming his fingers. "Wife missing."

Jake poured the hot water into the French press, let it steep then poured the coffee into two mugs. He set a mug in front of Kirk, leaving it black as they both liked it.

"What do they want with you?" Jake asked.

Kirk stopped drumming his fingers and picked up his cup.

"Formal request to attend the scene."

"Since you're out of Toronto Division, how did they know you were even local?"

"Probably because we bumped into that Officer Manks yesterday by the liquor store."

"Right. That would be it."

They drank in silence until Kirk fixed his eyes on Jake and studied his face.

"Come with me," Kirk said. "Let's go together. Like old times. What do you say?"

Jake shook his head. "Not me. Have you seen the case files I have to read out there in the living room?"

Kirk slapped the table and stood. "Forget about that." He moved closer to Jake. "Come with me. Walk through the couple's house. Examine everything with me. Make mental notes like you used to. Bounce ideas off me. Then come out to the murder scene. Walk me through a scenario just like the old days." He raised a finger as if dramatically making a point. "If it's the last case we walk together, at least make it more memorable than the Maytag death."

Jake chuckled, but he cut it short. Kirk had a point. He'd missed being in the field. To walk a crime scene, to feel the area out. He could *smell* it, hone his new skills. Who knew what would come of it?

He set his coffee cup on the counter beside the sink.

"I'll shower and dress. I'll go. But you're buying lunch. And I want a fucking prime rib."

"Shit man, you can have the cow. Just come with me and

deduce as only Jake Wood can."

Jake walked by him, headed for the bathroom.

"My old pal Jake, attacked by a snake, comes out of recluse, to attempt to deduce, the murder and the crime, that happened in the time, that it took to blink, but can he think, of what would make, someone so vile, to take …"

Jake yanked the knob on the shower and the water's stream drowned out Kirk's prattling. The rhyming shit wasn't something Jake had missed.

When they got in the car fifteen minutes later, Jake punched Kirk in the arm.

Just to let him know that with every rhyme going forward, a shot in the arm would accompany it.

CHAPTER FORTY

When Edwin arrived home, the car securely backed into his garage and the door down, he opened the trunk.

Megan was still unconscious but breathing steadily. Blood covered most of her face and where it didn't, she was ash-pale. The skin on her cheeks had split and her entire lower lip was double its original size. Blood had pooled under her head, his trunk a crime-scene tech's dream. A thick scab was already forming over her cheek. She was a mess with blood matted in her hair as well. It would take weeks for her pretty face to become something less grotesque.

He held the trunk open momentarily, staring down at his new wife. She was his, fair and square. Only Terry had seen him, but Terry was dead. There had been a moment when he'd thought his entire world was crashing in around him, but then it was over.

He would rest. Wake at noon. Then he'd come up with a believable reason to need to see Jake and Kirk, and call Detective Aiken to arrange it.

He grabbed Megan's arms and lifted her out of the trunk. Being too heavy to carry in his exhausted state, he pulled her far enough over the lip of the trunk and let her go. Megan dropped like she was dead onto the garage floor.

A grunt escaped her lips at impact. She rolled onto her back, her eyes trying to open.

Edwin slammed the trunk closed, wrapped a hand around Megan's wrists and dragged her hundred and twenty pounds toward the door that led inside.

She moaned and kicked in a dazed state. Once inside, he only had to go five feet until he reached the basement door. She was almost fully cognizant by then, so he opened the door and shoved her down the stairs.

He prayed she wouldn't break her neck in the tumble. He wouldn't want her to die so soon. Not after all that he had gone through to get her.

At the bottom of the stairs, he realized he had gotten his wish. She wasn't paralyzed, but her right hand was scrunched up under her.

He rolled her over and saw the damage. In the fall, her baby finger had twisted back like a broken pretzel, snapped at the second knuckle. On that same hand, her wrist hung at an odd angle. She wouldn't be using that hand for a few months.

Before the rush of pain, before the realization of what was happening settled over her, Edwin snatched up her feet, wrapped his meaty hands on her ankles and dragged her toward the bookcase. Once the door to the safe room was open, he pulled her inside.

She moaned softly, then moaned steadily louder. But what did he care? The safe room was entirely soundproof. She wouldn't hear him and he wouldn't hear her. No one would ever hear Megan again except Edwin when he came for his visits to either beat her or fuck her.

Two backward steps and he was clear of the safe room door. Tonight—or rather this morning—she would be spared a beating. She would also be spared a rough session of violent sex. He was simply too tired. He needed sleep and he needed to fulfill his end of the deal made on the side road, south of Huntsville.

Once Jake Wood was dealt with, Megan was officially his, free and clear. Then he would begin his treatment, his special husbandly duties.

"We're going to have a splendid time together, my love."

Megan screamed, her broken hand held above her head as she lay sprawled out on the safe room floor.

"You're in pain now, but it'll subside."

She screamed louder.

He smiled, knowing his smile lacked enthusiasm due to fatigue. "You're a lucky girl, Megan Radcliffe. I'm sure you will have at least one orgasm a day for the next year—wait, I should say, one orgasm a day for the rest of your life."

He barked a short laugh at his own joke, then suppressed a yawn, a hand over his mouth.

Megan twisted to her side, examining the room. She turned and started to crawl for the door.

"No, no, my sweet little toy. There's no escaping here. You're mine until you leave this planet." He started to close the door. "You're all mine, wifey."

When the door clicked and the lock snapped in place, it held the sound of finality. It gave him a sense of closure. This deed was done, it was over. He was safe once again. The police wouldn't come and cart him off like they had to his father. Edwin was a thinking man's man. Even if he made a mistake, it mattered little because he was free and clear.

Of course that still involved one telephone call. One meeting.

But that was the easy part. The hard part was done.

He climbed the stairs to his bedroom, the house as silent as a crypt. Megan was probably screaming and pounding on the door to be let out, but he couldn't hear a thing.

The joy overwhelmed him in that moment and he shivered.

"I love being me," he whispered. "There's nothing better than being me."

His sleep was fitful, with dreams of men in Armani suits tearing him apart.

Edwin woke in a cold sweat, wondering what had gone wrong, waiting to be rended asunder.

CHAPTER FORTY-ONE

Kirk pulled up to the Radcliffe's house and jumped out of the car the second it stopped moving. Despite the fact Jake had a jacket on, he kept the heat up, the vents aimed at him. To Kirk's credit, he hadn't complained for the fifteen minutes it took to get there.

Once Kirk had walked away from the car, Jake sat by himself for a moment, watching the flurry of people coming and going, listening to the tic of the engine as it cooled.

The murder hadn't taken place at the Radcliffe house, so only a few officers combed the grounds. People from last night's party were being interviewed as detectives attempted to put the pieces together. The process, the investigation, the paperwork, something Jake was all too familiar with.

Kirk talked to a uniformed officer at the front door. After a moment, he turned and gestured for Jake to come.

Jake waited another heartbeat until the sun broke through a smattering of clouds, then opened the door and stepped out, enjoying its rays.

He would do this exercise with his old partner because Kirk would help him with his problem. Kirk had resources that Jake didn't have. He would do this because it was the right thing to do. But he would do this because a part of him couldn't deny how good it felt to be back in play, to be walking a crime scene, to be doing *something*.

At the front door, Kirk pulled Jake inside the house and gestured toward an empty alcove.

"Apparently," Kirk started, wrapping an arm around Jake's shoulders, "no one saw either Megan or Terry Radcliffe leave the house. The kids were the last ones to see their mother when they were picked up to go to their grandparents' house. They're pulling Megan's and Terry's cell phone records as we speak."

"Then why are we here?" Jake asked. "There's nothing to go on right now. Let these guys handle the details of interviewing witnesses, tracking records, fingerprinting, making lists of the party guests and so on. Is someone specifically asking you to work this case?" He shook off Kirk's arm. "Why are we here?"

Kirk shrugged. "Don't really know. Let's just look around, offer a thought or two, then go to the murder scene, evaluate and leave."

"And food. I want meat. I'm hungry. You promised lunch." Jake felt like a whiny child.

Kirk slapped Jake's arm as he stepped away.

"You'll get your meat," he said.

Jake headed down the hallway toward the bedrooms. He entered the master bedroom, did a quick scan of the furniture, looked out the window at the yard, then moved into the kids' rooms. Minutes later in the kitchen, he took in the smells, the aura of the home. Multiple people had visited last night and now at least a dozen more people had roamed the premises.

But through all that, he detected one familiar smell.

He opened the back door and moved outside. On the back patio, most of the scents wafted away with the breeze. Back inside, he meandered through the uniformed and plainclothes cops, diverting his eyes from their strange or awkward glances, and exited the house at the front door. He gravitated to a bench on the side of the front lawn and sat to wait for Kirk.

There was nothing here for him except that one familiar scent. One scent he couldn't place. This ability was too new for him to be able to really own it yet. He was confident that in time he would be better equipped to manage the scents he took in, logging them in a part of his reptilian brain for later retrieval.

"Let's hit it," Kirk shouted to him as he stepped out of the house.

Inside the car, Kirk started away from the Radcliffe's house without Jake identifying the scent. He had no clue as to who he could've come into contact with that would've been here at the party.

Unless it was one of the four punks who had broken into his house. But he dismissed that thought as soon as it popped up. He knew their smells. It wasn't them.

Maybe he'd bumped into Megan or her husband at the grocery store in Novar. Maybe she worked there for all he knew. During lunch, he'd tell Kirk to see what he thought.

If the scent was important, then maybe, just maybe, Jake would be key in helping to solve this case.

For now, he would log that smell and wait until it came up again. Kirk would be not only the first person he would tell—he would be the *only* person he would tell.

There was no way anyone would understand that Jake could smell people with his tongue as good as, or better, than any dog.

CHAPTER FORTY-TWO

Kirk parked on the shoulder of the road six cars back from the crime scene. White walls had been erected around Terry Radcliffe's body in a makeshift lab that billowed in the light wind. Crime scene techs were already scouring Terry's car while gloved officers examined the nearby terrain for any further evidence.

"You coming out?" Kirk asked. "Or should I leave the car on, the heater blasting."

Jake studied the investigators milling about inside the cordoned-off area.

"I smelled something at the house."

Kirk turned in his seat to look at Jake.

"Like what?"

"Someone."

"Someone? Really? A lot of people smell, Jake."

"No, I smelled someone I know. Someone I've smelled before."

Kirk watched Jake with inquisitive eyes.

"Like with your new abilities?" he asked softly.

Jake nodded. "The person I detected wasn't in the Radcliffe house when we were there. That person was there last night."

"Who?"

Jake shrugged and turned to meet his partner's eyes. "I don't know. But it's someone I've been around since coming out of the coma. What's confusing me is I don't have a process to log scents, or to memorize who smells like what. I can just smell something and remember that scent."

"Not good enough for the courts, but good enough for me." Kirk tapped the steering wheel for a moment while he stared out the windshield. "Any chance it's random and means nothing?"

"Absolutely."

"Any chance it's our killer and you're onto something?"

"Absolutely."

"Then get out of my car and go smell this crime scene. If you detect the same smell, you're onto something. If not, then it probably doesn't matter."

Jake gestured at the men outside. "The wind is ruffling their hair, the walls of the tarp. With this much wind, the smell will be gone."

"And if it isn't?" Kirk asked. "You won't know until you try." Kirk opened his door and stopped to look back. "You coming?"

Jake followed Kirk to the officer with the murder log. Time to sign in and speak with the officer in charge.

Once they got the all-clear to examine the scene and the body, Kirk moved to look at Terry. Jake wandered over to Terry's car. He moved around the car, his mouth open, taking in the air, the scents.

Lavender air freshener. Terry's cologne, Megan's perfume. The smell of children came from the backseat. Someone had recently spilled chocolate milk on the floor in the back.

He pulled his head out of the backseat and moved to smell the trunk. Oil scents wafted up, along with the rubber of the spare tire. Gasoline was evident and a light mildewy smell.

There was nothing similar to the smell he detected in the Radcliffe house.

When he straightened up, a man in a Tommy Hilfiger suit

was staring at him from the opposite side of the car.

Jake closed his mouth.

"You okay, buddy?" the man asked.

Jake nodded.

"You the guy with Kirk?"

He nodded again.

They looked at each for a few more seconds, then Hilfiger turned away. It was obvious he'd been watching Jake's process, sniffing the car, mouth wide, tongue sticking out to get all the scents.

It was weird to have someone watching him, but embarrassment didn't come into it. If he caught the murderer because he smelled him out of hiding, it didn't matter how many people watched him sniff with his tongue.

He stepped away from the car and moved closer to the shoulder. Something crackled under his shoe. He looked down to see a small black piece of plastic. He bent to pick it up, knowing he shouldn't be touching it without a glove on.

The small plastic chunk denoted no weather damage. It hadn't been lying in the road long. He brought it to his nose and smelled deep, his mouth slightly open so it didn't look weird to casual observers.

Metallic smell, like it was from something electronic. The hint of human oil on it, but he couldn't tell if it was male or female. He needed more.

Kirk called his name from the other side of Terry's car. They were done here already. It was time to go.

Jake dropped to the ground. Tiny bits of black plastic converged in one area, so small they were barely detectable. He slowly moved his eyes toward the shoulder of the road and noticed another piece of plastic in the small stones that made up the shoulder.

"Jake?" Kirk said behind him. "We're done here. They've got it under control."

Jake stayed on his haunches, examining the ground. He edged closer to the shoulder, closer to slightly larger pieces of plastic.

"Jake? Let's go." Kirk stepped around him. "Unless you're onto something?"

Without preamble, Jake picked up the largest piece of black plastic in the small stones and examined it. Then he brought it to his mouth.

"Jake? What is it?"

"Cell phone pieces. Someone smashed one of the Radcliffe's cell phones into the cement over there," he pointed, "and kicked the rest of the pieces into these shrubs over here. This piece"—he held up the tiny black plastic chunk for Kirk to see— "is from a Nokia or a Blackberry."

Kirk took the piece and held it up. He examined the ground where Jake had pointed, then straightened.

"Hey, Brian," he called to the Hilfiger-suited man. "Got one of their cell phones here."

Hilfiger—Brian—came over and Kirk handed him the piece of black plastic.

"You'll find what's left of the phone in the bush there. Jake showed me that the phone was broken here"—Kirk pointed— "and shoved over this way."

"Wow," Brian said, shaking his head. "I don't know how my guys missed that."

"Very small pieces," Jake whispered as he rose to his feet.

He waited a moment, nodded at Brian, then headed for Kirk's car. Less than a minute later, Kirk joined him in the car.

"You okay, Jake?" Kirk asked.

Jake stared out the side window, watching the breeze spin the leaves on the trees into a frenzy.

"Jake?"

"Yeah, just thinking."

"About what?"

"I know who that smell belongs to now."

Kirk shifted in his seat. "You do?"

Jake turned to his partner. "Yeah, but it doesn't make sense."

"Why not? I'm not following you."

"It's that guy we bumped into yesterday at the liquor store. The medical examiner. He's all over this crime scene and the Radcliffe house."

Kirk frowned. "That's impossible." He scrunched up his brow. "Really?" Kirk stared at nothing through the windshield. "Sure, we saw him in town, and he could've been at the party, but—"

Kirk's cell phone rang. He brought it to his ear.

"Detective Aiken here." He waited a moment, cast a glance at Jake, then said, "Okay. When?" Another moment, then, "Got it. On our way." He hung up.

"That was the strangest call ever," Kirk said.

"How so?" Jake asked.

"That was Edwin Gavin, the medical examiner you were just talking about. He's in Toronto, at his office. He's apparently discovered something and claims I have to see it immediately. I'm supposed to be at his office by six this evening. But what's really strange is that I'm supposed to bring you, too. Why you?"

Jake eyed his old partner, taking in his words.

"He was here yesterday," Jake said. "I guarantee it. He is a part of this investigation somehow and he wants you to come to Toronto to absolve himself or admit his guilt. Either way, going to meet him is the right thing to do as it forwards this case. The way I see it, you have no choice and I wouldn't miss it for the world."

"What about lunch?"

"We can eat in the car."

Kirk started the car and pulled away. Once they were on Highway 11 heading south toward Toronto, Kirk turned to Jake.

"Could he have done something he shouldn't have?" Kirk asked. "Could Edwin have been thwarting Detective Joslin from the beginning? He's the one who handles and oversees all the autopsies on the BEK killer case. This could be huge."

"All I know, Kirk, is that Edwin was here yesterday. When he was buying alcohol, he seemed off somehow. He was at the Radcliffe house last night and his scent is on that small piece of plastic on the shoulder of the road by Terry Radcliffe." He cleared his throat. "If you want my opinion, treat Edwin as a suspect and enter his office prepared to arrest him."

"How? On the evidence that you smelled him? No one would enforce that. Sorry, Jake, I know you're trying to help, but I'll need something more concrete."

"Something tells me we're heading to something more concrete. Whatever's waiting at Edwin's office will offer clarity. He was here last night and what I detected on that plastic wasn't just his scent—it was his nervous scent, his fear." Jake turned to Kirk as he drove. "Edwin was afraid and did something out here and now he wants to talk to you about it. Don't worry, we'll learn what he did before the day is over."

"That's what I'm afraid of."

Kirk flicked his emergency lights and dropped the accelerator down.

As the car shot forward to over a hundred and fifty kilometers an hour, Jake turned the heater a little higher.

CHAPTER FORTY-THREE

Edwin set down the cell phone. He didn't want to touch it again. It was almost over, wasn't it? He suspected Kirk and coma man would know he was a part of whatever ambush Adam had planned for the two detectives. He was the one who had summoned them to Toronto, knowing they were driving down from Huntsville.

It was reckless to enter into this kind of arrangement with a man like Adam, but Edwin had been left with no other choice.

It was even more reckless to set up this meeting without knowing Adam's plan. If the man meant to take out both Kirk and Jake, Edwin would be protected. Unless Kirk told someone else that Edwin had called him to his Toronto office. Then, when two seasoned detectives went missing and were later found murdered, people would turn to him. The ensuing investigation would include phone records. The call he'd just made to Kirk would come up and he needed a reason for having made it.

Edwin rubbed his face with both hands and grunted. All this because he hadn't followed his normal Gathering routine. Deviation from the routine wouldn't happen again. It wouldn't even enter his mind.

He had a few hours until Kirk and Jake entered his office. Adam had assured him they would be dealt with and then their arrangement would end, leaving Edwin with Megan in his basement.

Then, finally, life could return to normal. Married life was good for Edwin. They said married men live longer and Edwin planned on living a very long time.

He rose from the desk in his home office, made a cup of coffee in the kitchen and started downstairs. Megan might want some company. He should check her broken hand. See how swollen it was. With that kind of break, bones twisted up, she might be useless to him for a while.

He entered the code on the keypad and waited for the audible click of the door's lock disengaging. The bookcase slid away from the wall. Edwin stepped back and peeked inside the soundproof safe room. He admired the work Safe Roomz Inc. had done. Silently, he thanked them for their professionalism and expertise.

Megan lay on the bed, her broken wrist dangling over the edge, as if she was trying to keep it as far away from her as possible. Her fingers and knuckles were large, grotesquely swollen, a purplish red, matching the swelling on her face.

"Oh my," he said in a breathless whisper. "What have we here?"

Megan rolled sideways and glared at him.

"I'm going to kill you," she said, each word spoken through a clenched jaw, teeth tight together, barely moving her lips.

Edwin entered the room. "Now, now, little girl." He sipped from his coffee. "No need for hostilities. We're married now. It's time to set the rules."

"We're not *married!*" she shouted, wincing at the pain when she opened her mouth too far. "You're insane and I'm going to kill you."

"How it works is like this," he continued as if she hadn't said a thing. "Reward and punishment. Everything is reward and punishment."

"Reward this." With her good hand, she flipped him the bird. "Punish my ass. Fuck you, Jeffrey. Just fuck you."

"Do or say anything negative. Act in a mean way. Mistreat me. Disrespect me. These things create a punishment. Do the opposite, like nice things, say nice things, tell me you love me. These things create a reward."

He smiled, then sipped from his coffee, knowing she wasn't listening and not caring. Sometimes punishment was far better than rewards. For him, rewards simply meant making love to his wife. Punishment was where the real fun lay.

He scanned the nearly empty safe room. There was really nothing available for Megan to hurt herself with. But if she were to overpower him in some way, what would stop her from running out the open door, past the bookcase, up the stairs, and outside? She could knock his hot coffee into his face, break the cup against his cheek, jamming a shard into his eyeball. Megan could do a lot of damage if she were so inclined and if he wasn't better prepared.

This had to be the last time he entered the room without the Taser. He would make a point of not bringing in anything else. Maybe he should even remove his belt for her visits. What would he need it for, anyway?

He stepped closer to her. She moved away from him.

"Being in close proximity bothers you?" He offered her a half smile, then pursed his lips. "By this time tomorrow we'll be closer than you could ever imagine. So close in fact, that I'll be inside you." He let out a sharp, short bark of a laugh.

She screamed, leaned on her good arm, and tried to get up off the mattress.

He bent forward and jerked the hand holding the coffee toward her. The coffee splattered on Megan's face, quelling her violent scream instantly. Her head snapped back, her arms flailing at the hot, brown liquid. She wailed in pain as her broken wrist smacked her face.

Even though the coffee had cooled slightly in the time he'd been in the safe room, it was still quite warm. Her cheeks reddened where it had hit, spots of color on her neck.

She inhaled like she was breathing through a screen door, all wet and noisy. Her eyes were wide and staring at him.

"You'll learn," he said. "My new wife."

She curled into a ball on the mattress, shaking with pain.

Edwin moved toward the open door. He needed to get to his office, meet Adam and set up for the coma man ambush. There were other things to attend to. The duties of a husband could wait. His new wife could wait.

At the door, he looked back at Megan, admiring her athletic body, her long hair. She would be a good wife—he just needed more time with her, more time to break her. It was only her will that stood between them. Once he broke that, she would be his, free and clear.

"I'll be back tonight to mete out your punishment. Be ready for me." He typed in the code to close the door. Before it was completely shut, he said, "Tonight, I will break bones with my hammer so you can't move without pain, thereby erasing any thoughts of escape." The door crept closer to being shut. "You will never be able to walk again after tonight, but that doesn't matter. I only need you on your back."

The door closed, sealing off sound.

"Damn it. I was just getting started."

He went upstairs, rinsed out his coffee cup while humming "Paint it Black" by the *Rolling Stones*, then left the house, thoughts of his new wife and the fun they were about to have on his mind.

He tried not to think of Adam and why he would want to

trick Jake Wood into coming to Edwin's office. He kept his mind far from what they were going to do with Kirk Aiken as well. He couldn't come up with any answers that made sense and allowed him to stay on as chief medical examiner.

No answers at all.

So he brought his Taser along with him in case he needed it.

CHAPTER FORTY-FOUR

Kirk stopped for a coffee twice on the way south to Toronto. Once at the Tim Horton's coffee shop just south of the Gravenhurst exit—where he gassed up as well—and again at a Timmy's near one of the north Orillia exits. If it hadn't been for the amount of caffeine in his system, he would've fallen asleep on account of how warm it was in the car. Jake had the heat on high the entire ride south, even though he'd slept for over two hours of the ride.

Navigating downtown Toronto, Kirk pulled off Front Street and drove toward Edwin's office five blocks away. After successfully steering the car into a parking spot two blocks short of Edwin's office, Kirk turned it off, laid his head back and waited a moment to catch his breath and thoughts. With the engine off, the heater had stopped its relentless blasting. Even though the car was equipped with duo air and Kirk had closed the vents on his side, it hadn't prevented the heat from Jake's vents from wafting toward him, making him break out in a sweat.

But what choice did he have? Jake was his friend, his partner, his brother from another mother. They had been through a lot of shit together and whether he believed in this turning-into-a-snake shit or not, if Jake needed the heat cranked up in the car, Kirk would not deny him.

As Jake stirred, Kirk asked, "Got your beauty sleep?"

"Fuck you."

"Nope. Doesn't sound like it. You're still fucking ugly."

"Fuck you. Twice." Jake sat up and rubbed his face. "Where are we?"

"Two blocks from Edwin's office."

"Why are we here? Pull up closer." Jake yawned, then licked his lips. "What's up? What's bothering you?"

"I don't know. Something doesn't feel right."

"Like what?"

"Edwin has always been a behind-the-scenes man." Kirk checked the rearview mirror, then looked at Jake. "He does his autopsies, fills in his reports, does what court appearances are required of him, and keeps a meticulous office."

"And?"

"He *never* calls me. Whatever relationship he had with Detective Joslin, he doesn't have with me. Hasn't in the year plus I've been on this case."

"So, he's changing his role, making it more proactive."

"I know what you're doing and I appreciate it. Playing devil's advocate usually draws it out of me, but not this time because there's nothing specific I can pinpoint. Just a gut feeling."

"About what? That he wants to quit? That he doesn't like you? That he's gay? Or are you thinking he killed Terry Radcliffe and kidnapped Megan? I mean, that's what I would be thinking based on what I smelled at the crime scene and his nervousness the day before."

Their eyes met for a brief moment. Kirk broke off first because staring into Jake's eyes with their new bluish hue creeped him out.

"After that murder scene, I will tell you this. Something is bothering Edwin or he wouldn't call about some bullshit case file. And it has to do with what he was doing in Huntsville this weekend. No doubt about it. He did something or he saw something and he wants to talk to us—"

"Because we saw him there and during your investigation you'll discover that he was a guest at the party and at one point or another, he touched the Radcliffe's cell phone. The one that was destroyed on the road by the body of Terry Radcliffe." Jake paused. Kirk felt his partner's eyes roaming his face. "Something like that?"

"I can't imagine he's involved. It doesn't work like that. Not in real life. Only in fiction."

Kirk checked his phone. No calls. No texts. Nothing. It was just after five-thirty in the afternoon. They were supposed to be at Edwin's at six.

"Well, I say we go talk to him," Jake offered. "But be wary going in. Be cautious. If he did do something and we saw him in Huntsville, he's either going to come clean or do something else he'll regret."

Kirk shook his head. "Again, he's not the type. I've met the type, as you have. Edwin's a pussy."

"You want backup going in?" Jake asked. "Make the call."

"On what grounds?"

"Exactly." Jake opened his door. "Let's go."

Kirk got out, locked the doors and started up the sidewalk with Jake at his side. Just like old days, the two of them shoulder to shoulder, working on a case. After what happened to Jake over a year and a half ago, Kirk had thought this day would never come.

Edwin's building reminded Kirk of the front of a factory where accounts receivable and payable would be quartered. The building was three stories high and contained several government offices on each floor. Edwin's was on the third floor and took up two large areas. One was his office and the other his file storage. Edwin's situation was unique in that he kept his office offsite, away from where he worked on dead bodies. Kirk recalled Edwin saying once that one was completely separate from the other. Bodies were for cold metal tables. Paperwork was for well-ventilated offices with large desks and a coffee maker.

Kirk had been to Edwin's office on several occasions but not for over six months as there had been nothing new on the BEK killer for some time.

He led Jake into the building and walked up to the elevator. Finger on the button, he scanned the empty lobby.

"Nervous?" Jake asked.

Kirk frowned. "Really? This is Edwin Gavin, our medical examiner, our autopsy guy. Why would I be nervous?"

"Maybe because it feels like an ambush."

"An ambush? How so?"

"After bumping into Edwin at the liquor store in Huntsville, I asked you about the burnout rate of morticians?"

Kirk nodded. "And?"

"Edwin *smelled* nervous. It bothered me. As soon as that cop showed up asking about me, Edwin smelled scared." The elevator door opened. They stepped on. "Being scared and being in attendance at a party isn't criminal."

"Hell, I know that. But this, calling us in, is out of character."

"Then act as if it's hostile," Jake said. The elevator dinged for the third floor. "Be prepared."

Kirk nodded.

The doors opened.

Both men remained inside the lift, not moving. They waited. The second the doors began to close, Jake stuck his arm between them. Open again, Jake eased out of the elevator and looked both ways. Kirk followed Jake out of the elevator, his right hand hovering near his weapon.

The hallway was empty.

"This way," Kirk whispered.

He started down the narrow corridor toward Edwin's office,

which was around a corner on the left. No doors opened as they walked, no sounds seemed out of the ordinary. But yet something still felt off even if it didn't make any sense.

He stopped at Edwin's door and listened. When he heard nothing, he glanced back at Jake and shook his head.

Jake reached past him and knocked.

"Coming," Edwin yelled from behind the door.

Kirk eased his hand away from his weapon. Edwin's voice sounded normal. This was a routine visit. They'd bumped into each other in Huntsville. They had worked themselves up over Edwin's call. Without Jake's new ability to *smell* things, nothing that Edwin had done up to this point would seem out of the ordinary.

The door's lock clicked and Edwin opened it from the inside.

He stepped back, and waved them in.

"Please, come. I've got coffee on."

Kirk entered first with Jake following him slowly. They waited at the door as Edwin closed it and locked it again.

Kirk and Jake exchanged a frown. Why lock the door?

Kirk scanned Edwin's body for weapons. Nothing protruded in odd places.

"What was so important that we needed to be here by six?" Kirk asked.

Edwin walked past him and moved toward the center of his massive office space. To Edwin's left was a door that led to his storage area, which was dark at the moment.

"You were in Huntsville," Kirk said. "When did you come back to Toronto?"

Edwin smiled awkwardly, showing teeth. He went to say something, decided against it, closed his mouth, then moved around his desk and took a seat. Once seated, he steepled his fingers and offered Kirk a lopsided grin. Neither Kirk nor Jake moved or said a word.

"I think I've linked the cases of the BEK killer by something other than MO," Edwin said.

"And you couldn't tell me this over the phone?" Kirk asked.

"It's something I have to show you."

"Why are you so nervous?" Jake asked. "I can smell the fear radiating off you. Just like at the liquor store."

A muscle twitched under Edwin's right eye when he turned his attention to Jake. Kirk wondered if Jake had noticed it. Now that Jake had said something, Kirk saw Edwin's fingers shaking, his mannerisms jerky, nervous-like.

"Smell the fear?" Edwin asked, saying the words slowly. "How is it you can smell that? Bad deodorant? Perspiration?"

Jake stepped closer to Edwin's desk. "You were at the Radcliffe party last night. And you were at the site where Terry Radcliffe was killed last night, just south of Huntsville—"

Jake stopped suddenly. It was enough for Kirk to reach for his weapon. Edwin had become a stone statue, frozen to his chair, his expression rigid.

Jake looked at Kirk, wide-eyed. "He's got Megan."

"What?" Kirk muttered.

"That's ridiculous," Edwin shouted.

Jake pointed at Edwin. "I can smell Megan on him. Same smell from Megan's house. Her pheromones. Very strong. She's either here in this office or at another location." Jake opened his mouth, closed his eyes and stuck his tongue out. He rolled it around, flicking it several times. When his eyes reopened, they grew wider than before. "She's not here. He has her elsewhere. But someone else is here. Several others."

"Who?" Kirk shouted as he pulled his weapon.

Edwin leaned back in his chair, his face a mask of shock and disbelief.

"What the fuck is this?" Edwin muttered.

Jake dropped to the floor, planted his hands flat on the carpet, and closed his eyes.

"Don't move," he said.

Kirk waited, his weapon out and aimed at the ceiling tiles above him.

Jake shot up from the floor and pointed toward the storage area.

Kirk looked that way just in time to see the muzzle flash. At the same second, something punched him in the calf muscle.

Kirk stumbled sideways and fell to the carpet. He rolled so his weapon aimed at the storage closet, but then something jolted him from behind as Edwin screamed. The gun was knocked from his grasp.

He vibrated as volts of electricity shot through him. When it was over, Kirk calmed, taking the time to breathe and mentally inventory his body. Pain came from several areas, his leg being the worst.

A man emerged from the storage area, followed by two others. The man stopped at Kirk's gun, then kicked it into a corner.

Warm, wet blood oozed out of his leg wound, soaking his pants. They had walked into an ambush, after all. He'd been shot in the leg and then tased by Edwin. A thousand questions ran through his mind.

Who was Edwin Gavin? Who was behind this attack? Why go after Kirk and Jake? Was it about the Radcliffes, the BEK killer, or something else entirely?

Hands gripped his arm and violently flipped him onto his back. The polished black shoes man stepped into view above him. He'd seen him before. It all came back in a rush. The Royal Victoria Hospital in Barrie on that fateful night so long ago.

"Hello, Detective Aiken," the man known only as Adam said. "We meet again."

CHAPTER FORTY-FIVE

Jake had been hit from behind by an electrical charge. At the moment Kirk was felled by a bullet and Jake had reached for him, Edwin tased Jake in the side, just above the waist.

It had been strong enough to knock him down, but strangely, its effects had worn off immediately. He stayed on the ground to avoid being shot and waited.

A well-dressed man stood over Kirk, talking to him like they knew each other.

"Edwin," the man said. "Step over here."

Jake rolled his eyes to Kirk who lay on his back now, bleeding from the bullet wound to his leg. His partner needed an ambulance. This had to end quickly, but the man looking at Kirk still held a silenced weapon. Two other men stood back by the wall, each holding a baseball bat.

Unsure of his new abilities, his strength, Jake waited to see what was going to happen next before he decided to act.

Edwin stepped around Jake, Taser still in his hand. A sudden urge to lunge, to grab Edwin's throat and squeeze it until it snapped came over Jake, but he couldn't. They needed Edwin alive to tell them where Megan was being held.

"Take this," the man said, handing Edwin the silenced weapon. "And kill Detective Aiken. We'll handle Jake."

Edwin stepped back. "That wasn't the deal, Adam."

"The deal?" Adam said. "What deal?" He raised a finger to his lips, closed his eyes, and appeared to contemplate something. "I removed Terry from your situation. I now have a situation with Jake that I will deal with. You must remove Kirk to make our arrangement complete." His voice had gone monotone, his words spoken with a measured evenness. "Or would you like me to explain how they know you were with Terry last night?"

Edwin nodded in a short spurt. "Please do, because I would hate to learn that you told them."

"They were called in to observe the crime scene. These two detectives walked the Radcliffe house. They examined the area where I shot Terry." Adam pointed at Jake. "Jake here found the cell phone you smashed and kicked into the shrubs on the side of the road. Now, here's the special part, the section that puts all the pieces together." Adam stepped closer to Jake until he was standing by his side. "Jake here has a special ability. He can sense things, smell things that ordinary men cannot."

"What?" Edwin said. "How's that?"

"Long story, but it involves the snake venom and coma he endured. We were the anonymous donors for his treatment. We saw every examination Dr. Sutton performed. We know all about Jake's special abilities. Nevertheless, Jake was our target and now we have him." Adam gestured for his colleagues.

The two men with baseball bats came to stand beside Jake. Kirk turned his head until they exchanged a glance.

"Your job, Edwin, is to eliminate Kirk. If you choose not to, he will see you in prison for the kidnapping and murder of Megan Radcliffe." Adam stopped. Cleared his throat, then added, "So what will it be? A long investigation with you in jail at the end of it, or your freedom with Kirk dead?"

Edwin surveyed the gun in his hand. His other hand still held the Taser. Whether it was the resolve on his face or his defeated scent, Jake saw that Edwin was going to do it.

Jake could not allow that.

Edwin aimed the gun at Kirk's face, the end of the barrel shaking, and began to squeeze the trigger.

Jake shouted as he launched off the floor. He turned sideways and pushed upward to dive at Edwin.

The gun fired before he made it, turning Jake's shout into a guttural cry as he smacked into Edwin, knocking both of them over Kirk and into the wall beside him. They landed in a jumble of arms and legs, with Jake fumbling for Edwin's throat. He would kill him for shooting Kirk. He would snap Edwin in half for killing his best friend. Edwin would be unrecognizable for the mortician who tried to put him back together again. A closed-casket funeral.

As they struggled, the medical examiner screamed for help. Jake sensed the two men with baseball bats closer. He spun around just as a bat swung down and whacked him in the small of the back. The man pulled the baseball bat back and swung again, this time with more force, and something in Jake's back snapped.

He grunted with pain and rolled off Edwin.

The bat came down a third time on Jake's left arm, snapping it at the elbow, then a fourth time, breaking his right wrist.

"Stop!" Adam yelled.

It all happened so fast. Someone was moaning. Jake wondered if it was himself. He breathed deeply, minding the pain, tolerating it, hoping consciousness would stick around.

He couldn't feel his feet, his legs. Could the bat have damaged his spine? Both arms were aflame.

The moaning got louder.

Adam was doing something on the floor. Edwin had moved back toward his desk, red splotches on his face and neck.

When Adam stood, he was supporting Kirk, who seemed whole and alive. Kirk looked down at Jake and whispered that he was sorry. Tears slipped from Kirk's eyes as Jake watched, paralyzed, blinking rapidly, breathing away nausea.

"The gun was empty," Adam said. "It was a test of faith." He shoved Kirk away from him. With the leg wound, Kirk dropped in a heap. Jake felt the vibration in his shoulder and head, but not his lower body. "Edwin passed the test of loyalty. You, on the other hand, you will be dealt with like the animal you are. Or should I say, the animal you have become."

The men with bats moved in and stood over Jake. He looked up at them, helplessly. This was it. He was supposed to have died that night in the rainforest, but had awoken to this. They were going to kill him and there was nothing he could do about it. Paralyzed from the waist down, he lay motionless and waited for the blows.

The man on his right was familiar. He blinked and stared at the man.

Of course—the Manaus cop. The one who followed me from my hotel and disappeared by the Opera House.

"Bash his body, bash his skull," Adam said. "But start at the feet and work your way up. Let's see how long Jake can stay awake while the body I created is destroyed."

The body I created?

What did that mean?

The bats began pounding on him. His head jerked each time the weapons crunched down. He was surprised at how little pain he felt as his legs were pulverized, his knees shattered to bits of crumbled bones. Maybe pain would come in time. Or maybe he would be dead before the intense pain started.

He tried to breathe, but that proved more difficult as the bats pounded on his ribcage now. At one point, he heard Kirk scream for them to stop, while Edwin gagged in the corner.

Both bats, painted red with blood, hovered over his face a

moment, gripped tight by his murderers.

Jake opened his mouth, licked his lips and blew a kiss to each man, then closed his eyes. A big fuck you. In another life, he would find them, hunt them, and destroy their bodies in the same fashion—or worse.

Kirk begged them to stop, his voice taking on a high-pitched plea.

"Don't kill him," Kirk shouted.

It sounded like Edwin had vomited in the corner. Jake pictured Edwin throwing up, standing by his desk, a hand on the wall. Edwin could work on dead bodies, but watching the bodies *become* dead this violently would make anyone toss their cookies.

A sharp white light raced across Jake's vision as a baseball bat connected with his skull.

Then all the lights went out.

CHAPTER FORTY-SIX

Someone knocked. Someone was swimming. It didn't make any sense. Who would be swimming in the dark? Why knock?

It dawned on him that he was swimming. In the dark. But why? A pool? A lake? He couldn't tell.

Nothing made sense.

Piecing it together was useless. He was in the car. Sleeping. Heading to Toronto. Gotta meet Edwin.

Something about Edwin. Edwin Gavin. Nervous. Smell of Megan Radcliffe on him. Terry's body. Edwin guilty, but would need evidence. No court would convict on smell alone.

Jake jolted at the memory of Kirk being shot. Edwin held a gun over Kirk's face and pulled the trigger. But that was a test. Kirk was still alive. They were going to make it out of this. Something to talk about years later over beer. Laugh with a future wife about how close they had come to biting a bullet that day.

If only he could stop swimming.

Images of Cindy assailed him. Her smile, her soft skin, her smell. Pregnant now. Married to another man. A man named Derrick.

A tear slipped from his eye, tickling as it rolled down his face.

If he was swimming, wouldn't the tear mix with the water?

He sniffed the air by opening his mouth.

That man was nearby. Adam. Kirk and Edwin weren't there.

Adam's baseball bat men weren't in the area either.

Baseball bat men. The Manaus cop—fake cop. It all came back in a rush and his breath caught in his throat. He choked on it a moment, then tried to open his eyes.

He wasn't swimming after all. Consciousness was returning. After what they had done to his body, why was he still alive—*how* was he still alive? And where was the pain, not that he wanted any, but it didn't make sense.

He tried his eyes again and realized they were open. Wherever he was had no light. Absolute black. He tried to raise a hand to pass it before his eyes, but his arms were secured to something. He tried to move his feet but they were secured, too.

He could move his toes. He could feel them again. The bats hadn't paralyzed him after all. There was still no pain. Was he dead? Or had everything been a dream? Could he be paralyzed from the neck down, feeling no pain and moving imaginary toes?

Nothing made sense.

Something Adam said came back to him.

The body I created.

Adam hadn't created Jake. Jake had been born December 28, 1980. He was in his mid-thirties and liked bands called Blue October, Moxy Fruvous, Fairground Attraction, and Slipknot. He'd attended police college in Aylmer, Ontario, and worked Homicide for the OPP. His longtime friend from grade eight was Detective Kirk Aiken, also his partner.

So no, Adam had not created Jake. Jake had created Jake. Jake had made himself into the man he always wanted to be and had lost that in an accident that had cost him eighteen months.

The new awareness, the ability to smell and feel things. The strength, the healing from the baseball bats—maybe that's what Adam was referring to. Luke's green liquid must be some sort of healing agent. Like an immortal serum.

Adam.

Had Adam killed Luke? If so, was Jake going to be another casualty? Had that been Adam standing by the SUV on the highway, watching when Jake had caught up to those four thieves who had broken into his house and stolen his computer? Had Jake been targeted from the beginning?

Adam is Fortech Industries.

His energy waned. Soft tickling sensations rippled through his body as things moved, came to life. In the blackened room, a heat vent churned warmth over him. Jake closed his eyes and drifted off.

Thoughts of Cindy calmed him as he went under. He would always love her. Even if she was with another man. Cindy would always be his in his heart.

Then his thoughts died as suddenly as a TV being switched off.

CHAPTER FORTY-SEVEN

A strike across the face snapped Jake awake. He blinked rapidly into the lighted room, then closed his eyes. It was too bright.

"Wake up," Adam said.

Jake recognized the man's voice from Edwin's office. His firm tone could be recognized in an instant. Like Morgan Freeman's voice, or Christopher Walken's.

Adam slapped him again.

Jake flapped his eyelids and managed to open them slightly as his sensitive eyes adjusted to the light.

"He's alive," Adam said in a boisterous voice, mocking Dr. Frankenstein.

The body I created flashed through Jake's mind.

He focused on Adam. The man wore another expensive suit. Adam rubbed his five o'clock shadow below the chin, surveying Jake.

"You've done well," Adam said. "I'm impressed. Haven't seen this kind of talent since, well, since my days."

"What have I done?" Jake asked, his words clipped, measured. The anger he felt, the violence and rage he wanted to spew on Adam echoed from every fiber in his body. His limbs began to shake with anticipation.

"You have to let that go," Adam said.

"Let. What. Go?"

"The repulsion for me."

"Why?"

"It'll do you no good where you're going."

"Where am I going?"

"Dust to dust ..." Adam stepped away.

Jake tried to follow him with his gaze, but a restraint on his forehead limited movement.

"We had been working on gene therapy at Fortech for quite some time," Adam said. "I've been working on it since the seventies, actually."

"Bullshit. You don't look a day over forty."

"I'm not. Well, the truth is." Adam stepped back into view. "I was forty-one when I injected myself with the I.G. serum." He scrunched up his face into a scowl, then released it. "They didn't want human trials. I didn't care. I believed in it that much."

"Did it work?" Jake asked. "This I.G. serum."

"It did. I'm still forty-one."

"When was this?"

Adam looked up to the left as if he was thinking. "1995. I've been forty-one for over two decades."

"Bullshit. You're lying."

Adam produced a large needle filled with a blue liquid. He held it up.

"This is death in a syringe."

"You gonna do the world a favor and inject it into yourself?" Jake asked.

Adam shook his head. "You won't be so lucky. No, this baby is for you. Think of it as an antivenin for the I.G. serum."

"What's the I.G. serum?"

"Immunity Gene, or as some refer to it as The Immortal Gene."

Jake frowned. "Immunity? Immortal?"

"Yes. With the serum in my blood, it gives me immunity from all known diseases, colds, and otherwise fatal conditions humans succumb to. Even aging."

Could Adam be telling the truth?

"Even the aging process is stopped?" Jake asked, doubt in his tone.

Adam nodded. "Anything that can harm my tissues, even aging, is arrested. Therefore, I'll live forever. The only way for me to die is to sever my head and make sure the two pieces aren't put back together for an undetermined amount of time."

"Undetermined?"

"Yes, the amount of time has never been tested so I don't have conclusive results with a human test subject on that yet. When I did it with snakes, their bodies didn't decay for months after we severed their heads. Once the body and head were set in the same cage, it took less than an hour for the snake to reform and look as if nothing had happened."

Snakes?

"Are you talking about the snakes Luke was supposed to test in the Amazon Rainforest?"

"The same ones."

"Like the one that attacked me?"

Adam nodded.

"Have I got this immunity gene in me?" Jake asked, already knowing the answer.

"That's why you're not dead. Those baseball bats broke your spine, paralyzed you from the waist down. Over half of your two hundred plus bones were broken only twenty-four hours ago, yet you lie on this table as good as new. Not even a bruise. Amazing isn't it?"

The tickling sensation he felt before made sense now. How he couldn't feel his feet, then he could when he'd thought he was swimming in the dark. Even now, no pain. Nothing.

"When the bats were hitting me, I felt the contact, but hardly the pain."

"That's normal. In your new condition, pain is an inconvenience better not felt. The I.G. serum was meant for soldiers. It still is, but the government doesn't take well to immortality so they're constantly reworking it. Just like GMOs, created with the cells from fish and spiders, our serum was created by nature's best. The way a crab can regenerate a claw, you too can regenerate a limb—even a new stomach if someone was to tear it out and stomp on it. Wherever you were on the evolution of your body's lifespan is where the serum halted your journey toward death. Although, you have a slightly different case than mine."

"How's that?" Jake found this hard to believe, but it explained the changes he'd endured since the coma.

"You received the I.G. serum in its purest form. When it was added to the snake venom and your unique reaction to the antivenin, you became something we could never have predicted. Our mistake."

"Are you saying I'm immortal?" *There goes Dr. Sutton's theory that I'm terminal.*

Adam nodded again, waving the needle in front of him. "Yes, immortal, unless someone who knows how to kill you can do it and I happen to be one of those people." Adam walked around Jake until he was on the other side of the table. "You've experienced changes to your body. A better sense of smell by using your tongue. Just like a snake. The inside of your body has changed, as a snake's would. You're becoming more efficient, more streamlined. Your strength has increased to at least five times a regular man. There are many more changes, but we won't belabor the point because you'll be dead inside an hour."

"Why? If I'm such a marvel of science, let's go do further tests. Let's show the world what I can do."

Adam faced him. "Never. The world would hunt you down and kill you like they would Dracula. You're an abomination. A mistake. Your bite alone can knock a man out for up to a half hour with all those neurotoxins floating around in there. And this is just the beginning. In a year, maybe two, your talents would be fully realized. I can't let that happen."

"Where's Kirk?" Jake asked, trying to keep him talking.

"Kirk's dead. Edwin dealt with the body."

Jake stared up at the ceiling. Grief swept over him like a blanket of hammers, heavy and pulverizing. Without seeing it for himself, he wouldn't believe it. How could Kirk be dead?

Jake struggled with the restraints, but his arms and legs remained locked down to the table.

"You can't get out," Adam said, a laugh in his voice. "A pair of handcuffs would seem like a Lego toy to you, but these reinforced steel cuffs aren't as forgiving."

"Why? Why kill Kirk?"

"He was close to you. He knew too much. You told him things you shouldn't have in your home."

"You were listening?"

"There's no need to investigate this matter any further, my little snake man. You're Jake the Snake. Forty percent snake, sixty percent human. In a month or two you were supposed to shed your first skin after your eyes turned a milky blue. But that day will never come."

Adam slipped the needle inside a tube.

"How did I become part snake?"

"We're not entirely sure. Think about it like this: our serum mixed with the venom and changed you when it thought you were a snake. The serum that altered the human part of you was just doing its job."

"Why would it think I was a snake?"

"We feel that has something to do with the reaction to the antivenin. Since you're allergic to it, the serum worked on you like you were a snake and replicated the DNA found in the venom to enhance your organs. Ultimately, you turned into a modern day Frankenstein."

"What's in that?" Jake gestured at the needle.

"Euthasol."

"Isn't that what veterinarians use to put animals to sleep?"

"The same. Although this is over four hundred milligrams. This amount takes out cattle, horses. I should be wearing gloves, but for me a little prick wouldn't matter. All four hundred milligrams would matter, though."

"If what you just told me is true, this won't kill me."

"Oh, it'll try its best. Administered like this, through an IV, Euthasol is an anesthetic drug with the barbiturate pentobarbital. It would make your pet fall asleep, then cause the animal's breathing to stop, and finally the heart stops." Adam met Jake's gaze. "It's a fast-acting drug. From mere seconds to a full minute and the animal is dead. In some cases, little animals are dead inside ten seconds. Make no mistake, this amount will kill you, but Jake the Snake will not stay dead for long. Not with the I.G. serum in his blood. That's where my two friends—you might remember the men with baseball bats—will enter the room and slice your head from your body. Then piece by piece, your body will be incinerated at separate facilities in Ontario. Once the flesh is burned to ashes, the serum dies with it. Spread out all over the province is the surest way to guarantee that you can't put the pieces together again." He chuckled. "That made me think of Humpty Dumpty. Funny, eh?" Adam adjusted something on the IV and a warmth entered Jake's left arm. "Hey Jake, did you know that Humpty Dumpty might not have been an egg? I mean, nowhere in the story does it say that Humpty was an egg."

The warmth spread fast, racing through his blood. Panic swelled as his heart beat faster in his chest.

"Goodbye, Jake. Shouldn't be more than a half minute left of consciousness, then death. My men will be here in ten minutes to decapitate you and your body will burn by sundown. No one will ever find you. Ashes to ashes, Jake, dust to dust …"

Jake closed his eyes and focused on his breathing. Consciousness seemed to hang on as if the Euthasol couldn't turn off his brain. The pounding in his ears reverberated through his head. He listened to it, felt comforted by it.

The pounding slowed, became irregular for a moment, then stopped.

Jake lay there, unable to move, unable to breathe.

He waited for something else to happen.

Nothing did.

Except a door closed somewhere to his right.

Adam had left.

Jake was alone. He was dead. But somehow still awake.

A murmur of movement fluttered in his chest.

The thump in his ear started up again.

I'm alive!

CHAPTER FORTY-EIGHT

Jake's heart pumped stronger than ever before, a resurgence of strength racing through his veins, firing him up. He opened his eyes. Adam hadn't killed the lights this time. His men were coming at any moment and they wanted Jake's head.

He focused on his right hand, pulling it upward, against the restraint. The steel dug into his flesh, the pain no more than an inconvenience. He pulled harder until the steel moaned in protest. Using the strap on his forehead as leverage, he lifted his entire body against its confines in an effort to bend inward, focusing all his strength on the right wrist.

Maybe he'd break his wrist, slip out of the steel cuff, then heal it again. But how long did broken bones take to heal with the immunity gene in his body? How fast could he regenerate the cells and get his wrist to fuse? Two minutes? Two hours? Two days?

Whatever it was, now was not a good time to test broken bones. Adam's men were coming and he needed to be able to fight.

The steel creaked as it twisted. Jake grunted with the strain and redoubled his efforts.

Then something unexpected happened. His head shot forward as the strap on his forehead snapped off.

He sat up and examined the steel cuffs on his wrists. He was almost through the one on the right. A little more negotiation and he could break it.

A door closed in another room. They were coming and he was still virtually locked to the table.

He pulled upward, leaning into it, took one deep breath, held it, then yanked and pulled again.

The steel snapped and his wrist was free. Blood dripped from two lines where the edge of the cuff had bitten into his skin, but the wrist was not broken.

He started in on the other wrist as another door closed and he heard footsteps coming closer.

He tried harder and was bending back the steel when the door to the room opened.

Jake dropped back to the table and closed his eyes. The sweat beading on his forehead could be explained away. His body had protested the Euthasol and fought but had succumbed to the death the drug guaranteed. That's what they would assume. He hoped.

He sensed the men coming closer. The sound of a blade sliding along another blade gave him chills. Everything he'd just learned about himself and his new reality gave him chills. That he was virtually immortal and becoming part snake. That he basically couldn't die. That he would be in his mid-thirties for the rest of his life. What would that look like? Would he see the end of the world? Would he survive a nuclear holocaust? So much to think about, to digest, to comprehend. But right now he blocked all that and focused on the two men who meant to kill him.

One man stood to his left. The other man hovered by his head. He had to be the one with the blade. The decapitation was about to take place.

Jake waited, heart pounding, every cell in his body screaming self-preservation signals to his muscles. The urge to open his eyes and sit up was overwhelming, but he had to wait until the time was right.

The blade slipped in beside his head. The cool touch of its

deadly edge rubbed the flesh on his neck near the collarbone.

It was time.

As the blade closed in on his skin and began to slice, Jake jolted up, deflecting the blade away. With his free hand, he grabbed the man's hair in a vise grip and yanked downward. The blade entered the center of the man's throat and disappeared in his flesh at least five inches before the man's partner took one full gasping breath beside the table to Jake's left.

As the man fell to the floor, jerking and spasming in death's throes, Jake spun to the other man who hadn't moved, the sudden action paralyzing him beside the table. Jake reached for him, but the guy jumped back. He almost missed but managed to snag an inch of the man's jacket.

The man reached for something inside his jacket as Jake drew him close to bite him—the knock out solution. A gun came out of his jacket. The man aimed his weapon and before Jake could get him close enough, he fired it rapidly.

Bullet after bullet entered Jake's abdomen. He felt each one as if a small girl delivered tiny punches to his solar plexus.

The shock of being shot almost paralyzed him with fear, but it was the anger of losing Kirk to these predators that fueled him. His body might have changed but his mind was slow in that realization.

Jake lunged forward and closed his mouth on the man's collarbone. He bit down so hard, he heard the man's bone crunch under his teeth. It felt like biting into a chicken leg. The skin split in a half oval, bones crushed, and the man yelled out in agony and dropped to the floor beside the steel table.

Jake examined his stomach. Blood seeped from multiple holes. He rested his head back and focused on his breathing while gingerly touching the exit wounds in his back. The man on the floor wailed in pain for another dozen seconds, then quieted and finally stopped moving altogether.

A tickling sensation in Jake's stomach made him look at the wound again. The bleeding had stopped. His shirt had holes in it—four in total—but the holes were merely rimmed in blood. Breathing became less a chore and more natural. His head cleared quickly and within another minute of rest, his stomach felt whole again.

"Holy shit," he muttered. "What the fuck is happening to me?"

As shock settled in and he felt the blood leave his face, he knew it wouldn't kill him. A state of shock could kill a man, but not Jake Wood, the man with the Immortal Gene who could regenerate any part of his body when it needed mending.

It took him ten minutes to free the rest of his limbs from the steel table. He dropped beside the man on the floor and bit him again, then began to rifle through his pockets. He came up with the man's wallet. The ID said his name was Bruce Barns.

In the billfold, Jake found several hundred dollars. He shoved the bills in his pocket and checked Bruce for extra bullets but found none. He relieved the man of his weapon and saw that it was empty.

He got to his feet, took a deep breath, feeling more alive than ever before, and turned his gaze to the man with the blade jammed up under his chin.

Blood covered the protruding blade. It had run down the length, over the hilt, and onto the man's hand. His eyes had bulged in the final moment before his heart stopped.

Jake didn't care to close the man's eyes. He just wouldn't look at him as he went through the man's pockets. More money, but no bullets. But this man also had a gun, and it was fully loaded with a bullet in the chamber.

Jake stuck both guns in his waistband and ran for the door.

He had to locate Edwin Gavin.

The door was locked.

He stuck his ear to the cold steel and listened. Then he placed his hands on the floor and listened again. Nothing. No movement and no pheromones. He was alone.

Since there were no windows in this room, the door was his only option. It was possible one of the men on the floor had a key, but Jake didn't bother to check. Smashing bodily against the door felt too good to stop. It helped with the anger, the internal rage building at what Fortech Industries had done to him.

When his mind turned to Adam, he ran at the door one last time, violently smashing the dented steel and breaking through to the other side.

In the corridor, he got to his feet and ran for the stairwell, his rage so thick he could taste blood. He made it to the lobby and ran outside into the sunlight.

CHAPTER FORTY-NINE

As soon as Jake bounded out of the building, he stopped to take in his surroundings. He was still in downtown Toronto. Cars raced by as Jake hailed a taxi and gave Edwin's office address on Front Street to the driver.

Thirty minutes later, Jake paid the driver, hopped out and looked for Kirk's car. It was right where he'd parked it earlier.

Before Kirk had been killed.

Jake stared up at Edwin's building, holding back tears.

Adam had made a mistake. He hadn't guaranteed Jake's death himself. And now Jake was coming for him. He would find Edwin, then Adam.

He started for the building thinking about his so-called terminal diagnosis. Dr. Sutton had told him the human body couldn't manage the changes Jake was going through, that the changes were killing him. Sutton had said it wouldn't be long before Jake died. Months, maybe six at the most.

Knowing what he knew now—if Adam was correct—then Jake wouldn't be dying anytime soon. Actually, Jake wouldn't be dying at all.

As he strode toward Edwin's building, Jake decided to visit Dr. Sutton in ten or twenty years to show him Jake hadn't aged a day since Sutton gave the dire news of Jake's upcoming death. The shock would be unbearable.

Jake entered the building and got on the elevator without being noticed. Just as before, the lobby was empty and all was quiet.

On the third floor, he stepped out of the elevator cautiously, pulled the loaded gun and started toward Edwin's office door. Déjà vu set in and for a moment he thought Kirk was right beside him, edging down the hallway.

Jake fought back the bitter taste of regret in his mouth, swallowing his grief and channeling it into rage.

At Edwin's office door, he listened. As before, he knelt and closed his eyes. When he was certain that the office on the other side of the door was empty, Jake got to his feet, slipped the weapon back in his pants, and tried the knob.

It was locked. He hadn't expected otherwise. There was one thing he learned years ago in police training and that was never break down an unlocked door.

He opened his palm and placed it on the door beside the lock. Lowering his center of gravity, he brought his hand back to his waist, then thrust his open palm forward with as much power as he could muster. The lock shattered in the doorframe, its bolt shoving the frame's rim out of alignment. All it took was that one hit and the door popped open.

Jake slipped inside and left the door slightly ajar. He flicked on the lights and cleared the office in under twenty seconds, confirming he was completely alone. Phantom smells of Kirk and Edwin, Adam and his men, floated through the air. He detected the anger, the fear, their perspiration.

At Edwin's desk, he ripped open the drawers and flipped through papers he found inside. The Rolodex on Edwin's desk didn't have his home address.

Jake didn't want to have to resort to calling in a favor from a known colleague at the police station. That would leave a record.

He had to get Edwin's address on his own. There was no other way to handle this.

In the corner of Edwin's second drawer in his desk, Jake located a business card for a safe room company. It advertised how the rooms were soundproof and could be designed to reflect the panic room in the Jodie Foster movie.

Jake held the card a moment, then sniffed it.

Safe Roomz Inc.

It listed a telephone and fax number, plus an email.

Could Edwin have used this service? Had he installed a safe room? If so, it had to be in his house.

That's where Megan would be.

As soon as Jake thought it, he was sure he was right.

He lifted the phone on Edwin's desk and dialed the number on the card, then waited while it rang, watching the office door.

After two rings, it picked up.

"Good evening, Safe Roomz. How can I help you?"

Jake held the card up to his face. "I'm looking to speak with Steve," Jake said, deepening his voice.

"With the number on my screen, I can tell I'm talking to the one and only, Edwin Gavin," the man said. "It's Steve. How are you liking your new safe room?"

Jake swallowed, then cleared his throat. He had to handle this delicately.

"Actually, that's why I'm calling." He coughed. "Sorry, excuse my voice. Picked up a cold somewhere."

"Hey, no problem. Fill me in, Edwin. What's up?"

"The door isn't closing properly. I thought it was a lock issue, but it's an alignment issue of some kind."

"Oh well, that can happen. Because you went with the bookcase option as a door, the weight of the books might be pulling on it in a way that just needs an adjustment. It's rare, but it can happen. I'll swing by on my way home and take a look at it if you want. It's still under warranty."

That's right, blame it on the customer's choice of door.

"No need to come tonight. Tomorrow would be fine. Afternoon."

"Perfect, see you then."

"Wait. Steve," Jake said, hoping he caught him.

"Yeah?"

"Can you confirm the address you have on file?"

"I was just there a few days ago."

"Yeah, I know. I just had a delivery go to the wrong house so I want to double check."

"Sounds good," Steve said, trying to sound cheery even though he probably felt this was a waste of time. With a defective door this soon, Steve could assume his customer had lost trust in Steve's word. He read Edwin's home address out loud. Jake memorized it on the spot.

Without another word, Jake hung up.

Then he ran for the door and Kirk's car, hoping Kirk had left the spare key in the wheel well like he always did.

In less than an hour, Edwin would be surprised to see him. In less than an hour, if all went well, Edwin Gavin would be arrested.

Or dead.

CHAPTER FIFTY

Jake pulled onto Edwin's street and cut the headlights. He parked a block away from Edwin's house in the older part of Toronto, south of the 401 Highway.

The entire drive over, he'd thought of Kirk, the years they'd spent together, the arrests, the danger, the good times, and how it was all gone because of Adam and Edwin. Jake felt Kirk's loss more than he expected. Probably because it was so *unexpected.* They had just spent the night at Jake's place going over case files and now Kirk was dead.

Jake lowered his head, tightened his hands into fists until his bones cracked, and cried. Now he'd lost everything. Completely. Absolutely.

Cindy, his dog Athina, his house, his job, his career, his life, and now Kirk.

He raised his head and stared at the roof of the car.

"What else?" he shouted at God. "Huh? What else are you going to take?"

He thought of verses and stories from the Bible. The snake in the Garden of Eden with Adam and Eve. Temptation and loss. Knowledge. The story of Job. Could he have done something to deserve this? Was it all his fault? Had everything been taken from him to serve a purpose, deliver a message?

If so, he hoped he had learned it because he just couldn't take another loss. And hadn't he flipped to the dark side now? Killing that man with his own blade.

He wiped his eyes, took a deep breath, flicked the interior light switch off so it wouldn't illuminate when he opened the car door, then got out silently. He slipped away from the car and moved behind a row of bushes to observe the street.

If being part snake with inhuman strength and virtually immortal meant he was evil, then he would take it any day. In fact, he felt more God-like than anything. This power allowed him to stop people like Adam and Edwin. Imagine such a man as a cop, on the streets, never needing to fear death. Never fearing the bad guys, guns, bikers, terrorists. The damage he could do to the Mafia, street thugs, punks, and murderers. If that was evil, then he would take it any day. He'd rather be evil and eliminate crime on the streets than good and allow the assholes to thrive.

As he strode up the darkened street, keeping to the shadows between streetlights as often as he could, he knew in his heart who he was. He knew that he wasn't evil and that God, whatever higher power reigned above human existence, hadn't forsaken him. He couldn't have because Jake's heart was clean. Deep down inside, Jake was a good person. His first thought, his first goal, now having an even better understanding of what he was capable of, was to solve crime.

Also, he wanted to locate Fortech Industries and stop their work. Fortech Industries would regret the day Jake Wood was born. As would a multitude of assholes in the days and years to follow.

In Kirk's honor, Jake wouldn't stop. He wouldn't love again. He wouldn't have a dog again. He wouldn't have a life. He would only exist after this. Exist to make things better from the shadows. Better for little girls who went to sleep at night with teddy bears. Better for little boys reading scary books under their blankets with tiny penlights. Better for their parents and better for the next generation. He was no Superman, no Spiderman, but Jake felt in his bones that he was a good cop and he had been given this gift for a reason. And that reason started tonight with his arrest of Edwin Gavin for the murder of Detective Kirk Aiken and the kidnapping of Megan Radcliffe.

Jake understood that he couldn't kill Edwin. It wasn't in him no matter how much he wanted to. It would be better to see Edwin in prison, suffering until he died a lonely old man behind bars.

The lights were out at Edwin's home. Jake walked by and continued to the house next door. At a row of bushes, he took a left and walked the length of them until he got to the corner of the house.

He squeezed through a hole near the base of the dense foliage and crawled onto Edwin's property. He took a moment to sniff the air, feel the ground for predators. When the air was clean and the ground still, Jake got up and started for the rear of Edwin's house, staying as quiet as possible.

He tried the rear door, but it was locked.

Of course.

After a look over his shoulder, Jake gripped the knob, tightened the pressure until he was afraid he'd dent it, and began to turn it. He continued even after he met resistance. The device inside the door creaked. He added pressure by degrees. Then more.

Something snapped quietly, muffled by the door's outer frame, and the knob slipped off in his hand. Jake tossed the broken piece into the bushes and slipped his fingers inside the hole in the door. He forced the lock's parts to the left, away from the door frame.

The door popped open a crack.

He leaned forward and breathed.

Edwin was home.

The smell of the man was too strong to be a residual odor. But there was something else. The faint smell of Megan Radcliffe and a stronger smell of Kirk.

Kirk? He frowned. *Why Kirk?*

Could Kirk's scent be from Edwin's clothes? Or had Edwin brought Kirk to his house?

A funny thought occurred to him. Why all the stealth? Why not just break down the front door and tear through the house until he found Edwin and forced the truth from him, broken bone by broken bone? There was nothing Edwin could do to stop the immortal Jake. It would be a lot faster and simpler. Maybe not as quiet, but faster. And if a life was in jeopardy, Jake needed a sense of urgency.

Old habits died hard. He preferred to stay the same, to remain a man and think like a man. Not act and think like the immortal he had become. To be that way would be boasting, reveling in the fact that he was better than everyone else. This Immortal Gene needed to be his backup card and not the first card he played.

He stood in the dark kitchen, closed his eyes, and listened.

Nothing. Not a single sound.

Edwin's odor grew stronger. The smell of fear, anxiety, mixed with excitement. He was definitely here, hiding somewhere. Awake, but in the dark.

Aware?

Did Edwin expect him? How? Why? Wouldn't Adam have assured him that Jake was dead? Hadn't that been the deal? Adam handled Jake and Edwin dealt with Kirk?

Maybe not. Maybe Edwin was supposed to handle Jake, too. That would explain why Adam left Jake alone with enough time to break loose and kill his men. If so, it was a risky game Adam was playing. A dangerous game for an immortal man.

Perhaps Adam hadn't had this much fun in years. How long

would it have been since Adam had another immortal man to spar with? Edwin was simply a pawn in Adam's bigger game. The world needed to know and Edwin needed to suffer in prison.

Following Edwin's scent, Jake left the kitchen and stopped by the stairs to the basement. Edwin had gone down there.

To test the strength of the scent, Jake moved into the living room. The strong scent diminished. He stepped into the dining room. Diminished. Back in front of the stairs, the scent was strong. But so was Kirk's smell. And even Megan had a stronger scent.

What the fuck was down there?

He nudged the basement door open and stopped on the second stair. The smell of fear was pungent. Anxiety was mixed with seething rage. Edwin was waiting and he meant to do Jake harm. But what could he possibly have that would be a threat? Jake didn't think Edwin would bother him, but something inside Jake, the human element, still warned him to not move forward.

He placed his hand on the light switch beside his head and waited another heartbeat, then flicked on the lights, illuminating the entire basement.

CHAPTER FIFTY-ONE

A comfortable leather chair, a recliner, was placed directly at the bottom of the stairs. If Jake had walked down the stairs in the dark, he would've bumped into it.

Edwin sat in the recliner, a huge gun cradled in his hands. His face glistened with sweat, eyes bulging.

"Adam said you'd come," Edwin whispered, his voice deep. "I thought you'd be dead by now. But I guess not. So Adam told me to kill you."

Jake dropped one step. "You could try."

He anticipated the gun blasting into his abdomen with each step, but he dropped another step anyway.

Could he ever get used to being shot? The initial shock, the pain, which almost immediately subsided. How could he get used to that?

"Not one step farther," Edwin warned. "Sit on the stairs. Wait for Adam. He'll come. He wants to talk to you."

Jake stopped with six stairs separating them. He gripped the wooden bannister.

"Where's Megan Radcliffe?" Jake asked.

"None of your concern."

"Did you kill Terry?"

"Adam did."

"Why?"

"None of your concern." After saying those four words a second time, Edwin smiled. "My business is my business and your business is with Adam. Sit down on the stairs and wait. Or move closer and die. It's not mathematical. It's actually rather simple."

Jake stared at him a moment, his mouth open, taking in the scents. Kirk's deodorant, his aftershave, his pheromones, were all stronger down here. Edwin had brought Kirk to the basement alive, he was sure of it.

"Where's the safe room that Steve put in here recently?"

Edwin's mask broke and he tilted his head. When he scrunched up his brow in thought, a series of lines formed large crow's feet beside each eye.

Jake sat on the steps slowly to be able to take in more of the basement. On his left, a large book case had been placed up against the wall. From where he sat, the bookcase looked brand new. It had to be the bookcase Steve had referred to on the phone.

"Behind that bookcase," Jake said as he nodded toward it, "what will I find?"

Edwin raised the gun higher. "Shut up. Stop talking." The distinctive sound of the safety clicking off could be heard throughout the basement. "Just shut the fuck up!"

He had hit pay dirt. Edwin had them in his soundproof safe room.

"Edwin Gavin," Jake said, his voice non-threatening, his tone even. "I'm going to get up now and approach you—"

"I said shut the fuck up!" Edwin raised the weapon to his eye to put Jake in his sights.

"And you're going to open that safe room door."

"Shut UP!"

"Do you understand me?" Jake shouted back.

Edwin's trigger finger moved.

Jake pulled upward with his hands and launched off the stairs in a perfect dive as the weapon in Edwin's hand fired. A bullet struck his chest, knocking him sideways and causing him to smack into Edwin's shoulder. They lay sprawled on the floor.

Edwin mumbled to himself several times as he scrambled to his feet, but Jake didn't move. The bullet had torn into his chest and hit something vital. A lung was punctured, or the bullet lodged itself in his heart.

Jake closed his eyes and waited.

And tried to breathe.

Edwin's foot stirred him. Jake opened his eyes. Edwin stood over him, staring down, a smile pasted to his lips.

"They came for my father once," Edwin said. "He died with a smile." Edwin pulled his foot back and kicked Jake in the side hard enough to crack a rib. Jake grunted, blinked at the pain, then refocused on Edwin. "You're a cop, Mr. Coma Man, and you came for me. But you're the one who's going to die along with your old partner, Kirk. You'll both die painfully."

What was he saying? Kirk is still alive?

"Payback for what happened to my father. Payback for making me kill him all those years ago. I didn't care about my mother." Edwin shook his head so hard, sweat dripped off his face. "No, fuck her. She's a woman. It was my father that mattered and he's dead because of men like you, men who *matter* in society. Men who try to stop me. Well, guess what? You don't matter."

The confession would reopen that case. The kidnapping of Megan Radcliffe and Kirk and now the attempted murder of Jake would create a host of charges. If only he could get his body back under control.

Edwin walked around Jake and set the gun down. He picked something else up, walked away, did something over by the bookcase, and then came back to stand over Jake.

"Kirk's alive, but barely. I have him in the other room. In the safe room—" Edwin stopped talking and stared off into space, unblinking. He refocused and blinked rapidly as he lowered his head and looked down at Jake. "How did you know about Steve? Did he tell you about the safe room?"

Jake tried to move his mouth but nothing worked yet.

Edwin kicked him in the side. Jake winced.

"Tell me," Edwin shouted. "Did Steve blab about me? Huh? Who else knows about my safe room?"

Jake couldn't talk yet, so he mouthed the word *everyone.*

Edwin grabbed his hair in a frantic gesture.

"No," he whispered. "It can't be. It can't be. No one was supposed to know." He stopped moving, let go of his head and glanced back at Jake, squinting. "You're lying to me. You're trying to scare me."

Edwin lifted the Taser to his face, pressed the button once to display its power, then tased Jake in the side. Jake vibrated with the volts.

Edwin turned off the Taser.

Jake took a deep breath. He could breathe again.

Edwin tased him once more.

Whatever Edwin had done, he'd restarted Jake's system. When Edwin stopped the Taser the second time, Jake was fully awake, fully aware. All his energy was back, his strength, his ability, and his anger, which rolled over him like a sheet of sandpaper, stimulating his skin.

Edwin grabbed Jake's arms and dragged him along the floor. Jake allowed himself to be dragged across Edwin's basement floor, eyes open slightly to monitor his progress. They passed through a door. The walls were different. The lighting was different, too.

They were definitely inside the safe room now.

Was he strong enough to break down a safe room door? Whether he was or not, he didn't want to be put to the test.

Edwin let Jake's hands go and moved around him, headed for the door. Jake arched his head back and saw a woman on a bed, her head dangling over the side of the mattress, eyes closed. Based on the smell, that was Megan Radcliffe.

Beside the bed, strapped to a chair, his head resting on his chest, was Kirk.

Jake couldn't contain the anger anymore. He sprang off the floor and landed on his feet. Edwin was already at the door, stepping outside the safe room, mumbling something to himself. Edwin walked around the thick, solid door, and began pushing it back in place.

Jake ran. Two steps, three. Then he leapt. At the second the lock was about to engage, Jake smashed his shoulder into the door, jolting it open a few feet.

Edwin yelled, startled.

Jake fell to the floor in a heap, grabbed the outer edge of the doorframe, and pushed, forcing the door open as Edwin screamed from the outside.

Once Jake secured his feet on the doorframe, he shoved as if he was doing a squat at the gym, using the power of his thighs to open the door all the way. It moved so fast, Edwin was knocked aside.

Jake rolled away from the open door, and, like a cat, got on his feet and hands and lunged at Edwin. He tackled the whining man, grabbed him around the throat with his left hand, and punched Edwin with his right.

"I thought I shot you," Edwin shouted as blood spurted from his mouth.

Jake punched him again.

"I tased you," Edwin said as more blood shot from a broken tooth.

He didn't try to fight back, just struggled and protested.

"I thought you'd die," Edwin mumbled through his broken mouth.

Then Jake punched him one more time, breaking more teeth and knocking Edwin out.

He let the murderer drop where his blood began to stain the carpet. Jake angled Edwin's head so the man wouldn't choke on his own teeth.

After a couple of deep breaths, Jake wiped his knuckles off on Edwin's pants and got to his feet. He grabbed the back of the leather recliner and pulled it to the bookcase/door of the safe room, blocking the door in the open position. Once the door was secure, he entered the safe room and went to Kirk.

Under Kirk's neck, Jake found a weak pulse. He was alive, but barely. Kirk had been beaten. A tourniquet had been fashioned on Kirk's leg where the bullet had hit him. Kirk needed a hospital and by the looks of Megan, she did, too. He checked her pulse, got a strong one, then made his decision.

Not wasting any time, Jake ran from the safe room and looked for a phone. He found one on a table beside a reading chair. Exhausted and relieved, Jake plopped down in the chair and blew out a long sigh.

After a quick glance at Edwin to make sure he was still unconscious, Jake grabbed the phone and dialed 911. He was transferred to Ambulance and requested they attend to the house on call display. Three people were in need of medical services, one of them being Homicide Detective Kirk Aiken. He told them to bring the police, too. Edwin Gavin needed to be arrested for kidnapping and murder. Then he hung up without waiting for a response.

He rubbed his face and got up. He pulled the two guns from his waistband and wiped his prints clean, then wrapped Edwin's hand around both, making sure to leave solid prints. He tossed both guns in a corner behind the reading chair. Let the police find those and match it to the bullet in Kirk's leg.

He was done with this case and didn't want to be here when the police arrived. He didn't want to be here if Adam arrived, either. He'd fought enough for one day. Kirk and Megan needed a hospital. Let them be tended to. Edwin could be arrested. Things needed to settle down. Then he would find Fortech Industries and deal with Adam.

Upstairs, Jake walked through the house, turning on lights as he went, careful not to leave his fingerprints. At the end of the hallway, he entered a bedroom. It looked like a young boy's room. Could Edwin have kids? Jake didn't think so.

A scrapbook sat on the desk in the corner. Jake moved closer, examining its cover. He brought his fingers to the lip of the book and eased it open with his knuckle.

Inside were pictures of a woman and a boy. Pictures he recognized from somewhere. He flipped the book open further and saw a page with locks of hair.

Jake frowned. What was this book? A scrapbook and a photo album put together?

Then he read the names and memories of a distant past began to form. Memories of the case files he'd reviewed from the other night.

- Jeff Lucas, Rosa Lucas, 2013.
- Janelle Hapstead, Paula Hapstead, 2010
- Christine Reilly, 2008
- Sally Boyd, Marie Boyd, 2006

Hands shaking, Jake flipped back a page and nearly dropped the cover of the book.

- Melissa Marcello, Jason Marcello, 2015

These were the names of the victims of the Blood Eagle Killer. Their locks of hair were compiled in the scrapbook like trophies, their sketched drawings taken from the pictures Edwin had stolen from each family's home.

Jake spun around and opened the bedroom closet. Inside, he came across more pictures. Family members from several of the houses the Blood Eagle Killer visited. A box on the shelf in the closet contained wedding rings that Jake knew would match Edwin's victims.

The thought of Edwin killing so many people, then adding the safe room to start a new venture of kidnapping women like Megan, made Jake boil over with rage. He fought every nerve in his body to not walk downstairs and rip Edwin apart.

Jake set the box back in the closet and brushed his fingerprints from it. He moved to the center of the room as the realization of what he had discovered settled over him.

A blinding white-hot rage urged him to seek justice for the victims. The humanity in his reptilian brain slowly lost its grip as the predatory nature of a snake made him yearn for Edwin's destruction.

The only way to stop himself would be to leave the house. He had to get out. Exit the back door the same way he entered and disappear into the night. Let the police handle it. Let the authorities make their arrest. Edwin would never see the light of day. Killing him would only be a moment's pleasure.

Jake turned for the door, fully intending to walk down to the basement to murder Edwin, but knowing he had to leave. To stay in this house one more second was to commit murder. Jake couldn't physically be around Edwin. He had to leave. He had to leave right now.

He stepped into the hallway and headed for the kitchen.

"I have to leave," he whispered to himself. "Get out, Jake. Run."

The urge, the *need*, the *draw*, to run down the stairs to the basement, actually made him turn toward the stairs, but humanity won out by a thread. He entered the kitchen, then stopped short.

The kitchen light shone on Edwin's face grotesquely. His face had changed to a mask of smeared blood and deformed teeth. Edwin's smile resembled something a Halloween mask strived to imitate.

In Edwin's hands, raised above his head, was an ax, in his eyes, insanity.

"You'll die …" Edwin stammered, his speech altered as the landscape inside his mouth had changed, "for what you did to me."

Then Edwin threw the ax.

At the sight of Edwin with the ax, Jake lost that thread of humanity. The names of the dead families echoed in his head as he jolted forward and ran into the ax's blade. At impact, every smidgen of kindness toward his fellow man departed.

Jake hollered an inhuman cry as the ax penetrated his left shoulder, digging deep. A second later, he plowed into Edwin, his right hand gaining purchase around Edwin's neck, his left hand deflected by the ax.

As one, the men backed up to the wall, hitting it hard enough to daze Edwin. His eyes rolled back and he slipped down to the linoleum floor mumbling gibberish to himself.

Jake eyed the ax, the blood starting to drip down his chest and stomach.

Without wasting another moment, he gripped the ax handle, took a deep breath, then reefed upward and out, yanking it from his flesh. After a moment hovering over the Blood Eagle Killer, Jake had full use of his left hand again.

He grabbed Edwin by the hair, lifted him upward with one hand, spun him around to face the wall, and drew the ax back.

"For the Reilly family," Jake shouted. "For the dead children."

In one strong forward thrust, he impaled Edwin to the wall,

the ax going straight through Edwin's shoulder blade and into the wooden stud behind the drywall.

Edwin wailed, his cheek pressed against the drywall. He moaned *No* over and over, his eyes trying to find Jake behind him.

"For the Marcello family," Jake muttered.

He grabbed a kitchen knife from the block on the counter, not thinking about the consequences, simply not caring anymore. The names of all the men, women and children raced through his mind. The fathers torn apart because of this sick fuck. The women raped and then ruined with acid. The children with lives ahead of them, dreams and hopes. All ruined because Edwin had felt like it. All destroyed because Edwin was fucked up in the head.

"Be fucked up on your own time!" Jake shouted as he jabbed a knife into Edwin's back on the left of his spine. Then he repeated the procedure on the right.

Edwin screamed, sounding like a scared teenage girl at a horror movie.

"For the women ..." he whispered to himself, his teeth locked together, jaw tight.

Jake worked quickly, reaching inside Edwin's back. He broke rib bones out on either side of Edwin's spine. Somewhere along the way, Edwin quieted, but Jake didn't care. He was honed in, working on his task, the color red all he could see.

"Live by the Blood Eagle, die by it," Jake said in his rage.

Then he did what the Blood Eagle Killer had done before him. He pulled Edwin's ribs outward to expose Edwin's vibrating lungs.

Before Edwin died suspended by the ax to his own kitchen wall, Jake grabbed both lungs simultaneously and pulled them out of Edwin's body cavity to place on the exposed ribs.

They fluttered a few times as Edwin's body shut down, then stopped their movement in response to Edwin's inactive heart.

Sirens wailed in the distance. The authorities were coming.

Blood was everywhere, covering Jake's hands and sleeves.

Jake spat on the corpse and glanced one last time at Edwin's face. Even in death, Edwin smiled.

"Fuck you," Jake said, his head pounding with rage. "I'll see you in Hell."

"Jake?" a soft voice said behind him.

He threw his hands up in defense and spun around so fast he almost fell over.

At the opening to the basement stairs, Kirk tried to stand, still tied to the chair. Fresh blood seeped from his bullet wound, glistening a deep red in the kitchen light.

"What are ..." Kirk tried. He swallowed and tried again. "What are you doing?"

"Edwin Gavin is the Blood Eagle Killer," Jake said. "The proof is in the bedroom at the end of the hall." Sirens stopped out front. Jake edged toward the back door. "Tell them you caught the bastard."

"How do I explain?" He nodded toward Edwin's corpse. "That?"

Jake opened the back door with the broken knob and stepped outside.

"I don't know, partner. I don't know." He lowered his head as humanity seeped back and he felt the full weight of what he had done. "I don't know. I'm sorry."

"It's okay, Jake. Go. I got this."

Someone knocked at the front door.

"Go, Jake. You were never here. And hey."

Jake stopped and peeked back inside.

"Thanks for saving my life," Kirk said.

Jake turned and ran. He ran and ran and ran, his new body replenishing tired muscles as he sprinted. He didn't stop until he got to the beach five kilometers away where he ran into Lake

Ontario and cleaned himself of the evening's battle. He washed away the dirt, the blood, and the stench of Edwin Gavin.

But he couldn't wash away the guilt, the loss, or the pain.

Even his new body couldn't save him from grief.

Nothing could.

CHAPTER FIFTY-TWO

Exhausted and frustrated, Jake entered his house in Novar the next day and dropped onto his couch. He put his face in his hands. How close had his partner come to being murdered? And discovering the killer of Ontario families made Jake feel good, but he regretted killing him in a blind rage. If Edwin had lived, he would have faced the full wrath of the law. The extended families of the people Edwin had killed could have had closure.

But all that was gone. And Jake was a murderer. At any moment the police, his colleagues, would roll up and arrest him. After what Edwin had done, it would be Jake who spent years in prison. It was all on Jake.

But how could he have controlled that searing rage? Maybe it would take time. Maybe he needed to get used to his new body. Maybe things could still work out for him.

He sat back and raised his face to the ceiling.

What next? Where should he go? What should he do? Find Fortech Industries? How? An organization like that was well hidden behind shell companies and titles with government security up the wazoo.

The phone rang beside him. He checked call display then picked up.

"Kirk?" Jake said.

"How you doing, Jake?" his friend asked.

"You calling to give me a time?" Jake said, ignoring Kirk's question.

"A time?"

"When I'll be arrested."

"No. They're not looking for you." Kirk said. Then added, "Yet."

"What do you mean by *yet*?"

"They're dusting for prints in Edwin's house. They know someone else was there. Sure we found all the evidence to implicate Edwin going all the way back to the first family. We even discovered a few notebooks where he wrote the dates and times of the things he did to thwart Detective Joslin on this case, his own case, going back ten years. Having the murderer in charge of processing the bodies was a huge mistake. Heads are going to roll over this."

Jake listened, but only heard bits of what Kirk was saying.

"You said *yet*," Jake reminded him.

"They found a partial print on a light switch. Also, on the handle of the ax. But they had nothing conclusive until they found the doorknob in the bushes. Was that you?"

"That was me," he said.

"Okay, I'll do what I can with the results. I should warn you, though. If they pull a good print off the knob, my cover story is out the window."

Jake closed his eyes and rubbed his forehead. "What was your cover story?"

"Better you don't know all the details, just that they know I was locked in the basement and someone, obviously not me, attacked Edwin. They're surmising it's a vigilante. Someone attached to one of the cases. At this moment, everyone's looking for a violent vigilante. Someone with extreme strength as Edwin's bones were broken by hand."

"They can tell that? What about a strap or something?"

"The bones were pulled on, snapped. They weren't cut with a blade. The profile is a monster of a man fueled by rage."

"They have no idea how close they are to the truth."

A silence stretched between them. Jake waited, breathing calmly. If they came for him, he'd deal with it, as he'd done with harsh realities in the past. If they didn't, maybe he could help Kirk look for the vigilante. Just like Edwin, he could help on the case to catch himself.

"Jake, you going to be okay?" Kirk asked.

"Yeah. Just keep me up to date."

"Keep you up to date?" Kirk said, surprise in his voice. "Shit man, you saved my life. I'm going to save yours here. Then together, we'll go after that Adam guy. I want Fortech Industries as bad as you."

"Good to hear."

"You should think about staying somewhere else for the time being."

"Why?"

"Adam knows where you live."

"So? I hope he comes here. I'll get the answers I want, then kill him. He'd be doing me a favor."

A moment of silence on the phone again.

"You're different, Jake, but somehow still the same."

"Come see me soon," Jake said. "I could use the company. And pick up the files you left behind. We won't be needing them anymore."

"Okay."

"Hey, Kirk?"

"Yeah?"

"Did Megan get cleaned up and taken home to her kids?"

"Cleaned up, yes, but her kids were brought here to be with

317

her. The husband's funeral will be in four days."

"Okay. Just wanted to make sure she's okay."

"A broken hand that was set and casted today. Otherwise, he didn't do anything to her, sexually or otherwise."

"Okay. Kirk, call me."

"Done."

Jake hung up. The phone rang as he pulled his hand away. He snatched it up.

"Forgot something?" he asked.

"I wanted to say thank you," Adam's voice came on the line. Jake froze, tightening the grip on the receiver. "For dealing with Edwin. He was such a nuisance."

"Let's meet."

"We will, but not yet. I want to watch the police solve their case of the vigilante on the loose. In the meantime, as you're the target the police are looking for, you can be my target as well."

"Fuck you, Adam. I'll find you and when I do, I'll bleed you, slice your head off, and then burn the remains."

"I gave you a gift, Jake Wood. Yet you fail to see my brilliance. Because of what I gave you, the BEK killer has been found and murdered in an appropriate fashion. Jake, you should be thanking me."

"Fuck you." He gripped the phone tighter.

"Since you are now my target, I will aim to hurt and kill any and everyone close to you. Anything you hold dear is now mine."

"You'll die," Jake shouted as the familiar anger raced through him. "Come now, motherfucker. Come now. I will eat your face off and shit down your throat. I'll pop your eyes out and shit in your skull."

"Cindy will be first," Adam said as if Jake hadn't spoken. "And her new baby girl. Then your house will burn. Kirk will have a work accident. Slowly, piece by piece, I will take your life apart from the shadows until you're a withered piece of mucus, begging me to kill you. Do you understand, Jake? You are *The Target* and I will stop at nothing to destroy you."

Jake slammed the phone down, breaking it into chunks of plastic under the force of his hand.

He ran for his cell phone. He needed to warn Cindy. He needed to call Kirk. He needed to hide, go underground.

Adam had to be found and killed before he found them.

Jake would be nobody's target.

Jake would stop at nothing to protect his family, his friends. Nothing.

His cell phone rang from the kitchen as he ran to it.

Call display said it was Cindy.

His heart sank as he picked it up.

"Cindy, are you okay?" Jake shouted into the phone. "Please tell me you're okay."

"Yeah, Jake," her voice was calm, nasally, as if she'd been crying. "I'm fine. Just wanted to tell you I had a baby girl this morning. We haven't talked much since you left the clinic in Brazil and I was thinking of you as I held my baby." She hiccupped and sobbed. "Just thought I'd be holding your baby one day, but life happened and well, I'm sorry, just thought you should know."

Jake held the counter so he didn't collapse. How had Adam known Cindy had had a baby girl this morning if he wasn't at the hospital already?

"Cindy, there's something I have to tell you. Where are you right now?"

"Orillia Hospital. What, no congrats? Are you still mad at me?"

"Cindy, please. Listen to me …"

AFTERWORD

Dear Reader,

Wow, what a ride. I've enjoyed every moment of it. The idea for *The Immortal Gene* first came to me over a year before I wrote the first word. I had been quite involved with Sarah Roberts' life at the time and I wasn't sure if *The Immortal Gene* would translate well to the readers of the Sarah Roberts Series.

For me, in the beginning of the idea for this novel, I was thinking Jake would be a new version of a vampire, without the traditional bloodsucking part. He would end up being a snake-man as in this novel, but with more anger, more horror. In the end, I wanted to have someone like Jake, a kind, good-hearted man, who was chemically altered with modified snake venom. I wanted Jake to become part snake, but not enough that his human side diminished outwardly. Jake is everything I wanted him to be. He's a strong, powerful man who can't die—unless torn apart and burned—and has a good heart, but piss him off, get in his way, or hurt the weak, and he'll exact justice his way.

Now that Jake has been explained, I want to mention a few things from the novel. In Chapter Six, I mentioned Naughty by Nature and their song, "O.P.P." Find it on YouTube and enjoy a song from the early nineties that was big in my youth.

Also, in Chapter Six, I referenced the movie *A Few Good Men*. I loved that movie. I'm a major movie and music buff. When writing novels I listen to original scores of movie soundtracks and I've been told that I write my manuscripts in a cinematic way that the reader *sees* the action taking place. For the record, that is and always will be my intention.

In this novel I mentioned Moxy Fruvous, Fairground Attraction, and Blue October. If you haven't experienced these bands and are interested, check them out on YouTube. Moxy Fruvous is a Toronto-based band and my favorite song is called "My Baby Loves a Bunch of Authors." Fairground Attraction is from the late eighties, early nineties, and their song "Perfect" is probably the one most readers would recognize. Blue October has several albums that are hot, but my favorite is the passion-fueled album *Any Man in America* from 2011.

Fortech Industries is a fictitious company. In the first full-length novel I ever wrote back in year 2000 called, *Bad Vibes*, Fortech Industries was experimenting with a shock-wave bomb, another fictitious kind of killing device. *Bad Vibes* isn't available for sale at this time. That story is collecting dust on my hard drive. But Fortech Industries has always stewed in the back of mind, as if it held a power of its own. Something devious and dark. Like the radiating seepage leaking out of the crack in a nuclear reactor, I couldn't ignore Fortech anymore and decided to make them the villain in this book. In the next book, (potentially titled, *The Target*), The Jake Wood Series Book Two, Fortech Industries will be summarily dealt with or live on for years to come. I guess we will both have to wait to see what happens with Fortech.

Two readers' names made it into the book. I hope Tammy Feltz, the officer at the Marcello Family massacre, didn't mind her bit part, and Detective Keri Joslin didn't mind me taking the BEK case away from her. Thanks for letting me use your names and being good sports about it.

A special thanks goes out to all the readers (that means you) for taking a chance on me and this book. It's the first in a series that will span quite a few more books. I appreciate you and I'm eternally grateful that you're in my life through the medium of reading the words I string together.

For the record, whether the Ontario Provincial Police call their homicide officers detectives or inspectors, I've elected to call them detectives.

If there are mistakes in this manuscript, they're all mine. They are never the result of my fabulous editors, whom I thank with enormous gratitude for the work they have done. I couldn't do this without them.

I'm looking forward to the release of *The Target*.

Until then, talk soon, and get caught reading.

Love you all,

Jonas

ABOUT THE AUTHOR

Jonas Saul is the bestselling author of the Sarah Roberts Series and has sold over two million books. Upon several occasions, Saul has outranked Stephen King and Dean Koontz in the Top 100 Authors on Amazon list. His most recent release, *The Future Is Written*, is published by pioneering media company Adaptive Studios.

Saul has traveled extensively throughout the world to scout settings for his thrillers, spending several years between Greece, Italy, Denmark, and Hungary. He is regularly invited to be a guest speaker at international writing conferences.

He currently resides in British Columbia.

www.jonassaul.com